BOLD
PASSIONATE
WILLING

Rachael Jobe came as a stranger to Devil's Ridge. She was eager to begin a new life, hungry to find love and determined that no man would hold her cheaply again. When she met Adam Warden, she thought she had found her match. But Adam believed she was Elisha's woman and contemptuously called her a whore. Insulted and enraged, she resolved to teach him a lesson about women that he would never forget.

ELISHA'S WOMAN
BY NORAH HESS

PLAYBOY PRESS

ELISHA'S WOMAN

Cover illustration by Betty Maxey.

Copyright © 1977 by Elsie Poe Bagnara. All rights reserved. No part of this book may be reproduced, stored in a retrieval system or transmitted in any form by an electronic, mechanical, photocopying, recording means or otherwise without prior written permission of the author.

Published simultaneously in the United States and Canada by Playboy Press, Chicago, Illinois. Printed in the United States of America. Library of Congress Catalog Card Number: 76-43401. First edition.

Books are available at quantity discounts for promotional and industrial use. For further information, write our sales-promotion agency: Ventura Associates, 40 East 49th Street, New York, New York 10017.

For Emilie

CHAPTER 1

It was early spring in Jamestown, 1782. The day was half gone and Rachael Jobe still lay in bed. She rolled over on her back and groaned.

"This life is going to kill me," she muttered.

The old gentleman she had entertained last night had left her exhausted. Not only had he been demanding, but there was a bit of cruelty in him also. She was thankful that he came but once a month.

She glanced at the stack of money on the table and wondered if it was worth the abuse her body took. Leaning on an elbow, she examined her shoulders and breasts. Teeth marks and bruises liberally sprinkled the white flesh. "Damned old bastard," she mumbled.

She sighed and threw herself back on the bed. She would have to turn away a lot of customers while they were fading. Her gentlemen of the upper class would not care to see the marks of another man on her. Moreover, there were a couple who, she suspected, would upon seeing the marks get the idea that they too could handle her harshly.

She smiled grimly. It was a costly privilege to lay rough hands and lips on Rachael Jobe.

She counted the money. Satisfaction curved her lips. As always, he had been quite generous. She would be able to take several days off.

"I certainly earned the right," she thought. "I know how he put three wives in the grave."

And yet her body trembled as she remembered, with a somehow pleasant revulsion, the pleasure the old gent gave her once his own appetite was sated. She had learned early that the older man had a knowing way about him when it came to loving a woman. She thought it a shame that the young men with their firm and muscular bodies were so fumbling and eager. They went at a woman as if she were some wild creature that had to be subdued and brought rapidly to acquiescence. In their rashness they were a long time learning, if ever, that a woman properly made love to would more than repay the time and gentleness given her.

Her stomach rumbled, reminding her of its emptiness.

Last night she had left orders that a light supper be brought to her room around midnight. But when it was announced through the closed door, her impatient lover had sworn angrily and heaved a boot at the voice.

She reached for the small bell. Almost before the tinkle died away, a large black woman, wearing a wide grin, entered the room.

"You ready for your bath, honey, or do I bring you something to eat first?"

"Food, Beaulah, food. I'm starved."

Loud laughter boomed from the black throat. "I reckoned you'd be hungry after entertainin' 'old randy dan.' I watched him leave this mornin' and that old codger could hardly put one foot in front of the other."

She paused and waited for Rachael to make some disparaging remark. When Rachael smiled in agreement, she continued.

"That old rooster was so wrung out, his driver had to help him into the coach."

"I wish he would have crawled . . . he made such a pig of himself. He's an inconsiderate man."

"I know. Around midnight when I made a trip to the privy, his little driver was sittin' up on that coach, shiverin' and shakin'. You ought to have heard him cuss. He was rackin' you over the coals for keepin' the old gent in here."

Rachael gave a short laugh. "I sure as hell didn't encourage the old reprobate. I'd had my fill after fifteen minutes. Besides, I felt sorry for the horses out there in the cold. But when I mentioned it, the old goat just growled, 'Get on with your work, girl. Get me up there.'"

"Wasn't nothin' you could do, honey, 'cept earn your wages."

Rachael sighed. "I earned them alright."

A twinkle appeared in her eyes and she teased, "Why didn't you take the driver into bed and warm him up?"

The big woman shook with laughter. "Not that little fellow. I saw him out back once and that little thing of his wasn't long enough to matter. He'd just be a teaser to Beaulah."

"You still have a yen for Roscoe, do you?"

"Oh, law yes. When that big stud comes at me, I just shiver. Roscoe, he's a humpin' man and I likes to feel it hit home."

"I thought it was all over between you two. Didn't you tell me that he wanted you to go to bed with his friends and that when you refused, he moved out?"

From the rosy flush that flooded Beaulah's face

and the fast shifting of her eyes, Rachael knew that she had given in to her lover's demands. How deeply it must have hurt her. She hoped fervently that she would never love a man so.

Speaking with a false bravado, Beaulah was answering, "That's what he wanted me to do, but I told him plain out I wouldn't do it. He tried to scare me by movin' out, but when he saw I was firm, he come back."

"Good for you, Beaulah. You handled it just right." She didn't add that it was common knowledge that Roscoe spent most of his time with a younger, prettier girl these days.

As though afraid of the conversation going further, Beaulah left to prepare lunch.

Rachael scooted farther into the featherbed and wiggled her toes against the silky sheets that a rough and crusty sea captain had gifted her with. She looked forward to his trips upriver, for there was always something special for her. From the many ports he tied into came fancy dresses and sheer underclothing, not to mention the jewelry and heady perfumes.

There was also another reason. He was a most knowledgeable man in bed. From the many countries he had visited, he had acquired erotic tastes and had taught her much. When she in turn used her new knowledge on her customers, business had boomed. Every day Beaulah made large deposits in the bank for her.

But it had not always been this way. Her green, almond-shaped eyes went blank in remembering. Thinking back, she absentmindedly fingered the black silky hair that framed her delicately boned face.

Until three years ago, she had lived in poverty. She had been the only child of Ben and Alice Jobe. Her difficult birth had almost killed her frail mother and had left her in permanent poor health. When Rachael was twelve, her mother died one night as quietly as she had lived.

Although Rachael loved the gentle woman, she had not grieved overly at her passing. She had watched too long the suffering on the wasted face and could only be thankful when at last the pain was finished.

She had a motherly, protective love for her father. While still very young she had realized that Ben was weak of character and not to be depended upon. She had also learned to meet him at the mill on payday. If she didn't, the first tavern he happened on would be the recipient of the better part of his wages. It would fall on her then to beg credit at the grocery store and put off the landlord.

Her waiting at the mill's gate one afternoon had led to the profession she had successfully carried on for the last three years.

Even at fourteen she had been a beautiful child. She had matured early, and her ripe body had soon filled her old dresses to overflowing. She was aware that men stared at her, hunger sharp in their eyes, but she had been only mildly curious.

On that eventful day that was to change her way of life, she walked to the mill and waited patiently for Ben. With interest she had watched two men, full of drink, swagger toward her. They seemed to find everything around them funny and were laughing uproariously. The younger of the two, husky and roughly handsome, had a contagious laugh and she had laughed with him.

Hearing her merry tinkle in sympathy with his own, he stopped and peered at her owlishly. The two men drew together, and after a whispered conference, the young one beckoned to her. In friendliness and innocence, she walked across the tall grass and smiled a greeting.

As she stood trustingly before them, the young one, grinning loosely, laid an arm across her shoulder.

"Ain't you a pretty little thing?" he hiccuped.

When the other one, pock-faced and hawk-nosed, added, "She's got some body too," she blushed and giggled.

They said many complimentary words to her and she drank it all in. Often they made remarks that she did not understand, but wanting to hear more of their flattery, she had pretended that she did.

Later, when the husky one complained of standing and his companion suggested they go sit under a tree some distance away, she agreed without hesitation.

But when they went under the tree's ground-hugging branches, her new-found friends turned into different men—men whose eyes devoured her body with such an intensity that she became frightened and cowered away from them. They began to stalk her as she backed away with trembling knees. Then suddenly and without warning, she was grabbed and sent sprawling to the ground.

The surprise attack held her dumb and motionless. Then her eyes stretched wide in horrified fascination. The young one stood over her, unfastening his trousers. Once she had secretly watched Beaulah entertain Roscoe and he had stood over her in much the same manner. She squeezed her eyes tight, remembering what had followed.

She felt him kneeling between her legs, felt his rough fingers tearing away at her encumbering clothing. It was then she opened her mouth to scream. But the ugly one had clamped a hand over her lips.

Then hot searing pain shot through her body as the man made his entry and started a rhythmic motion. She tried to scream again, but the hand was relentless.

Then suddenly his hair was brushing her throat and his lips, hot and soft, were covering a bared breast. Gently he drew the nipple between his lips and sucked. The unexpected sensation made her eyes fly open and she gasped.

Gradually the pain became a dull ache, and taking the place of the tearing horror, a tingling throb began. Unconsciously she pressed the dark head closer to her breast, helpless against the emotion that was building within her. But with a few more short, quick shoves, the man between her legs gave a moan and collapsed on top of her.

The hawk-faced one raised his head and laughed at her startled expression. "He's too fast for you, doll face," he murmured as he took his friend's place. Then guiding himself into her, whispered, "I'll give you plenty of time."

He had been savage in his attack, but had knowingly lingered until she clung to him helplessly, moaning her ecstasy. When he felt her shudder and lie still, he too went limp.

Later, when he would have risen, she wound her

arms around his neck, refusing to let him go. He chuckled and stayed with her.

When the men were ready to leave they did not go immediately, but stood around, shifting their feet nervously. They looked a little shamefaced and would not meet her eyes. They had raped a virgin and were none too proud of themselves, even though she had enjoyed it in the end.

The young one grinned down at her sheepishly and pulled some money from his pocket. Laying it beside her, he said, "That wasn't bad, little green eyes." He hesitated a moment then asked, "What about tomorrow night?"

She nodded her head dumbly and pulled her dress down over her knees.

The other one tossed some money into her lap and turned to go. Then he paused and turned around to study her fresh, young face a moment. "You go on home now and do something to yourself . . . so you don't get big bellied," he advised gruffly.

It was totally dark now, and by the pale light of the half-moon Rachael could hardly make them out as they reached the beaten path and moved out of sight.

"Everything is so different now," she thought. She felt so awake to the world around her. Looked at it through different eyes, it seemed. "I guess I'm a woman now."

She remembered the ugly man's advice and pondered on it. She knew that being big bellied meant being with child, but she had never known before just how it came about. She would have to confide in Beaulah and ask her what to do, she decided. Certainly she couldn't ask papa.

Papa. She had forgotten about him. The mill had been out for over an hour and by now most of his pay would be gone. She gave a ragged sigh. She was so weary of it all.

Then suddenly she became aware of what her fingers were playing with. She had money—money of her own. Never again would she have to worry about food and a roof over her head.

Giving a happy laugh, she jumped to her feet, kicked her torn underclothing into a nearby bush and ran for home. She would change her soiled dress, wash up, then go to the market.

"From now on, I'll eat the best and plenty of it," she vowed silently.

The next evening she went to the tree, and the two men, along with some friends, waited for her. In the early hours of morning her last customer had gone and her career was launched.

As the weeks sped by, she became very adept at the trade that provided her the security she had never known. In a box, hidden away from Ben, her little pile of money was growing.

She no longer bothered Ben about rent and food money. And although in his sober moments he wondered halfheartedly how the meals appeared regularly on the table and why they hadn't been set out upon the street, he never questioned her.

Then the warm summer evenings were coming to an end. Already most of her customers were seeking the pleasure houses that provided warmth and a bed.

In the beginning it had pleased the men's egos to lie with a woman on the earth's natural floor. They had derived pleasure out of knowing that just a few feet away other men were hearing their grunts and thumps and were envying them. But as Beaulah had warned, the first blast of cold air on their bare rumps had sent them scooting for warmer quarters.

One frosty morning she had sat at her kitchen table, staring out at the lowering clouds and worrying whether they would drop snow. A frown gathered on her forehead as she thought of the money she would lose. She sighed and poured another cup of coffee. Sipping it slowly, she relaxed in the cozy warmth and recalled how chilled she had been last night. And to worsen matters, only three men had showed up, hardly making it worth her while to have gone out.

She scowled into the coffee, musing on an idea she had toyed with for a long while. She would have done it long ago if Beaulah hadn't insisted that Ben wouldn't allow it. Sometimes she half suspected that it was Beaulah herself who didn't want the men coming to the house. Beaulah had loved Alice and maybe she felt duty-bound to look out for her daughter—to protect her reputation.

She rose and impatiently paced the floor. "To hell with my reputation," she thought. "Everyone knows what I am. Why should I worry what they think or say? They didn't feed me when I was pure and hungry, so to hell with them, now that I'm soiled and rich."

An hour later her mind was made up. After last night's small take and the winter weather about to bring business to a halt, she would argue the point no longer. She wouldn't even ask Ben's permission.

"I would starve to death if I depended upon papa," she defended herself.

Tossing a shawl around her shoulders, she took

some of her hoarded money and visited the local tavern. After purchasing several bottles of good whiskey, she stopped at Beaulah's on the way home. By the time she left, she had bullied the black woman into agreeing that she would serve the men their drinks while they waited their turn in the bedroom.

By late afternoon, everything was ready and she had only to tell Ben. When at last she heard his unsteady step upon the porch, dark had fallen and great flakes of snow danced and swirled in the wind.

She did not waste time breaking her news gently to the man who stood blinking at her. Guiding him to a chair, she told him bluntly what she had been about all summer and what she proposed doing now. Ben had put up a slight resistance—had shed a few tears over what his baby was becoming. But his whiskey-soaked mind was not capable of showing any authority over her and he dumbly watched her leave the house.

She had returned in a short time with five men she had encountered on the street. They liked sitting in her little parlor, sipping her good liquor, and in no time word had spread about her new quarters.

It was soon after this that Rachael met the river captain. She had gone for a walk in the park to clear her brain and lungs of the tobacco smoke that clung in the house. It was quite nippy out and she decided to go home when the sky turned dark and threatened to snow. She turned to leave and passed a stocky man about middle-age. He was oddly attractive, with a shock of gray hair and thick eyebrows over hot eyes that slid over her body. His gaze fastened on her face, then his eyes sent a question winging at her. She stared back a moment, felt an answering need and nodded silently. He took her arm, and without a word, escorted her home.

During that long afternoon, her education began on how best to satisfy a man in bed.

For five days he shared her afternoons and when it came time for him to ship out, she was accomplished in every way to please a man.

On his last visit, they had not gone to bed, but had sat before the fire and talked quietly. At one time during the course of their conversation, he leaned toward her and took her hand.

"You are a most beautiful woman, Rachael," he said gravely. "You have a face and body that I have not seen equaled in all my traveling. Do not sell it cheap. The rich man will pay any price you ask, so ask much. Save your money, then get out while you're still young."

And the rich men from the fancy part of town had heard of her beauty and knowing way in bed, and had been finding their way to her door in growing numbers.

Gradually her old customers were pushed aside, leaving only the original two. She was not quite sure why she clung to them. Perhaps it was out of a sense of duty, or maybe for old-times' sake. In any case, the hawk-faced one still brought her an overriding excitement that even the river captain with all his experience was unable to do.

She had remarked on this to Beaulah. "Do you suppose it's because he's so damned ugly?"

Beaulah had thought a moment, then giggled, "Ugly face, but something pretty."

* * *

While things had gone well for Rachael, Ben's path had been downhill. He was drinking more and his long body was becoming thin and gaunt. Every day Rachael prepared hot tasty meals for him but usually they were wasted. After a few bites he would push away from the table and disappear into his bedroom. Rachael knew that behind the closed door he would drink himself into oblivion.

Then came a day when her fears for him ended. It was winter, and the year's worst snowstorm was raging when a knock sounded on the front door. Rachael had frowned and muttered, "What damned fool is out in this weather."

But when she opened the door, she gasped and stepped back. Two men stood before her, holding her father's crushed and bleeding body in their arms. He had, they explained, stepped in the path of a horse-drawn vehicle and the animal's hooves had struck his chest.

They laid him on his bed and as Rachael knelt beside him, she knew that life was fast leaving his body. He groaned and began to mumble. She lay her head next to his and listened closely.

"Rach, honey . . . I've been a poor sort of father to you . . . but I've always loved you. You must quit this life . . . go to your grandfather in the hills. Do you promise, child?"

Her eyes glassed with tears as she gently stroked his forehead. Murmuring softly, she soothed, "I promise, papa. I'll go right away."

He had smiled a peaceful smile, closed his eyes and his soul was released.

* * *

But she hadn't kept her promise. Months later she still lay in her satin-covered bed . . . still entertained men in it. In guilt, she squirmed uncomfortably and tried to put her father's words out of her mind.

When Beaulah entered the room with a tray heaped high with food, Rachael welcomed the interruption. But even as she ate and listened to Beaulah's easy chatter, Ben's words continued to nag in the back of her mind.

Later, sitting in a tub of fragrant, steaming water, she relaxed and gave serious thought to her way of life and Ben's request.

She was seventeen. Still young and fresh. But if she continued her present lifestyle, how long would that freshness last? How long before her face became hard and coarsened? She thought of the prostitutes who had grown old before their time, and shuddered. In her mind she saw the ravished faces, heavy with powder and paint in the vain attempt to retain the glow of youth that had fled. But there was no way of hiding the forlorn and bewildered glaze that was fixed in their eyes.

The river captain had remarked once that if one looked deep enough into the eyes of a prostitute, one would be able to define hell.

Although she hadn't reached that point yet, a few more nights such as the one just passed would surely bring a terrible look into her eyes, she thought.

"Why do I live this life?" she muttered to herself.

Outside of her necessary need of a man, there was only one other answer. Money. She gave a derisive grunt. What had her money bought that was of any real value?

True, there were luxuries. Beautiful clothing.

Dresses that hung in her closet, unworn. Where could she wear them? Her money had not obtained invitations into the homes of the wealthy families. It had not even made the respectable poor accept her. There remained only the human dregs living on the seamy side of town. And rather than associate with them, she would remain friendless the rest of her days.

This state of discontent had not come on her suddenly. It had been building for some time. Seeing sweethearts together, in the park, had started it. Riding in her fancy carriage with her jewelry and finery on display, she would secretly watch the young lovers and regret what she was missing. The obvious devotion in the young men's eyes for the girls on their arms had awakened a longing in her heart.

Of all the men that shared her bed, not one loved her. Of course, she did not love them either. They merely filled a basic need. So lately, she dreamed of having a man of her own. Just one man . . . lusty as she was, and loving her completely.

She sat up in the water and began soaping herself. "There's a man for me somewhere," she thought. "The world is full of them. Here in Jamestown, or for that matter, in the wilds of Kentucky."

She stepped out of the wooden tub and into the warm towel that Beaulah held for her.

"I'm getting out of the business, Beaulah," she announced.

Beaulah gave her a long serious look, then smiled widely.

"I'm glad, honey. I've thought for a long time that your heart wasn't in this kind of life." She helped Rachael to dress, then asked, "What will you do now?"

When Rachael answered, "I'm going to my grandfather's," Beaulah exclaimed, "But, Rachael, don't he live in the wilderness . . . a place called Kentucky?"

"Yes. Papa said that he lives in a settlement in the Kentucky hills called Devil's Ridge."

"But, my land, child, what in the world will you do there? It's rough livin' on a homestead. Won't be no satin sheets and other comforts."

"You forget, Beaulah, I haven't always slept on satin sheets. I've slept on rough muslin more often than the other."

Beaulah busied herself at the fireplace, poking at it unnecessarily, sending red sparks up the chimney.

"What about your lovin'?" she asked hesitantly. "You're a gal that takes a heap of pleasurin'."

Rachael smiled at the big back and teased, "Really, Beaulah, are you trying to tell me that I won't be able to get a man in my bed?"

"Lawd, no," Beaulah laughed back. "They'll be lined up two deep. But I was thinkin' maybe your grandpa wouldn't like it."

Rachael went and stood beside her. "I wouldn't like it either, Beaulah. I'm leaving my old ways behind. From now on, I'll be looking for only one man."

Beaulah studied her earnest face and was convinced. She wouldn't badger her with reasons to stay in Jamestown. She would sorely miss her though.

It grew silent in the room, each woman busy with her own thoughts. After awhile, Beaulah stirred and asked, "What about business tonight?"

"Tell them anything you want. Tell them I've gone away."

Before retiring, she sat at her desk and penned a letter to the grandfather she had never known. As she wrote, she wondered about him. What kind of man was he . . . would they get along with each other?

Beaulah waited for her to finish the letter, then took it to the post on her way home.

Rachael walked to the window and looked out. The sky was shiny bright and she likened it to herself. That was how she felt, looking forward to a new life.

Last night was the last time she would ever go to bed with a man for money.

CHAPTER 2

In 1762 Elisha Jobe left Jamestown. Along with him went his daughter, Sarah, her husband, and two sons, Rafe, aged eight, and Dave, two years.

They, along with friends, traveled with Benjamin Logan into the newly opened territory of Kentucky.

Elisha and his son-in-law each bought a hundred acres from the Transylvania Land Company. They chose the hilly region, not unlike the terrain they had left behind.

Elisha's only son, a complete opposite of himself, had opted to stay behind with his expecting wife.

The new frontiersmen were a rough-and-ready lot . . . always spoiling for a fight, with the ever-ready chip on the shoulder.

They wore the regular garb of the pioneer—coonskin cap, buckskins or homespuns, and the long rifle accompanying them at all times.

The women were equally rough and tough, fitting mates for their men. They were of this nature out of necessity, for the trail they traveled was harsh and virgin. It was merely a buffalo trace, pounded hard by the herds on their annual migrations across the mountains. Long before Logan and his party infringed on the wilderness, Cherokee Indians had taken the same path on their way to the lush bluegrass hunting grounds.

From the suffering and privation that assailed the pioneers along the way, they had aptly named the trace The Wilderness Road, a name which has stood through the years.

The Virginians, who were mostly of English descent and of a clannish nature, had at first associated only with the people they traveled with. But gradually an acceptance of and friendship with the primarily Scottish pioneers sprang up.

The Scots had come in with Boone from North Carolina, and together the two groups had successfully kept the outsider, or *furriner*, from their part of the hills.

Elisha Jobe was the leader of the Virginia group, and Silas Warden headed the North Carolina clan.

Silas carried fourteen years on Elisha, and although no two men could be more different in temperament and nature, a strong bond of friendship existed between them.

But Elisha's boon companion was Nick Stone. Nick was eighteen years Elisha's junior, but they had taken an instant liking to one another the first time they met.

At the time, Nick had been living with an Indian squaw in the same locale in which Logan chose to settle. After several cups of rum had passed between them, Nick invited his new friend to move in with him. Elisha readily agreed, at least until he could build himself a cabin when the weather permitted.

Elisha brought along with him a young girl, Ruby Sieg. Ruby's husband had been one of the first left behind in a cold and lonely grave along the trail. Elisha had liked her comely face and soft shapely body, and within a week of her husband's death had had her sharing his blankets.

In the spring, when the weather had warmed,

Elisha, with Nick's help, erected himself a strong sturdy cabin. And Nick, tiring of his squaw, moved in with Elisha and Ruby.

After awhile, Elisha tired of Ruby somewhat and began to think of newer pastures. Eventually, he built her a place of her own a few miles away. And though he took many women throughout the years, he always visited her once a week. He told himself that he was duty-bound to see if she were well and had provisions. But in truth, he derived something from Ruby's presence that was missing in the loose women he associated with. He was a long time learning that it was love he felt in the little cabin.

For many years the inhabitants of Devil's Ridge saw some hell-raising escapades from the two burly mountain men. Indifferent to anyone's opinion, they rode the hills striking terror into the hearts of the timid and the law-abiding citizens. The decent women of the settlement never went far unless accompanied by a male relative. Needless to say, they guarded their single daughters jealously.

The people had lived and prospered in the hills for twenty years, raising their crops and tending their animals. Elisha was fifty-eight now, but looked forty-eight and was hearty and robust. And although he still wanted a woman regularly, the years had calmed him down and he was content now to visit only Ruby.

But Nick was only forty and still full of sap, and the hill women continued to keep a wary eye on him. The squaws were mostly gone now, and his source of pleasure greatly reduced. He complained often to Elisha that he sometimes had to ride several miles to find a willing partner.

Silas Warden looked his seventy-two years, but carried his big frame with dignity. His eyes were still a keen blue, showing a deep honesty of soul. His long white hair and moustache were always a welcome sight to his friends and neighbors.

He and his grandson, Adam, lived alone in the foothills. Silas had raised Adam, a bitter and unfriendly child, from the age of ten. The father, Silas's son, had been killed in a hunting accident when Adam was eight. Two years later, his mother deserted him, running away with a peddler traveling through the hills.

Silas had worked a long time at winning the boy's trust, and longer yet at winning his friendship and love. Sharing a liking for hunting and fishing had gone a long way in the final cementing of the lasting relationship that now existed between them.

Adam resembled his grandfather, their features and build the same, the eyes the same blue. But Adam's eyes were flinty and cold in expression, lending a look that was almost evil to the leathery face with the scar that ran from cheekbone to chin. He was dark of skin, whether by nature or weather, and his blond, shoulder-length hair was startling against it.

At thirty, he was a loner, wiley as a wolf, and a rakehell, or so said the hill people. Men feared him, even as they respected him, and women loved him, even as they feared him. But only he could handle the group of long-hunters that he headed.

Silas loved his grandson with a proud passion and had suffered deeply when in 1775 Adam joined the war. Adam had gone to Lexington, Massachusetts, and along with some other men of the settlement, fought the German mercenaries.

Finally, in 1779, Cornwallis surrendered to Washington and Adam returned home to a grateful Silas.

Nick Stone and Elisha's grandsons returned home also, but the boy's father was left behind in a nameless grave.

The hills and its people slipped back into the old routines, silently missing the ones who would not return. And the two men who returned not quite right in the head were accepted and cared for by the people of the hills.

One early spring morning, Elisha and Nick rode their horses down a narrow mountain trail. They were going to the grinding mill and Elisha balanced a bag of corn in front of his saddle.

Elisha was in a fine frame of mind, having just spent two days and nights with Ruby. But Nick was grumpy and complaining. Once when Elisha looked back and caught him rubbing his groin, he grinned and deliberately began singing an off-key ditty. As he had expected, Nick swore angrily.

"Hush up, 'Lisha. You don't have to rub it in."

Elisha's voice was all innocence when he asked, "Why, Nick, what are you trying to tell me?"

"You damned old reprobate, you know damn well what."

Nick swore at the horse for scraping his knee against a tree, then mumbled, half to himself, "I'm gonna have to go to Kate's, I reckon."

Elisha grinned sympathetically. "It's a sorry day when Nick Stone has to pay for his pleasurin'," he teased.

Nick grunted and Elisha added, "I think it's time you pick yourself a woman and just visit her. Whenever you get an itch, you'll be sure of finding a place to get it scratched."

Nick shook his head. "That's not for me yet. I still like variety."

They traveled in silence for the rest of the trip. When they entered the settlement, Nick turned his horse toward Kate's. Elisha called after him, "When you've finished, stop at the post and see if there's any mail."

Nick looked over his shoulder and grinned. "Who'd write to you, you old tomcat?"

"Nobody. Might be a paper from Jamestown, though."

They met a couple hours later, and on the trip home both men sang. Nick had paid for two women, but thought it well worth the cost.

It wasn't until they sat at the supper table that Nick remembered the letter in his coat pocket. Rising, he said, "I forgot to tell you, 'Lisha, I got a letter for you. Comes from Jamestown."

"Damn it to hell, Nick. How could you forget something that important?" Elisha demanded. "I ain't had but two letters in the past twenty years."

Nick laughed good-naturedly and held the letter to him. But Elisha did not take it at once. He had a premonition about it. He always received bad news in letters.

Nick jiggled the letter toward him. "After all that carrying on, ain't you gonna read it?"

Elisha gave a resigned sigh and took the wrinkled and soiled envelope. With stiff, nervous fingers he fumbled, tore it open and pulled out the single sheet of paper.

April 14, 1782

Dear Grandpa,

I know you will be surprised to hear from me after all these years. Papa has passed away, and his last wish was for me to make my home with you.

I am closing the house now and preparing for my journey. I don't know exactly when I'll arrive, so look for me when I get there.

Your dutiful granddaughter,
Rachael Jobe

For long moments, Elisha stared blankly into the flames of the flickering candle. Remorse that he hadn't been closer to his son flooded over him. Ben had been a big disappointment to him, and he had rejected the young lad who hadn't been of his own nature. When he had finally realized and accepted that Ben had inherited his mother's sensitive ways, the young man had already taken to the bottle and it was too late to help him.

Nick grew uneasy at his silence. "What is it, 'Lisha? Bad news?"

Elisha nodded and passed him the letter. Nick read it and handed it back. "I'm sorry as hell, 'Lisha."

Elisha nodded his thanks and wondered aloud how Ben had died.

"My granddaughter didn't waste any words."

After several moments of silence, Nick asked, "How old is your granddaughter, 'Lisha?"

Elisha took some time, mentally calculating the years. "I remember getting the letter from Ben when she was born. I think it was in sixty-five, so if my figurin' is right, she's seventeen, or thereabout."

Nick frowned. He hadn't known she was that old. Seventeen was a woman grown. He cleared his throat awkwardly.

"You think it's gonna work out? Havin' a female under our feet, I mean?"

Elisha picked up his cup of coffee and drained it. That disturbing thought had entered his mind too. He looked around at their messy bachelor quarters and mused aloud, "I wonder what she'll think of this boar's nest?"

Nick methodically packed tobacco into his pipe. He was unhappy about this young woman invading their privacy, yet he was reluctant to say so to Elisha. One was never quite sure how the old wolf would take some things. He puffed awhile, then ventured, "Maybe she should live with your daughter, Sarah."

Elisha's head snapped up and his answer was reproachful.

"She can't go there, Nick. You know that Sarah practically runs a whorehouse. You can't put a young, innocent girl in amongst a bunch of men comin' and goin' all the time."

Nick grunted, grudgingly convinced. "I guess you're right."

The fire crackled and a soft spatter of rain hit the window. Nick walked to the fireplace, spat into it and then said thoughtfully, "Maybe I ought to move out, 'Lisha."

Elisha shouted his reply. "No, by God. You ain't movin' nowhere. This is your home. Me and you ain't gonna change our ways nohow. Rachael will have to change if she don't like the way we live."

"Well, maybe," Nick answered doubtfully.

Long after Nick had gone to bed, Elisha sat in

front of the fire, thinking about his granddaughter.
He wondered how she had fared all these years. He
recalled his bitter disappointment when Ben's letter
announced that his grandchild was a girl. He had
remarked glumly to Sarah, "It don't look like Ben is
gonna keep the Jobe name alive. From the sound of
his letter, I doubt if Alice will bear any more babies."

He had put the matter from his mind, and now,
years later, a letter comes from that same baby.

He gave a start, came out of his reverie and
realized that the room had grown cold. He gave a
wry grin. Nick would be madder than hell tomorrow
morning when he had to waste gunpowder to start a
new fire.

He stood and stretched his wide frame and wished
that Ruby was there to warm his bed.

CHAPTER 3

Intermittently during the night, discreet knocks sounded at Rachael's door. But Beaulah successfully turned them away with a curt "Miss Rachael has gone away."

Rachael spent part of the evening going through her parents' personal effects. There was nothing of any material value.

However, in a corner of her mother's hose drawer, she found a packet of love letters, written by her father. She untied the yellowed ribbon that bound them and began to read. But midway through the first page, she stopped and laid them aside. The tender words of love had been meant for Alice's eyes alone. A glimmer of tears filled her eyes and she became more determined to find such a love for herself.

Later, lying in bed, it occurred to Rachael that she had no idea where Devil's Ridge was, and she pondered the question of how she was to find it. Before she fell asleep, she came to the conclusion that she would have to hire a guide.

The next morning, while Rachael worked steadily at packing and discarding, Beaulah walked around town trying to find someone who would act as a guide for Rachael.

As Rachael rolled the expensive perfumes and powders in her silken underwear and packed her fancy dresses, she wondered if they would be wasted on the backwoods hillmen. Certainly they would be out of place there. As for her money, would she really need it?

After much searching and inquiry, Beaulah found a husband and wife who were going in Rachael's general direction. They had, the man informed her, bought a farm several miles beyond Devil's Ridge, and for a fee would take Rachael with them.

Beaulah introduced the stern-looking couple to Rachael, and after haggling a bit over their price, an agreement was reached.

The next morning, after a tearful good-bye with Beaulah, Rachael and the pair set out.

The man chose the river trail, his boots squashing through the heavy clay of early spring. On either side of the wagon road, the grass was bent and brown and flattened by the winter storms. But deep down, at the base of the old grass, Rachael could see the promise of full spring in the tiny green shoots pushing up. A smile of anticipation of what was to come wreathed her lips.

They did not make the trip in short easy stages as Rachael would have liked, but pushed on as fast as the lumbering oxen could go.

Actually, it wasn't that fast at the beginning. As the day advanced and the sun became hotter, the frost line melted and the overladen cart sank deeper into the mire. Many times the man and his wife waded in mud past their ankles to help the oxen roll the vehicle out of a deep rut.

Fortunately, Rachael's mare and pack mule were able to walk alongside the road where the ground was quite solid.

At noon, they stopped beside a spring and the wife

hurriedly set out a few slices of cold beef and corn pone. Rachael tried to strike up a conversation with the taciturn pair, but when they only answered her in grunted monosyllables, she gave up the effort.

When they resumed the journey, the rutted road veered off through the woods, and the ground was firm with the leaves and needles of a hundred years. Cracking his whip, the man urged the animals on, anxious to make up the lost time.

It was almost pitch black when at last they halted for the night. Rachael was one big ache from the hours spent in the saddle, and she stumbled when she climbed down from the mare. Her arms felt dislocated from pulling the lead rope of the pack mule, and as she rubbed away at the soreness, she caught the sly grin that flitted across the woman's gaunt face.

When at last the woman had a fire going, Rachael pulled a blanket from her pack and spread it near the leaping flames. Stretching her weary body upon it, she thought, "What a dismal camp."

She stared up through the trees at the sky. A million stars were glittering, remote and cold, just like her companions. Then, to make matters worse, the rank odor of a skunk drifted into camp.

She turned on her side and watched the thin, angular woman bustling around the fire, preparing a meager supper. She was about to offer her help, then thought better of it. The woman appeared to be in a bad mood and kept throwing suspicious glances her husband's way. Rachael glanced at the man and found him staring openly at her. Then, startled, she noticed the bulge in his rough homespuns. Since he made no effort to hide it, she supposed that his wife saw it also. Quickly she turned her back to him.

When the meal was spread on the blanket, the wife muttered some word, and they gathered around the poorly prepared meal. And as the man wolfed his salt pork and beans, his eyes constantly roamed to Rachael's breasts. The wife grew angry and Rachael became uneasy.

Gulping down his second cup of coffee, the man turned and growled to his wife, "You got the bed ready?"

She gave a quick nod and glanced triumphantly at Rachael as she scrambled after her husband. He waited impatiently for her to lie down and hike her skirt up around her waist, and then, in full view of the campfire's flame, he mounted his unattractive wife. Embarrassed, Rachael looked away but not before she caught the significant leer he shot her way.

Later, when the wife crawled out from under him and began to tidy the camp, Rachael, rolled in her blankets, feigned sleep.

That night's action set the pattern for the rest of the trip. It never varied, only the scenery was different. But on their third night out, Rachael was beginning to get threatening looks from the wife. The husband was becoming more flagrant in his attention, and had of late taken to sitting next to her while they ate.

One night when the wife mumbled some word to him, he slapped her across the face, sending her tumbling backwards. When he turned back, Rachael noticed for the first time that the front of his trousers were open with a good part of hardness sticking out. And though it had disgusted her, still her eyes had flickered, and the man had seen and had smiled knowingly.

The following night began like all the others. But as the woman cooked and tended to camp chores, she became increasingly rude to Rachael. And when they were called to supper, there was no food prepared for her. She became angry and felt the color rushing to her cheeks. She had done nothing to encourage the revolting man, and the wife had no reason to treat her in this manner.

She turned to the husband and flared out at him. "Listen, mister, I paid good money for these miserable meals your wife has been serving, hadn't you better tell the bitch to fix me something to eat?"

He looked up at her sharply, then glowered at his wife, his brows knitted irritably. She fidgeted with a piece of bread and refused to meet his eyes. Silently, he reached across and took her plate of food from her lap and thrust it into Rachael's hands.

As she grasped the plate firmly and stared down at the piled beans in surprise, the enraged wife let out a squeal and lunged for her. She fastened her bony fingers in Rachael's hair and pulled her over backwards, screaming accusations at her.

For awhile, the husband watched the scratching, pummeling pair with amusement; then tiring of it, he grasped his wife by the hair, drew back his fist and clipped her on the chin. She gave a deep sigh and went limp.

Sprawled on the ground, Rachael stared in disbelief. He had knocked his wife unconscious. She opened her mouth to object and the words died on her lips. Slowly her eyes went wide in comprehension as she watched him unfasten his homespuns and drop them to the ground.

The next morning, Rachael scrubbed herself furiously at a nearby creek, muttering through chattering teeth, "The stinking bastard."

After a scanty breakfast with no talk between them, but many murderous glances sent Rachael's way, they broke camp and left on the last leg of the journey.

In the early afternoon, the man halted the oxen at the edge of the forest. To the north, a winding river reflected the glimmer of the sun, and along its banks several buildings dotted the area. Without interest, Rachael wondered who lived there.

She turned and looked from the husband to the wife where they stood uneasily shifting their feet about.

"What's come over them now?" she mused. "Afraid that I'll tell grandpa about his attack," she concluded.

The man cleared his throat a couple of times then spoke gruffly. "Why don't you get down and stretch your legs a bit?"

She sighed. That meant there was still a way to go. Climbing stiffly from the saddle, the thought occurred to her that it was out of keeping with the man's nature to be so considerate.

She walked some distance away from them, and in a spot of sunshine she spied a clump of purple violets. They were such a lively spot of color after the long drab months of winter, she hurried to pick them. She became so engrossed in pinching the slender stems and building them into a small bouquet, that she hardly heard the creaking of the cart.

Whirling around, she saw the oxen, followed by the man and woman, moving off through the forest. Jumping to her feet, she ran after them, yelling,

"Hey, you, where in the hell do you think you're going?"

The man looked over his shoulder and called back to her, "That's Devil's Ridge over there, miss. We got to get on."

She stared after them, unable to believe her eyes and ears. Then shrill and angry her voice went ringing after them.

"You rotten son-of-a-bitch, our deal was that you'd take me to my grandfather's door."

The woman looked back with a malicious smirk on her face. "Just spread your legs for the first man you meet and he'll take you there," she sneered.

For one wild moment, Rachael wanted to jump on the mare's back and race after them. To catch them and beat their hateful faces into a pulp. But that was foolish thinking, she knew. A fat chance she'd have of striking and hurting the burly farmer.

She leaned against Ginger's warm side, choking back the angry tears and pondering her next move. She couldn't believe that those few buildings she was staring at were really the settlement of Devil's Ridge. Straining her eyes, she studied the buildings more closely.

Besides the three important buildings that every settlement had, a church, tavern and post, there were a few others scattered about. She made out a mill straddling a fast-running stream, and from a low, open building the clang of iron on metal denoted a blacksmith. There was a building back of the tavern, but it was too far away to discern what it was.

Her eyes studied the people gathered in small knots or walking about, and she wondered hopefully if any of them knew Elisha Jobe. Taking a deep breath, she swung into the saddle and urged the mare forward.

The sun had become quite warm, but when she entered the settlement and met the suspicious and wary eyes of the hill people, she shivered. Their open hostility jabbed at her like knives and even the mare became uneasy and snorted nervously. She had not anticipated unfriendliness, and the thought came to her that this was probably the reason for her guide's hurried departure.

Guiding the mare along the wide beaten path that wound around fallen logs and tree stumps, and leading the mule, she approached a group of women. She was about to inquire if they knew Elisha Jobe when she caught the old familiar condescending looks of contempt on their faces. She smiled grimly. She had borne such looks for three years and they no longer bothered her. Beaulah had pointed out to her, "They just jealous and envious of you, child. Pay them no never mind."

Tilting her head proudly, she gave them a cool, sweeping glance and rode past. Her fast glance showed most of the women thin and stooped, with drawn faces.

"Overwork and childbearing," she said to herself. "And if I know the look, a regular demand from their husbands."

In front of the tavern, several men milled about and she halted the mare before them. They ceased their talk and let bold eyes ogle her face and body. Irritated at their rudeness, she lifted her chin and stared back at them coolly.

Mainly, they were older men, lean and bearded. Most chewed tobacco, the brown juice slobbering down their chins and onto their shirts. Disgusted by the sight, she thought how sickening it must be for the women who shared their beds. Masking her look of distaste, she broke the silence.

"Can one of you men direct me to Elisha Jobe's place?"

Knowing grins spread across their faces, and behind her she heard the women titter. Then suddenly, one of the younger men was standing at the mare's head. He was unbelievably dirty, and the stench of his unwashed body reached her all the way to the saddle. She stared down into his narrow, mean-looking face and saw a low intelligence in the pale blue eyes.

Insolently he stared back at her as he opened his tight slit of a mouth and asked in a nasal drawl, "You mean, 'Lisha Jobe, the whoremaster?"

She hid the surprise that swept over her, and while the women in the background giggled, she studied him impassively for several moments. Then with a withering look that silenced the snickering, she snapped, "That's the one."

Encouraged by her deceptive calmness, the simpleminded one became bolder and laid a grimy hand upon her knee. Startled, she looked quickly at him and black anger jabbed at her. Why were these hill people being so downright insulting?

The man's next words explained. Pressing her knee familiarly, he whined, "What do you want with 'Lisha? He's a old man . . . couldn't please a purty thing like you." His hand tightened and he urged, "You stay here with me. I got somethin' you'll like."

Rachael was becoming alarmed now and her fast glance probed the surly visages surrounding her.

There wasn't a sympathetic face in the group. If this crazy man should pull her out of the saddle and rape her on the spot, not a hand would be lifted in her defense.

For a frightening moment, she debated trying to flee the hostile village. But realizing that she didn't even know in what direction to run, she gave up the idea. Somehow she must learn where her grandfather lived.

The grubby fingers were tugging at her again. "Well, play toy, what about it? You gonna stay here with me?"

Her mind raced frantically with ways to escape. But her common sense told her it was useless. There was only one slim chance left. She would swallow her pride and tell them who she was. Even though they seemed to think poorly of Elisha Jobe, maybe they wouldn't harm his granddaughter.

Forcing back her fear, she met her tormentor's eyes steadily and retorted coolly, "You'll have to ask Elisha about that. You see, I'm his granddaughter and I do his bidding."

Blank astonishment filled their faces, and like lightning their manner changed. The grasping hand was jerked away as though her leg was afire.

Seeing the fear in their eyes, Rachael was glad. She had had nothing but insults heaped upon her head since leaving Jamestown. It was high time she got in some licks of her own.

It was a new people who pressed forward now, each trying to talk over his neighbor in giving her directions. The older women were suddenly friendly, spreading their thin lips in toothless smiles. The young ones, however, still held back, sending her dark, glowering looks. Rachael would be hard competition for them and they hated her for it.

Rachael sensed what they were thinking and thought inwardly, "If these men are all the hills have to offer, they needn't worry themselves about me."

Finally out of the hubbub of voices, directions were straightened out and she thanked them and prepared to leave. But as she turned the mare in the pointed way, one of the men laid a restraining hand on the bridle.

"Look, miss, we didn't mean no harm afore. Jake, here, he's kinda loose in the head . . . got shot in the war. We'd appreciate it kindly iffen you didn't mention none of this to 'Lisha."

"Like hell you didn't mean it," Rachael thought hotly. "Only your fear of grandpa stopped you."

While she studied him doubtfully, a woman, bent with age and rheumatism, added her bit.

" 'Lisha Jobe is a real cat-o-mount when he's riled up, miss. For sure this is gonna rile him aplenty. Ain't none of these men here want 'Lisha after them with his fowlin' piece."

"Nor his friend, Nick Stone," another added.

There was no doubt in Rachael's mind that the hill people feared her grandfather and his friend, but it was hard for her to believe that they would go after their neighbors with a gun.

"Do you really think that he'd shoot you?"

"He'd try," came the unanimous answer.

The old woman, her voice shrill and reedy, added, "That ornery 'Lisha, he's got a powerful temper. When it's up, he don't give two whoops in a whirlwind who he's shootin' at."

"His friend is worse than him," someone remarked.

Although she still had her doubts about the hillmen being shot, she smiled down at the hillmen and said, "There was no harm done, I guess, even though I still think you meant to. But most likely I could have handled old Jake, here. One good kick in the right place would have stopped him permanently."

Amid the relieved laughter Jake's face flushed and he gave her a dark look.

She lifted her hand in farewell and started the mare up the needle-strewn trail, the excited jabbering of the settlers floating after her. But soon she was out of hearing range and their voices were only a muted sound.

The winding trail, sometimes only a narrow path, was a thing of beauty. Spring's first new leaves on the oak and maple were startling against the dark green of the fir. She breathed deeply of the clean pure air and compared it to the reeking stench of the litter-filled streets of Jamestown.

The mare took the upward swing of the hills easily, as did the pack mule, their powerful and dainty feet nimbly avoiding the rocks and holes. Rachael looked up at the sky and noted that the sun was well in its westward swing and frowned. She hoped to reach her destination before dark. Someone had said it was around five miles to the Jobe place. She wondered how far she had already traveled.

A small lunge of the mare brought them on top of a hill, and a cleared level spot of an acre or so lay stretched before her. She drew rein at the edge of the forest and stared about at the little-known wilderness. The limitless silence that pressed in around her caused her breath to catch in her throat.

She noticed that the air was thinner and cooler up

here, and carried the scent of cedar and fresh earth. She shivered a bit, and debated donning the coat tied behind the saddle.

Then a crackling in the underbrush drove the thought from her mind. Her eyes moved swiftly to the sound as the mare, with a nervous quiver, moved back against the mule.

Fighting the reins, Rachael did not immediately see Jake step out onto the trail, and gasped in sudden fear when he grabbed Ginger's bit. Her voice trembled a bit when she demanded sharply, "What in the hell are you trying to do, Jake, scare me to death?"

His wide mouth twisted into an ugly grin and he snickered, "Hell no, purty play toy, I don't want you dead. I want you alive and kickin' when I get atween them purty legs."

Disgust mixed with Rachael's fear. This dirty bewhiskered thing still meant to rape her. She shuddered. She would rather die than have anything to do with him. Watching him out of wary eyes, she wondered why he wasn't afraid of Elisha like the others were. Then she remembered his head wound and imagined that his mind wasn't capable of working beyond the present moment. Later, he might think of Elisha Jobe and his fury, but right now he thought only of his hunger.

Her mind raced with ways to elude him. The awkward position of the sidesaddle hampered any sudden move on her part, and she silently cursed the society that frowned on the female straddling a horse. Grimly she promised herself that never again would she ride such a contraption.

In the meantime, Jake had jerked the mare's head

cruelly, causing her eyes to roll in terror as she reared and swiveled about.

Rachael leaned forward to grab the reins from him, and at that moment, his free hand shot forward. His fingers grasping the front of her dress, she was jerked unceremoniously to the ground. The animals skittered away and Rachael lay huddled where she had fallen.

Stunned and frightened, she stared up at him as he came and stood over her. His eyes fastened on her revealed breasts and she read his intent in his eyes. She commenced to struggle to her feet, but fast as a striking snake, he was upon her, forcing her back, pinning her shoulders to the ground.

His hand moved downward and she suffered his scaly touch upon her breast, silently praying that she would faint before he went further. But she was very much aware when his tobacco-stained lips came toward her. Closing her eyes tightly, she began to struggle fiercely, and with her last strength, pushed him away.

But her struggling only seemed to incense and make him more determined. Again his hands came upon her and she felt his nails bite deep into her flesh. In desperation, she began to thresh about, her frightened strength almost equaling his. And muttering his annoyance, Jake threw his body against hers, leaving her immobile. As his face lowered to her throat, she groaned in her helplessness.

But as his rough beard barely brushed her skin, a brown and sinewy hand came from nowhere and clamped on Jake's shoulder. Slowly, as if he were nothing, he was lifted from her.

An expression of dumb bewilderment flooded

Jake's face, but when he saw who handled him so easily, fear took its place. He began to back away from the menacing figure as it stalked after him. He held out a restraining hand and whined, "Now, Adam, don't go gettin' mad. I wasn't...."

A rock-hard fist hit him square in the mouth, and blood sprayed the air. Slowly his body folded, and he drifted to the ground.

Bewildered by the events that were happening so fast, Rachael stared at the tall giant who stood looking down at Jake. The buckskin shirt was unlaced at the neck, and the brown column of his throat hinted at the muscular strength the rest of his body held. An old, jagged scar ran down one cheek, and tiny crowfeet lines ran out from the corner of his eyes. Those eyes were hard and cold, and suddenly they were studying her in much the same manner that Jake had.

She squirmed uncomfortably under the raw hunger thrusting out at her, and finally had to close her eyes against it. When moments of quiet had passed, she opened them to find him squatting beside her. Startled, she gathered the edges of the torn dress together and started to climb to her feet. But he pushed her back and rasped out, "Lie still and keep your hands off that dress."

A stubborn defiance came over her at the crisp crackle of his command and her fingers tightened on the material as she glared at him.

Blazing green eyes burned into steely blue ones, and time was motionless as their gaze clung.

She lay perfectly still as his hand reached and released her fingers. Slowly he pulled apart her bodice, and for a moment a look of wonder overshadowed the cold of his eyes. His hand moved caressingly over her throat and breasts, and against her will she responded to his touch. She wanted this man with an intensity that frightened her.

Then abruptly, he was sitting back on his heels and asking bluntly, "Whose woman are you?"

She sat up, again pulled the torn seams together, and straightened her skirt before answering. Then, sharply, "I am nobody's woman."

He studied her a moment then grunted suspiciously, "What are you doin' up here in the hills ... a woman alone?"

Forgetting her unhappy experience in the village, she answered readily.

"I'm on my way to Elisha Jobe's place. I'll be making my home there."

Too late she remembered as she caught the quick, contemptuous look he darted at her. Anger mixed with disappointment built within her. He was like the others, jumping to the same conclusions. Well, let him, she thought angrily. There was no power on earth that would make her explain to him.

But his scornful laugh stung her like a whiplash and she clenched her hands into fists when he sneered, "It must have cost the old man a pretty penny to get you."

She didn't bother to answer him, but inside, she cried out, "Why does he have to be like the rest of these narrow-minded hill people?"

When he made no other remark, but only stared at her, she rose to her feet and untied her coat from the saddle. Shrugging into it, she buttoned it up to hide her torn dress. She grabbed up Ginger's trailing reins and climbed into the saddle. Then picking up the lead rope of the mule, without a word, she started out across the darkening field.

A dull emptiness gripped her, and helpless tears swam in her eyes. She was getting a very bad start in her new life.

CHAPTER 4

With a curious reluctance, Adam watched Rachael ride away. Puzzled, he tried to analyze the new and strange emotions she had stirred in him. Her wild beauty had evoked a tenderness in him that he had never known before.

And too, why was he so keenly disappointed that she belonged to another man? Such a thing had never bothered him before.

Softly, he cursed her for awakening new feelings in him and wished that he had never laid eyes on her. In a few short minutes, she had broken down his defense and he had wanted her in a way he had never taken a woman. Even now as he thought of her satin-smooth breasts, his breathing became heavy.

For an excited moment, he thought to ride after her; to jerk her from the saddle and make wild love to her. But angrily he pushed the thought away.

"It would please the little whore too much to have me chasin' after her like a hound after a bitch," he muttered darkly.

But the picture of raunchy old Jobe taking her yielding body into his arms flashed before him, and his flesh chilled as though a north wind had swept down from the mountains.

He sat on the ground and filled his pipe. As the smoke drifted up in thin spirals, he watched them and wondered gloomily why it couldn't have been he who had discovered her. Why did it have to be 'Lisha Jobe? That whorin' old bastard had had more women than a man could count. And what about Nick Stone? Would he also use her?

His thoughts became too vivid and he shook his head to clear them away. It was foolish of him to waste time thinking about a fancy whore. The women at camp satisfied him fine. He didn't have to think about them and get upset. Whenever he whistled, there was always one ready and eager to go down on her knees for him.

Jake was coming to. He moaned and broke into Adam's reverie. As he felt his mouth and grimaced at loosened teeth, Adam walked over to him and kicked him sharply in the side.

"You, son-of-a-bitch, what did I tell you about botherin' women? Didn't I tell you to use the camp sluts and the whores in the village?"

Nodding dumbly, Jake cringed away. Adam shook his head and turned away. "You stupid bastard, you're gonna get shot one of these days."

Adam swung into the saddle. He had a long way to travel yet.

Jake leaned on an elbow and glowered after him. "I'll get you, Adam Warden," he whispered.

Adam urged the horse on to a faster pace in the fading dusk. The mountain air was cold and the wind was going right through him. He wondered if *she* was cold, then swore angrily because he cared.

The stallion climbed always upward, and he snorted his displeasure at the darkened trail. Adam was equally unhappy because he was late. This would not set a good example for the wild bunch he controlled.

His men were long-hunters. Loud and rowdy, large on courage and small on manners. Mostly they were rejects from the surrounding towns and settlements. They were men who could not conform to society's idea of good behavior and had been, more or less, banished to the hills.

They had come together at the end of the war, and Adam had been elected as their leader. The combined efforts of their hunting and trapping experiences had provided them with a good living. And too, away in the wilderness with no eye to censure their actions, they could do as they pleased. That is to say, if it also pleased Adam Warden.

Adam was strong in his rules, and the man who didn't abide by them was soon ordered off the hill. The same principle went for the women. Their rules were hard and fast, with no exceptions. They were expected to do camp chores and be ready to lie down whenever some man desired them to. There, the slatternly, unloved women were used in a harsh and degrading manner.

And though their lives were hard in the permanent quarters, their suffering was even greater when the men went on the long hunt in the winter. The hunt usually lasted for several months, and in time, they became like the animals they hunted. It was the helpless women who bore the brunt of their rages and lusts.

But cruel treatment wasn't the only worry the camp women had to contend with. There was always the nagging fear of becoming ill on the hunt. There would be no turning back for them. No man in camp would waste his time taking a sick whore back to quarters. She either recovered, or died, with no one caring either way.

Many factors were involved in the length of a hunt. It depended on how plentiful the game was, the health of the hunter, and how well the men got on with one another.

Many times a hunt was cut short because of dissenting members. Mostly they fought over cards and whiskey, but occasionally there would be a vicious battle over some particular woman . . . a new one to the group, usually.

Adam tried to screen the new men and women who showed each spring, but once in awhile an ill-tempered or maladjusted one slipped through. These people would show fine in the easy, careless life of summer camp, but the proving of their worth and grit in a howling mountain winter was another story. The misfits soon learned that the mountains were a jealous and particular mistress. She would have only the bravest and strongest clasped to her breast, and would reject the weaklings in a harsh and unmerciful manner. The many who could not stand up to her rigors turned into blustering and argumentative people to cover their weakness.

But Adam felt that he had a good bunch this year. Besides the old bunch who had been tested and proven true, there were a number of new people, young and full of fire. He didn't believe there was a quitter among them.

He sighed and longed for summer to arrive and pass, and the chill of autumn to return. In the past hour he had decided that the next hunt would be a long one. Long enough, hopefully, to erase from his mind a small face with green, catlike eyes.

The stallion trotted into a clearing, and before him his people were gathered around a blazing campfire. He halted the horse and for a moment watched their silhouetted figures.

"Poor, rag-tail misfits," he muttered.

Unbidden came remembered words of his grandfather, Silas. "I wish you'd give up that wild bunch, Adam. You'll never live to be an old man, carousing with them."

He sighed deeply. No one knew better than he that his way of life was taking him nowhere fast. But to save his soul, he could think of no other way. The permanence and confinement of working a farm by day and sitting idly by the hearth at night was not his way.

He regretted deeply though that the fine old man was unhappy with him. He bore a great love and respect for the grandfather who had raised and taught him, and for a time dwelled with affection on the good times they had shared.

The hoot of an owl deep within the forest, a mournful sound in the hills, startled him. Coming back to the present, he settled his features into their usual grim mold, and spoke quietly to the horse.

The half-wild dogs that were so important to the hunter were the first to hear his approach. They came barking and snarling, their ruffs standing high. They were a treacherous bunch of mongrels and he hoped they would get his scent before sinking their teeth into him.

The hunters caught sight of him and followed the dogs, swearing and kicking out at them. Their greeting was boisterous as they gathered around him, and from the thickness of their speech, he knew they had been drinking freely of the corn whiskey that was always on hand.

Irritated about it somehow, he evaluated them with stern, probing eyes. A brief movement of disgust ran through him. Dirty and unshaven, they presented a front that made him ashamed for them. And the women, the joy of living wrung out of them, were worse.

He shook his head. What was to become of them? "What will the men do when they become too old to hunt the hills?" he wondered to himself. "And the women. What will they do when they can no longer lie down and spread their legs?"

Each and every one was an outcast with neither home nor acknowledged relative. "But hell," he thought, "why am I worrying? The majority of them will die young. Either raw whiskey, or a knife in some drunken brawl, will get them."

A small voice in the back of his mind whispered, "What about you? Don't you drink just as freely and fight just as hard?"

Reluctantly, he admitted that it was true. Only his respect for Silas kept him a little above his companions. When the old man was gone, might not he become as they?

His soul-searching left him in a state of angry hopelessness, and when one of the women staggered up and offered him a cup of clear liquid, his contemptuous eyes stopped her short.

The woman was short and thickset, and wore a coarse dress of homespun that hung past her knees. She was barefoot and her big toes splayed out in the earth. She smiled timidly at him and her widened lips revealed her two front teeth missing.

Unconsciously, Adam compared a slender body with firm jutting breasts to the squat, lumpy one standing before him. In his mind he saw a pair of small shapely feet, encased in dainty black slippers. And when the odor of the camp woman reached him, he recalled the faint perfume of Elisha's woman.

A repugnance for the creature with the cup in her hand swept over him, and he snarled, "Get the hell away from me, slut."

The smile still trembled on the woman's lips, but his brutal words caused tears to stand in her eyes.

Climbing down stiffly, Adam tossed the reins to the nearest man and strode purposefully to the whiskey keg. If he was to endure their company, he must become as roaring drunk as they.

The hunters followed him, all talking at once.

"What are furs bringin' this year, Adam? Better than last year?"

"Them was good pelts you brung to the post, ought to bring good money."

Adam siphoned a tin cup of liquor out of the keg before answering. Then, "I done real good, men. Top price this year."

His announcement was greeted with great whoops and much slapping of one another's backs. Excited, they followed Adam back to the fire, and squatting on a blanket, watched eagerly as he opened his saddlebag and brought out the money.

Each man had kept a list of the pelts he had trapped and hunted and was paid accordingly. When everyone had his pile in front of him, John, Adam's right-hand man, spoke up.

"Where's your pile, Adam?"

"Gone," Adam answered complacently.

"But how?"

"Whores and whiskey," he answered. Then added laconically, "Also a crooked dealer at a poker table."

"Lord, Adam, you don't mean you lost."

"Yep. Every damn cent."

John shook his head. "Six months trappin' lost in two days."

He waited until Adam brought the tin cup from his mouth, then asked, "What did you do to the dealer?"

"Him? He's six feet under by now."

As he walked away from them, the men started a poker game, quickly dealing the dog-eared cards. Some of them would lose their money in less time than their boss had.

Adam awakened the next morning with a horrible taste in his mouth. A stinging fire burned in the back of his eyes, and his throat felt parched.

He lay still, willing the throbbing in his head to cease its beating. Then, ever so slowly, he leaned on an elbow and gradually opened his eyes. His glance swung around the room. In every available place, dirty quilts were strewn, with sleeping couples lying upon them.

His eyes fell on Jake, and he wondered when he had made it back to camp. He lay sprawled on his back with his mouth gaped open, snoring loudly. "What a picture," Adam grunted.

He lay back and his eyes fell on his own bed partner. He gazed at her in disgust. The same woman who had offered him the whiskey. He must have gotten pretty drunk last night. He brought up a moccasined foot and pushed her roughly off his blankets.

She slid across the floor and came to rest against a chair. When she whimpered and cringed away, his lips curled contemptuously.

He sat up and immediately felt nauseous. He had to get out of there. The dead and smelly air was choking him. Disregarding his pounding head, he climbed to his feet and threaded his way through the sleeping couples.

Outside, he paused and breathed deeply of the aromatic air, trying to rid his nostrils of the stink that clung to them. Suddenly he felt unclean and made his way to a nearby creek, shedding his clothes as he walked. Wading into the deepest part, he scooped up the fine sand on the bottom and scrubbed his body furiously.

Tingling all over, he hurried, shivering, to his own cabin and donned clean clothing. The icy water had cleared his brain and soothed his body, and suddenly, hunger gnawed at him.

Squatting beside the fireplace, he piled twigs and small pieces of wood together, then snapped his flint lighter under it. When the fire was going good, he piled on large chunks of wood and filled a blackened coffee pot with water and coffee grounds. While it brewed on the flames, he sliced bacon from a side of pork, and soon it was spattering in an iron skillet.

When he had eaten his fill and was enjoying a pipe with his second cup of coffee, his mind, like a magnet, turned to the raven-haired woman. Angrily, he tried to push aside the image of slanted eyes and ripe red lips, but they persisted and his breathing became fast and hard as he dwelled on the scene of yesterday.

For a moment he determined that he would go to

Elisha and take her away by force. But his common sense laughed at him. He would only get a bellyful of lead for his trouble. Elisha Jobe did not fool around when it came to keeping his own. Besides, Silas would be down on him for such an act toward his old friend.

He forced himself to think of other things, and eventually the dread of the long summer ahead came to nag at him. Before his eyes marched the long, dreary nights and days ahead. There would be nothing to break up their monotony. The men would drink, brawl and abuse the women, in that order.

He shook his head. It would be impossible for him to spend another summer in that fashion. He would do something foolish if he hung around the hills.

His mind traveled back through the wilderness, to the camp of an old Indian. To Bear One Claw, chief to a tribe of Cherokees.

He had met the proud old chief in '75, just before the war broke out. For four months he had been alone, hunting and fishing in the wilderness, and was beginning to feel the loneliness that comes from too much solitude. One morning, early, as he tracked a deer, he debated starting back to civilization.

The ground was lightly frozen and Adam had no trouble tracking the animal, and thinking on something else at the same time was easy. In a short time he came upon it, paused for a drink at a fast-running spring. Quickly he brought the rifle to his shoulder and took careful aim. There was a belch of smoke, and the deer flopped to the ground, its neck broken.

Jerking the knife from his belt, he moved forward to gut the deer. But midway he heard the cracking of a twig, and as he spun around with all his senses straining, he cursed himself for not reloading the rifle immediately. Only a greenhorn would have pulled such a dumb stunt.

A feeling of hopelessness enveloped him as a group of Indians materialized out of the forest and stalked toward him. The rising sun glistened on their bronzed bodies and sent sparkles of light off the tomahawks in their hands. He felt the hair on the back of his neck rise in anticipation of the fight that was sure to come.

But a few feet away, the Indians had stopped and the leader beckoned a finger to him. "Come."

It had been about two miles to the Indian camp, and as they walked, Adam listened intently to the braves' speech as they talked amongst themselves. At first he could not understand their guttural babble, but bit by bit, fragments of their conversation rang a bell in his mind.

Years ago, when he was a youngster, Silas had spent long winter evenings teaching him the Cherokee language.

"You never know when it might come in handy, knowing their lingo," he had explained.

By the time they arrived at camp, Adam was able to understand nearly all the braves said. And knowing this had gone a long way in saving his neck. The chief had been pleased at his ability and had questioned him quietly. When he was satisfied that Adam meant them no harm, he was welcomed into their camp and called brother.

Adam's strength and courage appealed to the red man, and Bear's wisdom and honesty had drawn Adam. A close friendship built between them, and

Adam had spent the rest of the summer and part of the winter in the Indian camp.

He remembered now that the chief had been most generous with his squaws, and recalled with a quickening of his loins their slender bodies and willing ways. If anyone could drive Elisha's woman from his mind, they could.

But discounting the women, the simple and easy life of the red man was what he most desired now. It would be good to once again sit at Bear's fire sharing a pipe, or to wrestle a Cherokee brave. And God knew his stomach could stand a rest from the rotgut corn whiskey.

His mind made up, he knocked out his pipe and got to his feet. Working swiftly, he packed his gear and provisions. When all was ready, he wrote a note to the hunters, not knowing or caring if any of them could read. Leaving the cabin, he pinned it to the door and locked it behind him.

He took a dim, seldom-used trail leading straight through the wilderness. After three or four miles, he came to a rushing, white-flecked river. This still unnamed stream would be his starting point. Somewhere alongside it, Bear would be camped.

Following its winding course, he kept his eyes open for shallow parts. In the bottom of the stream where it was cool and gravelly, speckled trout would be lying. And when the sun shone directly overhead and his stomach rumbled, he pulled a length of string from his pocket and entered the chilly water. Trolling as he waded, he soon had several pan-sized fish.

On the bank in full sun, he built a fire and fried them crisp on a flat river rock. His hunger sated, he filled his pipe and smoked contentedly. Then anxious to be on his way, he shouldered his rifle and gear and moved on.

His spirits had lifted and his blood moved faster. When a man walked the wilderness, he never knew what the next bend in the river might reveal. His buckskins were still wet to the knees, but he hardly felt them. He was in his special domain now, and no hardship was too great.

In the late afternoon, the sky became overcast and a slow drizzling rain commenced. Knowing there would be no shelter along the river's edge, he turned back into the forest. He walked steadily, his moccasined feet making no noise on the water-soaked leaves, the whispering rain in the treetops the only sound around.

An early night was coming on and he stepped up his pace. Just before darkness settled, he spied a cave and breathed a sigh of relief. He didn't relish the idea of sleeping in the rain.

The cave was not deep, but fairly large, and high enough for him to stand. He noted that it had been used before. The ceiling was black from many campfires. Along one wall was stacked a plentiful supply of wood, and he hurried to it. He would use what he needed and replace it tomorrow morning before leaving. That was a law of the wilderness. Leave things as you find them for the next traveler.

In a short time he had a crackling fire going, and its heat felt good against the dampness of the weather. From his gear he pulled out a coffee pot, blackened and dented. Tilting a leather pouch, he measured water into it and added coffee grounds. While it brewed, he squatted beside the fire and munched on jerked venison and parched corn.

By the time he had drunk the last of the coffee, it was totally dark outside, and the rain still fell. He piled more wood on the fire and sat staring into the flames. A pair of green eyes appeared there and smiled mockingly at him. This time he did not fight them, but gave his mind free rein. Released, it recalled to him every detail of her face and body. He saw the high thrust of her breasts and the firm swell of her hips, and the desire to make love to her swept over him. Impatiently he jumped to his feet and paced the floor.

As he walked back and forth, he held himself tight against the hunger that grew in him until his body was rocked with the pain of it. On his clenched fists his knuckles grew white, and he ground out harshly, "You damn fool, wasting your thoughts on a whore."

He squatted again beside the fire, determined to put her from his mind. The fire had died low and he reached for a stick of wood. Then his hand stopped and he was listening intently. A stirring, scratching sound broke the silence. Then a whippoorwill flew off through the woods, its melancholy cry trailing behind, and he gave an embarrassed grin.

"Scared by a bird, by God."

He relaxed and bent to relight his pipe, then stopped and sniffed the air. Wafting into the cave came a scent he knew well. Uneasily, he reached behind him for the rifle. But as his fingers groped at empty air, a huge shape bulked in the cave's entrance. Swearing in alarm, he leaped to his feet as a seven-foot grizzly roared and lumbered toward him.

His scalp tingled from his fear as his hand went automatically to the knife in his belt. Slowly and cautiously, he circled the fire. From the corner of his eye he could see the rifle propped in a corner, and he cursed his folly for not having had it next to him. What were his chances, he wondered, of getting it in his hands and firing before the animal had him in a bone-crushing hug.

When Adam was midway to the mouth of the cave, the bear stopped and stood with outstretched paws waving angrily at the intervening fire. Deep roars continued to issue from his throat and his tiny eyes gleamed red.

With only the flames separating them—a bare four feet—he felt his fear reaching all the way from his stomach. He warned himself sternly not to panic ... to think straight.

What was his best course? Reaching the rifle in time would be a doubtful accomplishment. But then, outrunning the animal was just as unsure. He had never heard of anybody doing this if the bear was determined to catch him.

But there was always the chance that the bear wouldn't follow him in the rain. Maybe all the old grizzly wanted was a dry place to sleep. He would take his chances on running, he decided. Perhaps luck would be with him.

Carefully, he took a tentative step forward. The bear remained where he was and hope built within Adam. Step by nervous step, he edged nearer the opening. A rush of cold, wet air brushed against his face and he grew weak in relief. One more step to freedom.

Taking a deep breath, he took that step and placed his foot in a hole. A look of defeat passed over his face as his ankle turned and he lay on the floor of the cave.

His last remembrance was bringing the broad hunting knife up to meet the charge of the bear, and then his head connected sharply with a hard object.

Painfully, Adam opened his eyes and stared into a dying fire. A burning pain gripped his shoulder, and his head throbbed with a hundred tiny drums. What had happened? Then, fuzzily, he remembered the four-inch claws racking him.

Fumbling, his hand moved toward his shoulder, then was stopped by a firm yet gentle hand. He turned his head slowly and gazed at a thin, gaunt figure squatting beside him. He recognized the shriveled, leathery face instantly, and whispered, "Bear One Claw?"

"Yes, young brave, it is me."

"Did I get him?"

"You got him. The knife went straight into his heart."

"Good."

He felt a long, bony hand laid upon his forehead and drifted into darkness again.

CHAPTER 5

With hot angry tears burning her cheeks, Rachael urged the mare on. She had given Ginger her head, letting her pick the way. It would be useless trying to guide her in this utter darkness. Behind her, she heard the mule's tiny hooves scattering the gravel as it followed closely behind.

She swiped at her wet cheek, and for the dozenth time asked herself what she was doing here in the wilderness. Had she made a mistake in coming here? Would she be able to face up to and accept a life that would be totally different from what she had ever known?

And what if her grandfather didn't like her? Why hadn't she at least waited for his permission? What if they didn't get along? If he were like the rest of the hill people, she was afraid that they wouldn't.

In the dark, a low-hanging branch brushed against her face and she gave a startled exclamation. Then an owl let out with his noisy *whoo whoo*, and she jumped again. "Is there no end to the strangeness of these hills?" she fretted inwardly.

She buried herself deeper into the collar of the coat and concentrated on the comforting sound of the pack animal behind her as he picked his way carefully around the large rocks that speckled the trail. She would not look back, she decided. She had made her choice and would stick by it . . . if grandpa allowed her to.

After what seemed an interminable time, she smelled coffee and wood smoke, and heard the barking of dogs. She jerked erect and gripped the reins tighter. That meant that human beings were near, and she became almost giddy with relief. She spoke urgently to the mare, and suddenly, in the distance, a door was opened, spilling light into the darkness.

"Is this it?" she asked herself as a massive figure filled the doorway and cursed loudly at a pair of hounds.

Elisha Jobe was to remember that evening for a long time. The emerging of a granddaughter after seventeen years was to change his way of life.

He and Nick had been finished with supper for some time and were settled comfortably in front of the fire. When the dogs started barking in their usual vicious manner, he had at first reckoned that they had scented a deer or bear. Bears often came around the cabin and rummaged in the trash can.

But when the dogs neither ceased nor lowered the volume of their yapping, he said grumpily to Nick, "Who in the hell is the man foolish enough to come to these hills after dark?"

Nick looked up from the Jamestown paper he was reading and answered lazily, "Maybe it ain't human. Probably an animal."

"No, it ain't no animal. The dogs is barkin' different. It's human alright."

A humorous look came over Nick's face as Elisha took down his rifle and slipped to the door. "Ever cautious, 'Lisha. Still don't trust nobody."

Elisha stood to one side of the door and slowly pushed it open. When no shots blasted the silence, and no arrow came winging into the room, he peered out into the night. Dimly, he made out the shape of a horse and a pack animal some yards away. The slight figure on the horse's back didn't seem to present any danger and he stepped out onto the porch. Swearing the dogs into a reluctant silence, he watched the approaching horse and grunted in surprise to see that the rider was a woman.

She reined in and sat wearily while Elisha, from under lowered eyebrows, studied her haughty features and proudly tilted chin. What in the hell was a woman like this doing out after dark, he wondered.

She sat quietly bearing his suspicious scrutiny and after awhile her steady returning gaze unnerved him. Scowling, he asked gruffly, "Who are you, gal? What brings you to my part of the hills at this hour?"

She gazed at him a moment longer, then answered coolly, "I'm your granddaughter, Rachael, you old coot."

Elisha stared at her sharply, his eyes wide with disbelief. How could that be? He had received Rachael's letter only yesterday. But remembering the undependability of the post, she could very easily have arrived before her letter.

He leaned forward eagerly. "Are you sure about that, girl?"

"If you're Elisha Jobe, I'm sure," she laughed.

He liked the ring of her laughter, liked the way her eyes squinted tight, a trait of the Jobes. In fact, she had all the Jobe qualities now that he looked at her closer. The same pride, the arrogance, and the handsome good looks.

Letting out the breath he had unconsciously been holding, Elisha spit on the ground, then grinned, embarrassed. And Rachael, with a gnawing hunger in the pit of her stomach and an almost unbearable fatigue, shivered in the cold and wished that her beetle-browed grandfather would make up his mind.

Finally, in angry desperation, she snapped, "Like me or not, this is the way I am."

Elisha covered a grin with his hand. He hadn't been so pleased in a long time. He would meet his match in his high-spirited granddaughter. Chuckling softly, he roughly remarked reprovingly, "You've got a damnable tongue in your mouth, Rachael, you know that?"

But his warm eyes belied his gruff voice and she was quick to notice. She threw back her head and laughter pealed out, a sound of complete enjoyment. Elisha's lips moved in a wide grin.

Sharing their pleasure in one another, the ice was broken then, never to form again. Elisha reached his arms to her.

"Come out of that saddle. You look beat."

She staggered a bit when her feet touched the ground, and Elisha quickly took her arm and led her onto the porch.

"We'll get a bite of food in your stomach and you'll feel better."

His curiosity piqued by Elisha's long absence, Nick stood at the door. Elisha smiled at him proudly.

"Well, Nick, here she is. What do you think of my granddaughter?"

Rachael gazed into a face that was raw-boned and ugly, and yet, almost hypnotically, she was drawn to him. She smiled and murmured, "I'm happy to meet you, Nick."

His large hand gripped hers and he said softly,

"Rachael, you are lovely. Something tells me that you are gonna raise a lot of hell in these hills."

Rachael's eyes twinkled and Elisha chuckled as he said, "I don't know if these hills can stand another hell-raising Jobe."

Rachael joined in their laughter, then looked yearningly toward the fire. Nick noticed and urged her, "Go over by the fire and thaw out while me and 'Lisha make you something to eat."

Remembering her torn dress, she smiled at him anxiously. "That sounds good, but I wonder if I might freshen up a bit first? I've been in these same clothes for four days and nights and I positively itch."

"Of course." He opened a door behind him and stood aside. "You can have my room. I'll sleep in here in my bedroll until me and 'Lisha can build another bunk."

She looked up at him, objections rushing to her lips. "I couldn't take your room, Nick. Chase you out of your bed."

He quirked an eyebrow at her and she read his thoughts. He blushed when her eyes crinkled, blurting out, "That's alright. I won't mind 'Lisha's snoring too much."

Elisha joined in their laughter, then Nick went to fetch her bag.

When Rachael returned to the main room, her meal was on the table. The soft gown and robe she had exchanged for the travel-worn clothes clung to her body, and she saw desire flicker across Nick's face and linger in his shadowed eyes.

When he pulled out her chair, she lifted teasing eyes to him.

"I like your room, Nick. The bed looks inviting, too."

At the quick intake of his breath, she smiled secretly and dug into the stew and corn dodger with the appetite of a woodchopper.

Elisha, watching her, smiled. "She even eats like a Jobe," he thought proudly.

When she had cleaned her plate and smiled her thanks, Nick hurried to pour her a cup of coffee. She sipped slowly, savoring its strong, black bitterness, and remembered the weak concoction served by the woman on the trail.

Elisha reached for his can of tobacco and began filling his pipe. He tamped it tightly, then drew the candle toward him. Puffing great clouds of smoke until it drew to his satisfaction, he sat back and gazed at Rachael through the wispy spirals. Then at her questioning look, he took the pipe from his mouth and leaned forward.

"Rachael, I've been wonderin', how did you manage to keep body and soul together all these years ... what with Ben's drinkin' and all?"

When an immediate answer didn't come, he peered at her anxiously. She sat with bent head, staring into the coffee cup. Afraid that he had insulted her by speaking so of her father, he cleared his throat awkwardly.

"Your letter didn't say how Ben had died, and I kinda took it for granted that drink had killed him. Forgive me if I'm wrong."

Rachael sighed. The moment of questioning. About her father she could talk freely, but how much of her own personal life should she reveal? Actually she didn't want to tell him anything until she knew him better. Learned enough about him to know how much to safely tell him.

She would answer his questions about papa, she decided, and maybe that would satisfy him for the time being.

She toyed with her spoon for a moment, then said, "You could say that drink killed him, grandpa."

Elisha nodded his shaggy head, his eyes staring into space. "I figured as much. I guess he drank a lot?"

And while Elisha leaned back in his chair, listening quietly and puffing his pipe in quick, short puffs, Rachael talked of Ben's addiction and the events of his death.

When she had finished, he made no response, and to all intent, seemed to have dismissed the subject from his mind. But just as Rachael was about to draw a relieved breath, he spoke again.

"Did Ben leave you some money? I see you're wearing good clothes, and that mare out there is an expensive piece of horse flesh."

For an instant Rachael's eyes hardened stubbornly. These were awfully personal questions he asked in front of his friend, and she thought he had about as much tact as a mule. It was on the point of her tongue to tell him it was none of his damn business when Nick laid a silencing hand on her arm.

"Excuse me, Rachael, for butting in, but I'd best go unsaddle the animals and bed them down."

She looked up in relieved surprise and smiled at the understanding in his eyes. There was depth to Nick Stone. Suddenly, she knew that he would play a big part in her life.

She watched the door close behind him and

thought inwardly, "In a few short hours, I have met two of the most interesting men in my life."

She turned back to Elisha and found him watching her curiously . . . and waiting. Still half angry, she threw caution away and said bluntly, "I have been selling my body since I was fourteen."

Startled, he stared at her, his shaggy brows beetling. Her green glare challenged him back, even as she thought bitterly, "Here it comes. He'll order me out of his house now."

She gave a ragged sigh and looked away, regretting that she had told him the truth. She could have lied to him and given him a dozen reasons for her good horse and clothes.

Through the fringe of her eyelashes she saw him lean forward and take the pipe from his mouth. When his hand moved forward and covered her own, she looked up.

She was unprepared for the look on his face. Neither shock nor alarm showed there. Instead, amusement, sympathy and pity gazed out of his eyes. Amusement that she should follow in her Aunt Sarah's footsteps, and pity and sympathy that one so young had to fend for herself. His was a nature that could accept and understand that she would turn to her best asset to provide for herself, and he was proud that she had the courage to do it. Jobes would make their own way, whatever the odds. It went against their grain to beg help.

Elisha squeezed her hand and chuckled softly, "Were you good at it?"

Her eyes crinkled, and throwing back her head, peals of husky laughter rang through the cabin. Between gusts of mirth, she managed to say, "Grandpa, I was the best in all of Jamestown."

Together they laughed uproariously at her answer. Then wiping away the streaming tears, they gazed understandingly into each other's eyes, knowing that they were made from the same mold. When Rachael reached impulsively and laid a hand on his arm, Elisha was glad she had come. She would stir things up in his and Nick's humdrum world.

But when Elisha teased, "The hillmen are gonna line up in a row to get to you," he was warned by the darkening of her eyes that he had expressed an opinion that she did not care for.

When she answered him, her voice was very earnest. "Grandpa, I'm not going to continue my trade here. I intend to make a new life for myself. A life with only one man in it. One that truly loves me and wants to marry me."

Elisha was silent a moment, thinking that there was a bit of her grandmother in Rachael also. That bit made her different from a true whore.

He nodded his head sagely. "I can understand that, Rachael, but I don't want you wasted on some ignorant hillman."

She gave a small laugh. "I agree with you wholeheartedly. If I had to choose from the bunch I saw at the settlement today, I'd stay single for the rest of my days. But surely there's a man somewhere in these hills who is decent looking and halfway intelligent."

Her sardonic comment brought a dry grunt from Elisha. "There are some," he answered, "but they're mighty few."

He chewed on the stem of the now dead pipe, his brows puckered in thought. After a full minute had passed, Rachael decided to bring up the man on the trail.

"I saw a good-looking man on the trail today . . . an ugly one, too."

"Oh? Do you know who they were?"

"Not really. The ugly one is called Jake, and he called the other man Adam."

"Yeah, I know them. Jake is loose in the head; got shot in the war. Adam, Adam Warden, is the grandson of a friend of mine. He's a long-hunter, and Jake is one of his men. What did them two hellions have to say to you?"

She cocked a quizzical eye at him. How much should she tell him, she wondered. In the end, she decided to tell him everything. It would do her ego good to see someone else insulted and pushed around for a change.

"Oh, they had a lot to say," she began. "None of it nice I might add. The ugly one tried to rape me."

In the deadly silence that followed her words, Rachael watched, fascinated, the transformation that came over Elisha's face. It grew red and the veins in his forehead stood out. Like a maddened bear, he struck out at the table.

"I'll gut shoot the bastard," he roared. "I'll learn him to try that stuff on my granddaughter."

Alarmed at the hornet's nest she had stirred up, Rachael was sorry that she had mentioned it. She had best try to calm him. She grasped his hammering fist and exclaimed, "That's the point, grandpa, he only tried. The man Adam stopped him."

Elisha cut off another tirade on Jake by exclaiming sharply, "He did? That surprises me. It would be more like Adam Warden to use you himself. He's a womanizer if there ever was one. He don't take them natural either."

Rachael shot him a surprised look. "You mean never?"

"Never. They say he ain't took a woman natural yet . . . don't like them." He paused a moment before asking, "You sure he didn't make a move to you?"

"No. He did a lot of looking though." She gave a short laugh and added, "He thinks I'm your new 'toy,' come up here to sleep with you."

The look on Elisha's face was ludicrous, and the restraint Rachael used to hold back her laughter had little effect. When Elisha noted her mirth, his features straightened out and he began to see the amusing side of it. But even though there was silent laughter in his eyes, anger was still evident in his voice when he said, "That cold-eyed bastard thinks you're my woman, does he? I think it's time that wolf was trimmed a bit."

An intense glimmer came into his eyes, and Rachael knew that he was hatching some plan in his devious, contriving mind.

"What are your feelings about him?" he asked suddenly.

Rachael's hands stilled the spoon in her cup, and she gazed silently at Elisha. What exactly were her feelings for that cold and rude man? He had hurt her feelings . . . made her cry. Mostly in anger, she admitted. Even now she could feel the rage that had filled her when he had taunted her. Still, she had been so drawn to him. But then again, perhaps his attraction was the very rudeness he displayed toward her. She had never experienced this in a young man before.

But she kept recalling the softened look that had come into his eyes that one time, and she longed to see it again. That, too, was a new experience for her.

Under the table, Elisha nudged her foot. "Well, girl, what do you feel for him?"

"In all truthfulness, grandpa, I don't really know. But I'd like to see him again . . . get to know him better."

Elisha's eyes searched her face a moment, then he knocked out his pipe and got to his feet. He could understand how the hunter would appeal to Rachael's wild, passionate nature, but he deplored the idea of her ever marrying the man. The girl could have no idea of the life she'd lead, following a long-hunter around.

His plan was unimportant now. The most pressing matter was to make her understand that Adam Warden was a most unlikely man for a husband.

Rachael had risen also and followed him to the fire. Elisha sat down and pulled her into a chair beside him. "Put Adam Warden out of your mind, honey," he told her gently. "I told you that he's a long-hunter."

She made no reply, but looked at him questioningly. Elisha searched his mind for a moment, hunting for the right words that would impress upon her exactly what Adam was and how futile it would be to consider him as husband material. Finally, he began.

"A long-hunter, Rach, is a different cut from the usual man. He don't care nothin' for hearth or home. He don't want to be tied down by a wife or younguns'. He don't want the responsibility of tendin' land or raising his own food."

"But how do they live? Are you saying that they are outlaws?"

"No, I can't say that. They don't live outside the law . . . quite. They make their livin' by huntin' and trappin'. Sometimes they take huntin' trips that can last over a year. That's what I'm tryin' to tell you. You couldn't take that kind of life."

There was a long silence as Rachael sat with her chin in her hand, digesting Elisha's words. Then, taking Elisha by surprise, she remarked, "Adam Warden didn't strike me as the kind of man that would go that long without a woman. There must be women that go along with them."

"Oh, they have women with them alright. Camp followers . . . females of the lowest degree. Scum that has been driven out of the settlements."

When Rachael made no comment, he hastened to add, "You see, honey, that's the kind of woman Adam has been used to. He wouldn't know how to treat you. He's half animal from living in the woods so long."

Silence built again, and the ticking of the clock sounded overloud. It was a strange story grandpa had told. Silently she pondered the picture he had painted. Provided she wanted to, and could lead the wild man to the altar, could she endure such an existence? Would she be able to love him enough to overcome her aversion to his associates and to his way of life? She concluded that it would be a rough and shaky undertaking, but it was something that she would try if things turned out that way.

She glanced at Elisha now, and her voice was soft and serious. She said, "I wouldn't like his way of life, but if necessary, I would do my best in trying."

Resigned, Elisha nodded his head. "Well, Rachael, the genuine article only comes once. Maybe for you, that cub is it."

He rose and clumped to the fireplace and laid another log on the fire. He wouldn't worry about it now, he decided. If he could keep her away from Adam during the summer, the hunter would be gone with the first cold weather. In the meantime, maybe someone else would come along.

Nick entered the cabin, bringing along the rest of Rachael's gear. He stored it in his room, then joined them at the fire. He questioned Rachael about Jamestown, and as she told him how it had changed and grown, Elisha sat quietly, a dreamy, faraway look in his eyes as she spoke of places he remembered so well.

The clock struck nine and Rachael yawned. It would be so good to sleep in a bed again, she thought. She remembered the guide and wondered if she should tell Elisha about his attack. "I'd best not," she decided. "For sure he would go after the man, and in all probability, shoot him."

Later, snuggled down in Nick's quilts, she caught his male scent and wished that he were there beside her.

The balmy spring months had flown and summer was upon the hills, hot and humid.

Today marked the beginning of the fourth month since Rachael's arrival to the hills. On this late morning, she was in the chip yard, doing the family wash. With a long wooden pole, she jabbed at the boiling linens bubbling in an iron kettle. The pot straddled a steadily burning fire that Nick had kindled earlier. After awhile, she ceased the stirring and stepped back to wipe the perspiration from her flushed face.

She leaned against a tree and absentmindedly listened to the variety of sounds coming from the barn area. A cow in heat lowed her long, drawn-out call to the bull in the distant pasture. Her mare, Ginger, wanting to run, neighed unhappily every few minutes. And from the chicken house came the cackling of hens, a surprised sound, as they laid their eggs.

Rachael's mood was bad today, as it had been for some time. Her sleep was restless and her nerves edgy. She plucked at her clinging dress and grumbled, "I've done nothing but work ever since I got here."

She did not mention that the work she did around the place was of her own choosing. Being fastidious by nature, she had itched from the time of her arrival to get soap and water after the cabin. Once cleaned to her satisfaction, she had, however, found it difficult to keep it that way. At one point, she had nagged Elisha and Nick so about their slovenly ways, they had threatened to move out and leave her on her own. But in the end, they had conformed to her notion of how one should treat his home. On rainy, muddy days, two pairs of boots could be found on the porch, while inside, Nick and Elisha walked in their stocking feet, grumbling at women's fool notions.

But Rachael knew that the grumbling was only a pretense. Even sooner than she had expected, they had become accustomed to the new neatness and cleanliness, and she knew that they would be displeased to find the cabin as it once had been.

Elisha had finally remarked one day, "I bow to you, Rach. I admit that I like the smell of your clean sheets better than the stink of my sweat and dirty feet."

But he had ranted long and loud when she had first declared that every Saturday night was bath time. "Hell's fire, girl," he had shouted. "Do you want me to catch my death? I'll just wait till the weather warms and scrub myself at the creek."

Her hands on her hips, she had glared at him for a moment, then lashed out, "Dammit, grandpa, you stink."

A look of surprise came over Elisha's face and he turned to Nick. "Do I stink, Nick?"

Nick chuckled dryly, spat in the fire, and said, "Yep."

"I'll be damned," Elisha grunted. "I always thought it was the hound."

Nick had always followed the practice of bathing once a week in the winter, and his only complaint was having to take the tub into the cold bedroom. But in a short time, and Rachael couldn't remember how it had started, he was stripping and bathing in front of the fire again.

Hanging one of Nick's shirts on the line that Elisha had strung between the trees, she thought of those cool spring nights and regretted that Nick now bathed in the creek. She had enjoyed watching the play of the firelight on his muscular body as he lathered it with soap.

The magnetism between them had grown until the

intensity of it had her nerves drawn taut. She knew the effort that Nick was making to control himself. The undeniable truth that he wanted her leaped out of his eyes at all times.

She had given up on Adam Warden. She had seen him but that one time. At first, she had been desolate when Elisha informed her that Adam was off visiting his Indian friends, but when weeks passed without his return, she had become angry. It was plain that he hadn't been drawn as she had, and as time went by, she thought less and less about him.

However, sometimes in the evening, when she sat alone on the front step, her gaze would go absent, and she would wonder what he was doing at that moment.

She hung the last garment, turned from the line, and tripped over the hound lying at her feet. Swearing angrily, she scrambled to her feet and rubbed a scraped knee. The dog pushed a wet nose into her hand, and she reluctantly forgave him. A few months ago, she would have laughed at such a mishap. Her temper was so short these days. It seemed that she snapped all the time.

Elisha blamed the hot weather on her shrewish behavior, but she was aware that Nick knew better. She had caught a knowing gleam in his eyes one day when she had retorted sharply to some teasing word of Elisha's. She had blushed furiously and avoided his eyes for the next couple of days.

She eyed the sun and decided that there was time to take the men some fresh water before she started the noon meal.

Nick and Elisha were working the tobacco field, and the cool water was a welcome treat. Elisha poured a dipperful over his head and neck.

"That hits the spot, Rach."

Nick smiled his thanks and studied her over the rim of the dipper. Her short, straight shift clung to her damp body, and his eyes caught and held on her thrusting breasts. When a bulge appeared in his buckskins, Rachael noticed and smiled a teasing smile. Nick's face reddened to the roots of his hair and he strangled on a mouthful of water.

Elisha slapped him smartly on the back, and demanded, "What's wrong, Nick, old man, did the water go down the wrong pipe?"

He too had noticed Nick's predicament and was secretly amused. He had known almost from the beginning how it was between the pair and had wondered why they hadn't gotten together. He hoped that it would be soon, for he couldn't stand much more of Rachael's witchy behavior.

But now, to help his friend, he called Rachael's attention to himself. "You gonna have us a bite to eat pretty soon, Rach? I'm so hungry I could eat the ass end of a skunk."

A look of impatient vexation swept across her face, and without a word, she flounced off across the field. The two men watched her switch away, and Elisha remarked, "You know what she wants, don't you, Nick?"

It was on the tip of Nick's tongue to say, "Yeah, she wants me between her legs," but he ended by giving a little sound like a laugh. "I'm not sure what you mean, Elisha. Exactly what are you saying?"

"I'm saying, damn it to hell, that she wants you to take her to bed."

When Nick only stared at him, he snapped impatiently, "You want to, don't you?"

"Hell, yes. I've wanted to from the first time I

saw her. I just didn't know your opinion about it."

Elisha watched his granddaughter disappear into the cabin. "Ain't nobody I'd rather have bed her, old friend."

Nick gave an angry snort. "You sure as hell took your time informin' me about it."

Elisha grinned. "I enjoyed seeing you squirm every time she wagged that little ass of hers at you."

Nick glared a moment into the eyes that twinkled back at him, then laughed. "You damned old billy goat."

Elisha clapped him on the shoulder. "C'mon, let's stop work. By the time we get washed up, she'll have something on the table."

Quietly, they took their places at the table and cast quick glances Rachael's way. She banged plates of pork and potatoes before them, then went and stared out the window while they ate. The meal was silent, with Nick and Elisha exchanging knowing winks.

When they had finished eating, Elisha pushed away from the table and swiped at his moustache. "Them was good vittles, Rach," he remarked.

Rachael grunted, "Thank you."

When the men had gone back to the field, Rachael busied herself clearing away the table and washing the dishes. Noisily she slammed pots and pans, swearing inwardly at Nick. "He knows, damn him. I've done everything but ask him right out."

She hung the dish towel to dry and wandered aimlessly into her room. "God, it's hot," she muttered.

She pulled the single garment over her head and threw her naked body across the bed. She landed with a thud and cried a surprised "Ouch."

She had forgotten that the feather mattress had been removed for the summer, and that the straw tick replacing it had no resilience.

She lay on her stomach a moment, listening to a bottle fly buzz and bump against the window. She felt the sweat gathering between her breasts and flopped over on her back. Flinging an arm over her head, she sighed. How hot it was . . . not a sound stirring the silence. Even the bottle fly had exhausted himself.

Then suddenly she became aware of the soft whisper of moccasins gliding over the rough floor boards. She jerked erect and stared. Nick. The almost desperate hunger in his eyes seemed to devour her. Her heart began to pound as a strong excitement grabbed her.

Without words, he dropped down beside her and gathered her in his arms. His lips came down, covering and forcing hers apart. She made a small sound in her eagerness and caught his tongue with her own and sucked it gently and rhythmically.

They fell back onto the bed, their lips still clinging. Nick's hands began to move over her body, soothing the nerves that had been raw for so long.

His lips left her mouth and moved to her throat, lingered awhile, then moved on. She gave a short gasp as his tongue flicked out and captured a hardened nipple. With each urgent pull of his lips, she moaned and arched into him.

Then her breath stopped as he moved down and began to lick her stomach, and then to the inside of her thigh. Her breath coming in pants now, he pulled her to the edge of the bed and knelt on the floor before her. She bent her knees and spread them apart, pushing toward him.

He saw the pink lips surrounded by the curly hair and buried his face there, and she moaned, "Nick, oh Nick."

She stroked his head and brought one leg up against it, pressing gently. Breathing hard, he slipped his hands under her squirming buttocks and held them still as he slid his tongue toward her opening. He found his target and sucked hard. Then he drove his tongue deeper. She leaned on her elbows and her breasts heaved with her swift panting. Again and again, she stiffened in spasmodic jerks, and finally collapsed on the bed.

Swiftly, Nick rose and stepped out of his buckskins. He lay back down and Rachael opened her eyes and smiled at him lazily. Then she rose to her knees and started kissing him, her tongue licking a path down his stomach.

He groaned and squirmed, then grabbed her head. "Don't tease, Rach," he rasped, "I've waited so long."

Her hot mouth enveloped him, sucking as the riverman had taught her.

Later, exhausted, they lay in a half sleep, Nick's head heavy on her shoulder. Rachael smiled. Now she knew what Beaulah had meant by a "humpin' man."

Twice during the afternoon he had mounted her and pumped furiously, making her climax almost uncontrollably. She stroked the welts on his back where her sharp nails had raked him.

When Elisha returned to the cabin in the late afternoon, the fire was dead and no supper was on the table. Rachael's soft laughter drifted out of the bedroom and he grinned and began to prepare supper.

CHAPTER 6

The late August air was cool and sharp. Unusual for this time of the year. All signs pointed to an early winter.

Adam Warden leaned against a tree and watched the Indian children herding a group of goats onto a grassy pastureland. They made a game out of the chore, running and laughing and doing mock battle.

He mused to himself that there wasn't a great deal of difference between the red child and the white. Especially the white youngster born and raised in the hills. He, too, had had his make-believe battles ... fought his enemies, roamed the forest setting out traps and snares. And in the evenings, he had sat around a fire listening to the tall tales told by his elders.

But the two different groups of youngsters would grow up with different sets of values. Rarely would the white and red become friends. The lucky white lad would get to know his red brother, and benefit from it. But the number would be small ... hardly worth counting.

The childern ran off through the woods and Adam's eyes followed them. He noticed that the trees were already showing a tinge of color—the mighty oak was beginning to wear a russet brown. He turned his head and looked into the valley below. In its earlier gloom, he could make out the falling dew, sparkling and clear. Fall was about here, and winter would soon be upon the hills.

It had been his intention to stay in the Indian camp until the first snowfall, but lately his dark face had turned more and more often to the south. He pulled the brightly colored blanket tighter around his shoulders and thought, "I wonder what the wild bunch is up to? Most likely it's time I get back to them."

The summer months had been peaceful and fulfilling and he dreaded the thought of returning to the old and careless ways. For some reason unknown to him, the excitement of his old life had dulled.

He moved his shoulder against the tree and the bark scraped against a part of the still tender scar that lay there. According to Little Flower, it was a miracle that he still lived.

After Bear had carried him the long way to camp, he had hung suspended between life and death for several days. He vaguely remembered the old medicine men who had gathered around him, probing and poking, and directing someone to use this herb and that berry on his wounds. Then they had performed some kind of dance around him, he recalled, and chanted a wailing kind of song.

Something had worked. He was fine now, with nothing to show for his mishap but the long claw marks that he would carry to his grave.

When he had healed and regained his strength, Bear had presented him with his own teepee. It sat back in the trees, several yards from the main camp.

"You will rest better here," the chief explained. "Sometimes my braves get loud with their boasting and singing."

Adam had expressed his thanks and entered his new quarters. At first he could not see in the dark interior and stood still, waiting for his eyes to become accustomed to the darkness. When finally he could make out objects, the first thing that met his eyes was a young Indian girl sitting on a pallet of furs. She smiled timidly at him and he was aware of her beauty and knew why she was there. She was a gift from Bear, sent to comfort him in bed.

"Good Lord, she's young," he thought, his eyes traveling over her body, taking in the small breasts that barely pushed out the material covering them. He remembered another pair, large and firm, and felt himself grow hard in the remembering. He had been a long time without a woman, and desire built high within him.

He walked over to the girl and squatted beside her. "What's your name?"

Her head jerked up, startled at the cold hardness of his voice. Her smile trembling, she answered, "Little Flower. I'm daughter to Bear One Claw."

"How old are you?"

"I will be thirteen when the next snow falls."

"Good Lord," he thought, "only twelve." He studied the smooth and innocent face, thinking that he had never had one so young. "But hell," he reminded himself, "that's not young for an Indian squaw. Old Bear's third wife isn't much older."

He reached out a finger and traced it lightly across the childish breasts. "Why have you come to my teepee?"

"My father says I'm to tend to your needs."

"Do you know what that means?"

She bowed her head and nodded silently.

Adam gazed at the shiny, bent head with the long, black braids swinging on either side of her face, and asked quietly, "Do you want to?"

Little Flower's eyes traveled to his hardness that throbbed against his buckskins, and after a moment, whispered, "Yes."

"Don't be afraid. I won't hurt you," he assured her gruffly.

While Flower watched, wide-eyed, he sat back on his heels and unlaced the front of his trousers. Pulling himself free, he raised up on his knees in front of her, and ordered, "Suck it."

She stared up at him, thinking that she must have misunderstood his words. She had never seen a squaw do this to a brave.

As she continued to stare, Adam became impatient and slapped her sharply across the face. When she opened her mouth to cry out, he rammed himself through the red lips.

Before the evening meal was called, Flower had learned that she must use her tongue and lips, and must not draw away at that most important time. She must wait until *he* pushed her face away.

Being bright and eager to please, she learned within a few days to read his thoughts before he voiced them. The time came when he had only to look at her in a certain way, or lie down in a particular position, and she would be beside him, her hands going quickly to his laces.

Despite his cold treatment, Flower followed him around camp like a small puppy dog, anxious and happy to attend to his smallest wish. She picked the tenderest pieces of meat from the pot for him and sewed him the finest of deerskin shirts. Had Adam asked her to jump off one of the tall bluffs that towered into the sky, she would have, unquestioning, jumped.

Only one thing spoiled his lazy summer. Try as he would, he could not keep the image of Elisha's woman from his mind. He saw her face in everything he did. When he sat smoking with the braves, she would appear in the wispy spiral of tobacco smoke. If he sat before the campfire, her eyes would mock him in the flames. Even when he fished the river, he could see her face in the flowing current.

And at night when he stretched out on the furs, it was worse. At first he could not stand to have Flower next to him on the pallet. But his desire for the green-eyed beauty became so overwhelming, he finally forced himself to pretend that Flower's caressing lips and hands belonged to her.

Adam sighed and pushed away from the tree. There was no sense in postponing the return trip any longer. The woman would be on his mind regardless of where he was. He would go now to find Bear, tell him good-bye, and leave the first thing tomorrow morning.

He found the old chief resting in his lodge, a young squaw reclining on either side of him. Bear's first wife had grown old and fat and no longer appealed to him and now lived with the other old squaws. She was, however, treated with much respect from everyone. Bear would have it no other way. She was of his youth and his feelings for her went much further than the relieving of his male hardness. Where the young wives were very adept at that, it was to the old wife he went for counseling and comfort.

Bear rose to his feet and motioned Adam to the

fire that blazed in the center of the floor. When they were seated and the pipe lit and passed between them, Bear looked at his young friend and asked, "What brings you here at this hour, young brave?"

"I've come to say good-bye, chief. I'll be leavin' in the mornin', early."

Bear nodded his head and spoke gravely. "Yes. I watch you look homeward for some time."

"I want to thank you for your hospitality . . . and for saving my life."

"No give thanks. You would do the same thing for me or my people."

"Yes . . . I'll see you again then."

Bear raised his hand, palm forward. "Good spirits go with you, long-hunter."

Adam's sleep was fitful that night, and he awoke in the still, cold hours of dawn, eager to be on his way. Flower lay curled beside him and he looked down on her sleeping form. He hadn't told her yet that he was leaving and he wondered how she would take to his news. "Hell," he thought, "what difference does it make? A squaw is used to the white man leaving her."

A bitterness grew in him as he continued to gaze at Flower. Why wasn't it Elisha's woman lying here . . . anxious to do his bidding? Then angrily, he reminded himself that she was a whore and would do a man's bidding only for money.

He slipped quietly from the furs and climbed into his buckskins and pulled one of Flower's shirts over his head. The leather moccasins went on next and he moved across the dirt floor and picked up his shoulder bag.

As he moved about gathering his gear, rolling the

blankets, and filling a pouch with dried venison and coffee, Flower came and stood beside him. Her eyes were wide and full of anxiety. Her voice trembling, she urged, "You take Flower with you."

A feeling, almost of guilt, assailed Adam and he would not look at her. Impulsively, his hand went into his shirt pocket and pulled forth a length of red ribbon. It had once been tied in the black curls of Elisha's woman. It had loosened and fallen to the ground in her tussle with Jake.

He had found it shortly after she had ridden away that late afternoon. It carried her perfume and he had held it to his face, breathing deeply. Then becoming angry at himself, he had crumbled it in his fist and flung it away. He had ridden several yards up the trail before turning the stallion around and going back to retrieve the bright red strip.

He pushed the ribbon at Flower. "Here, a ribbon for your hair."

She stared down at the length of velvet, shaking her head. "Flower no want. Flower want to go with long-hunter."

He tossed the ribbon on the floor and snapped, "You're not going. You stay here with your people. There's no place for you where I'm going."

When he left the teepee for the last time, Flower was huddled on the furs, crying softly.

The unbroken forest stretched out in front of him, and with the swift supple step of the Indian, he climbed one hill after the other. If all went well, he should be home in three days.

In the late afternoon, near dusk, he climbed a steep footpath to the top of a hill. Below, in the mist rising from the river, a small herd of deer browsed. Peacefully they cropped the short grass, unaware of his presence. Then a large buck with widely spread antlers lifted his head and looked straight at him. He stared a moment, then in a flash he was plunging away, the others following at his heels.

Swiftly, with practiced dexterity, Adam raised his rifle, and taking careful aim, brought down a yearling. His sharp knife smoothly sliced away enough steaks for his supper, and the wolves would finish the rest within hours.

The second night out he camped beside the river that rushed and tumbled to the valley of his grandfather's home. He was in familiar territory now and tomorrow he'd be home.

They were in the thick of sorghum-cutting and every hand was needed. Even the grandsons, Dave and Rafe, had come to help Elisha.

The late summer day was hot and humid, and before Rachael had worked for half an hour, her clothing clung like an extra skin. At first the sorghum's musty, sweet odor had smelled delicious to her as the sharp cutting knife released the thick juice. But gradually it sickened her and before long an aching throb reached across her forehead.

Elisha approached her with a pail of water, and as she took a dipperful, he spoke with concern, "You're all flushed, Rach. I think you'd better go back to the cabin."

She shook her head stubbornly. "I'll be alright, grandpa. I just feel a little sick to my stomach."

Elisha felt her forehead and frowned. "You're much too hot. You'd better go take a dip in the creek and then go on home and lie down. I don't want you gettin' sunstroke."

She felt too miserable to argue, and dropped the knife with relief.

She reached the creek, stepped out of her dress and waded into its cool, soothing water. Eagerly she lowered her body and stretched out. Feeling its cold glide over her, the thought struck her that before long these waters would be locked tight in solid ice.

She relaxed and floated downstream until she hit the gravel bottom in a shallow place. A clump of willow grew out of the tall grass, edging the creek, and cast a shadowy pattern of shade over her and the water. She smiled lazily as small birds began to twitter and fuss in the tops of the trees.

Then suddenly, their noise was stilled and a qualm of unease swept over Rachael. Quickly she scanned the screening grass, then started. Had she caught a fleeting glimpse of movement behind the willows? For a frightened moment she thought of bears. They often came down and nosed around the scrap pail back of the cabin. The strong scent of the sorghum could have reached them.

Then there was a flash of color and she knew that a human watched her. Suddenly she was strongly aware that the clear water did nothing to hide her nakedness; that actually she was only half covered by it. She glanced at her dress lying on the shore, miles away it seemed. Then to worsen matters, she was becoming acutely aware of the icy water that waved and flopped about her.

Shivering from cold and nervousness, she debated what to do. Should she pretend ignorance of the homespun-covered leg showing through the grass, in the hope that the man would look for awhile and then leave, or should she rely on the swiftness of her long legs to carry her to safety?

Then it entered her mind that the spying man could be Jake, and her mind was made up. She would run.

She eased up out of the water and stood on shaking legs. Forcing herself to appear calm and natural, she began slowly to wade upstream. After what seemed hours, she came opposite to where she had tossed her dress. Several yards beyond was the cabin, and safety. She gathered herself for the sprint and set one dripping foot on the bank, then froze. A man had stood up in the tall grass and was coming toward her.

"Jake," she gasped.

Jake's thin mouth spread in an ugly grin, and a knowing dread spread through Rachael. She wanted to scream her fright, cringe away from him, but her inner voice was whispering, urging, "Don't let him know you are afraid. Bluff him."

And drawing on every ounce of her courage and cunning, she ran icy eyes over him and demanded, "What do you want, Jake? Why are you spying on me?"

Through tobacco-stained lips, he sneered, "What do you think I want, pretty play toy? I'm gonna finish what I started this spring. Adam Warden ain't here to stop me this time."

His eyes devouring her nakedness, he stepped down into the creek and grabbed out at her. She twisted her body and managed to evade his reaching hand, and began to back away from him. But his boots, churning the water, came closer and closer.

She became terror-stricken and tried to move faster, but in her haste a foot came down on a smooth, slippery rock, and suddenly she was sitting on the bottom of the stream.

Like lightning, Jake's taloned fingers came down and gripped her shoulder. All calm and reasoning gone, Rachael opened her mouth and scream after scream came tearing through. Indecision flickered in Jake's eyes as he gripped her harder.

"Don't open your mouth again," he warned menacingly.

She had already decided she wouldn't scream again anyway. It would be a wasted effort—everyone was too far away to hear her. She would need all her energy and strength to fight off the half-crazed man who tugged cruelly at her shoulder. As he raised her struggling body out of the water, she was amazed at the strength in his puny arms. For despite her swinging arms and threshing legs, he was steadily drawing her onto the bank.

He released her for a moment to grab her under the arms. She took advantage of the moment to twist away free, only to have him grab her by the ankle. She came flying up, her curved fingers reaching for his face. And fast as the weasel he resembled, Jake grabbed her wrists and slammed them, helpless, onto the ground.

As she lay panting, trying to catch her breath, he struggled to straddle her twisting body. But she managed to bounce him off each time, and finally he bored a knee roughly between her thighs and forced them apart. His breath coming in gasps, he flopped down between her legs and lay still.

Rachael watched frustration slowly build in his

face as he tried to figure out what to do next. At the moment he was helpless to do anything but maybe pump his body uselessly against hers. Then a mad cunning crept into his eyes and Rachael knew that he was going to strike her . . . knock her unconscious.

Her eyes went wide in denial and he grinned at her loosely. "Too bad, pretty play toy, that you ain't gonna feel my pumper, but I'm. . . ." His words stopped short and he gave a startled grunt. Rachael watched his scrawny throat work and his eyes bulge in alarm as he stared at the opposite bank.

Rachael turned her head and went weak with relief. On the other shore stood Adam Warden. His long rifle was cradled in his arms and its barrel was pointing at Jake's stomach. There was a strange stillness on his features, and fury stared out of his eyes.

Whimpering his fright, Jake scrambled to his feet and struck out running, his sodden clothes hampering and slowing his speed. Rachael breathed a shaken sigh of relief and rose to her feet. She looked across the creek to give Adam thanks, and the words froze in her throat. His rifle was nestled beneath his chin and he was drawing careful aim on the lumbering figure.

"Oh, no," she whispered, and splashed through the water to grab his arm. "Don't shoot," she insisted. "Don't shoot."

He jerked free of her clinging hand and demanded sharply, "What did you do that for, damn it? The hound is out of range now."

"You were going to shoot him," she stated more than asked. "One of your own men."

"That dog needs killin', and I'll do it one of these days."

Suddenly they were both aware of her nakedness and Rachael bent down for her dress. But his foot shot out quickly, pinning the garment to the ground. His sneer was shaky as he muttered, " 'Lisha surely wouldn't mind me just looking at his merchandise."

Rachael straightened up and looked at him coolly. "Look then, you bastard, look until your damn eyes fall out," she snapped.

He chuckled at her spirit and his eyes took a long, slow survey. Then his hand come out, and with gentle fingers he traced a path around her throat and then across her breasts. Against her will, she felt her nipples harden with a building desire.

Then his head was brushing her chin, and his warm mouth was covering a breast, pulling the nipple tightly between his teeth. She groaned and trembled as the kindled fire in her loins leaped with new warmth.

Then, just as suddenly as he had bent to her, he was straightening up and walking away, without a word or backward glance.

Rachael stared after him in disbelief. When he had moved out of sight, she threw herself upon the ground and pounded her fists into the dirt. "Damn him, damn him," she cried silently. "He's been in the back of my mind all along."

"Why did I do that?" Adam asked himself, over and over. Why had that uncontrollable desire come over him? It had rushed on him without warning and left him powerless to do anything else. It was only through iron determination that he had been able to walk away from her. He had ached with a terrible fierceness to let his lips slide all over her body. Even now it was all he could do not to return to her and do so.

"Damn it," he swore out loud. Kissing her wasn't all he had wanted to do either. He wanted to lie between her silky thighs . . . to push his hard self deep within her. He had never had this urge before, and as he stalked through the forest, he silently cursed the woman who had caused it.

The wind rustled the leaves and something stirred in a dense thicket some yards to Adam's left. He hurriedly checked the rifle, making sure it was primed. Anything from a bear to an Indian could be lurking there.

He stopped and listened intently, waiting for the sound again. Then he heard a sharp click and felt the breeze of a bullet whiz past his ear. Throwing himself behind a tree, he heard the ringing spat of it hitting a boulder.

He had moved so fast that he had scraped his knuckles and scratched his knees. Looking down at the long rents in each leg of his buckskins, he swore softly.

Carefully he peered from behind his cover and saw a mist of gray smoke drifting out of the thicket. "The bastard is probably gone by now," he muttered darkly.

Crouched behind the tree, he pondered on who had shot at him. Different ones ran through his mind, but in the end, he suspected that it might have been a renegade Indian. Although the settlers were mostly at peace with the red man, there were still some, outlawed by their tribes, who would still stalk a white man if they found him alone.

Still, he couldn't quiet the small voice that spoke

in the back of his mind. "It was Jake," the voice insisted. But he dismissed the thought with, "That hound wouldn't have the nerve."

When an hour had passed with no movement from the brush, and the birds returned with their busy chatter that preceded their roosting for the night, Adam decided that it was safe enough to leave his shelter.

There was still some light left in the sky when he walked into the clearing and the hunters came clamoring around him. A dozen questions were shot at him at once, and he sighed resignedly and answered their queries.

"Everyone been behavin' while I was gone?" he began his own questions. "Anybody been down to the post?"

A large man with bulging muscles pushed forward and answered. "We've been on this hill all summer, and me for one am sick to death of it."

Adam ignored his complaint and asked, "Is Jake around?"

"Yeah. I just saw him slippin' in the shed. Why?"

"I caught him wrestlin' Elisha's woman around this afternoon and I come close to shootin' the bastard."

" 'Lisha sure as hell will if he gets wind of it," the big man remarked.

"Yeah," Adam replied thoughtfully. "I'd better put the fear of God in that louse before he gets us all in trouble."

He turned to his favorite hunter. "John, go fetch him, will you?"

While Adam waited, he drank two dippers of water. The suspenseful waiting back on the trail had left his mouth as dry as a bone. Over the rim of the dipper he watched John returning, pushing a reluctant Jake in front of him. "I'd sure as hell like to get a sniff of Jake's rifle," he thought. "I'd bet a year's hunt it's been fired recently."

Jake stood before Adam, his shifty eyes looking everywhere but at his boss. Adam wasted no time coming to the point. His fist knotted and struck savagely, and Jake lay sprawled on the ground, a thin trickle of blood running from his nose. Standing over the cringing man, Adam demanded, "What did I tell you about her? Didn't I tell you to leave the outside women alone?"

Edging away and swiping at his nose, Jake whined, "I didn't mean to touch her, Adam. I only meant to look. But when I saw her all wet and shiny, I couldn't help myself."

Adam admitted silently that the half-wit was right. It would take a stronger mind than Jake's to keep his hands off that one. He hadn't been able to.

"If you'd kept your ass away from there, you wouldn't have been tempted," John pointed out. "We all told you."

Jake didn't answer but his eyes were full of hate as he glared at the circle of faces. He looked up, startled, when Adam demanded sharply, "Where's your rifle, Jake?"

For a moment Jake tried to stare back at Adam, then his eyes slid away and he muttered sullenly, "I lost it."

"Like hell you did," Adam roared. "You got it hid somewhere. You took a shot at me this afternoon."

Jake's arm came up to protect his face, expecting the smashing fist again. "I didn't, I didn't," he screamed.

With the toe of his boot Adam shoved his arm from his face. "You did it, you son-of-a-bitch. But from now on I'll be watching my back trail. The next time you try, I'll blow your brains out."

He spun on his heel and moved toward his cabin. Someone called after him, "Now that you're back, can we go down to the post?"

"You'd better not. 'Lisha Jobe is probably on the warpath by now."

As he unlocked the cabin door, he heard Jake let out a yowl. He turned, then grinned. The hunters were taking their disappointment out on Jake.

Dusk came on, and Adam made and ate his supper alone. And later, although he could see his men looking expectantly at his door, he remained inside. He was not quite ready to join them. Their wild ways did not lure him as they once had.

He spent some time straightening out the cabin, then with the first cry of the whippoorwill, sought his bed.

He was restless and could not get comfortable. After sleeping on the ground all summer, the bed seemed strange. And the vision of Elisha's naked woman wasn't conducive to sleep either.

The next morning after breakfast, he looked out the window to see if the hunters were up and about. But everything was quiet at the dilapidated building. He was not surprised. He had heard their drunken laughter long into the night.

To kill time, he decided to take his rifle and walk in the woods. A mess of squirrels would taste good, he thought. By late morning and several miles, he had six furry bodies hanging from his belt.

The autumn day had turned hot and he paused

beside a bubbling spring and drank deeply. Then wiping the sweat from his face, he turned toward home.

He was just skirting the Jobe place when he heard a woman scream.

CHAPTER 7

There was nothing to break the sound of the forest but Elisha's and Rachael's footsteps. They, too, walked the forest hunting squirrel.

The mornings and evenings of late August definitely carried a chill in the air, but by noon it was quite warm. Rachael pulled at her sweat-dampened dress and sighed. She was so tired and hot. They had been walking for hours and she longed to sit down.

Elisha had shot five squirrels and she watched them swing slowly back and forth on his back as she trudged along behind him. Finally he stopped beneath a huge beech and mopped at his sweating face. Turning to her, he grinned. "We're so near Ruby's place, what say we take a couple of these to her?"

Rachael gave a good-natured snort. "Did the itch come on you, grandpa?"

Elisha's eyes crinkled. "Yeah, I got me a fine itch."

Rachael plopped down on the ground and removed her moccasins. She had discovered how comfortable they were and wore them most of the time now. She rubbed an aching instep, thinking that going to Ruby's wasn't what she had had in mind. She would much rather go home and sit in the cool cabin.

She leaned back on her hands and stretched out her legs. "I don't know if I want to go to Ruby's. It gets awfully boring sitting there listening to you two bounce on the bed."

"Hell, why don't you watch us then? Bet you could learn some new tricks."

"You're impossible, grandpa, you know that?"

Elisha laughed and moved away from her slapping hand. "I expect that I am. Ruby is always tellin' me that I am."

"I don't know what Ruby sees in you."

Elisha chuckled significantly. "Come on, I promise I won't stay long."

Scuffing along behind him, Rachael recalled the first time she met Ruby.

It had come about with Elisha's accident. He had tripped and fallen over his favorite hound one day, and upon rising, discovered a badly sprained ankle. It had swollen until he could neither stand on it nor pull on a boot. Consequently, he was confined to the cabin with nothing to occupy his time. Within a few days his thoughts turned to Ruby, and in a short time he was insisting that she be brought to him.

He had chosen his grandson Dave to be his courier. "He's not so apt to wear her out before she gets here," he explained. "If I sent Rafe, she'd need a couple days rest before she could do me any good."

Ruby had come and stayed for two weeks. Elisha was always after the good-natured woman, openly fondling her. It was not unusual for him to interrupt her at some chore by calling out, "Hey, Ruby, come give me some kissin'."

Rachael had been a little surprised at his interpretation of "kissin'."

At any rate, Rachael had been glad when Ruby

returned home and things got back to normal. Grandpa beat anything she had ever seen.

They were soon out of the forest and standing before a small, well-cared-for cabin. Late-blooming flowers spread a riot of color around the place, and off to one side, the remains of a frostbitten garden lay baking in the sun. Rachael knew that inside there would be strings of green beans and peppers hanging from the rafters. It was so in their own place, along with pans of cut corn, slowly drying in the loft. Also, there would be piles of pumpkins and squash in every available corner.

They stepped upon the small porch and the door swung open. Ruby greeted them, a pleased smile upon her simple face. She was not simple in the sense that her brain was not strong, but rather, that she wasn't worldly wise. The bigger part of her life had been taken up with Elisha. She had spent twenty years in the mountain cabin waiting for his visits. And later, for his two grandsons.

Elisha had brought the boys to her when they had come of "age," and Ruby had initiated them to their first "pleasurin'."

Rafe had been thirteen, and Dave but eleven. Rafe, big and mature for his age, had enjoyed the session and had stayed with Ruby for two weeks, pestering her constantly. But Dave had been too young and allowed that he didn't know what all the crowing was about. He had, however, liked the sensation Ruby's mouth gave him and had continued to come along with Rafe on his weekly visits. Then one day, he was rewarded by his manhood and began to make his own private visits to Ruby's.

Now when Dave came and stood behind Ruby, fastening his buckskins, no one was surprised. Elisha's only comment was, "I hope you ain't been here long, boy."

Dave laughed a relaxed sound. "Just a short time, grandpa." He smacked Ruby on the rear and added, "Didn't even heist your dress, did I, Ruby?"

Elisha grunted and propelled Ruby into the cabin.

Inside, the husk mattress began almost immediately to rustle, and Rachael, becoming embarrassed, fidgeted with the beadwork on her moccasions.

Dave looked at her and a grin spread over his face. "Ain't you got used to grandpa's ways yet?"

Rachael shrugged her shoulders. "Yes, I suppose I have. I just wish he'd hurry up."

"So do I," Dave agreed.

Several minutes went by and Rachael became impatient. She turned to Dave. "Is Aunt Sarah home?"

"Yeah. She's washin' and dryin' mushrooms."

"I'm going to go visit her. Tell grandpa, if he ever comes out."

Dave nodded and suggested, "Take Grizzly with you. Won't nobody bother you with him at your side."

She walked lightly, her long legs eating up the distance, the hound at her heels. About a mile from Ruby's, she entered a glen of mostly walnut and hickory trees. A few nuts lay on the ground, but the real harvest was still on the trees, waiting for the heavy frosts. She made a mental note to come here later and gather them. They would lend much nourishment to their winter larder.

In the distance she heard the rumble of a wagon and guessed that it was taking supplies to the post. She remembered supplies needed at home and was glad that she had the money to buy them. Hard cash was one thing that grandpa didn't have. He was not alone however. Most of the settlers were in the same fix. Grandpa said that only the long-hunters had any real money, and that they wasted it on drink and whores.

Once she was startled by a flock of pigeons flying overhead and she thought of the many dozen she and Elisha had netted during the summer. Ruby had taught her how to cook them and then pack them in their own juices. They sat now in great stone bowls on the cellar floor. They would be delicious this winter, along with the several crocks of pork sausage prepared the same way.

The path followed the river now. The wilderness pushed in to its very edges, casting a dense shadow. She stopped in the cool shade and leaned against a tree. It was farther to Aunt Sarah's than she had remembered. She leaned her head against a tree and listened to the countless voices of katydids. They had ground out their monotonous tuneless song all July, and she would be glad when cold weather arrived and shut them up.

A cloud slipped past the sun, casting the forest into a gloomy half-light. An owl gave its ghosty hooting cry and Rachael jumped and shivered. Sometimes the woods were downright spooky, she thought.

The hound nudged her leg and she reached down and patted his head. He licked her hand and wagged his tail, and she was reassured. "Come on, boy, let's get out of here," she murmured.

They turned a bend in the trail and a few feet away a large buck stood staring at them. Grizzly gave a yelp and sprinted after the animal as it bounded away through the trees. She wouldn't see him for awhile, Rachael knew.

Finally, the density of the forest was thinning, and up ahead Rachael could see her Aunt Sarah's apple orchard. She gave a sigh of relief. Her aunt's cabin was just on the other side.

Then a sudden move in the forest made her gasp and hold her breath. Just inside the boundaries of the woods she had caught a glimpse of a figure darting behind a tree. She immediately thought of Jake waiting to waylay her again.

She bent down and pretended to tie her moccasin as her mind raced in fear and indecision. If it were Jake, maybe she could outwit the simple fellow . . . scare him with the threat of Adam. But as her thoughts wavered back and forth, she heard a twig snap behind her and she froze. Springing to her feet, she wheeled around, her eyes passing swiftly over the area. Had she seen a movement behind that tree, or was it her imagination working overtime?

Then alarmingly, "Could it be Indians?"

She felt the hair prickling at the back of her neck and her mouth went dry. If there was also someone behind her, then all escape was shut off. She felt panic building and strove to compose herself, ordering herself to be calm.

If it were Indians, perhaps they only wanted to spy on a white woman and would let it go at that. She took a tentative step, another one, and yet another, and began to hope. Then from nowhere, a half-naked figure leaped in front of her, throwing her to the ground. Before she could scream out, a red lean hand was clamped over her mouth and she was staring wide-eyed into a bronzed, fierce face.

For a moment she lay motionless, too stunned to move. Then automatically she was biting down on the gripping fingers and heaving herself away, trying to rise. But two more braves joined the one who held her and she was pushed back to the ground and held fast. A piece of dirty rag was shoved into her mouth and her hands were jerked behind her back and tied tightly.

It had all happened so swiftly and silently. Only a slight scuffling noise had disturbed the forest. Even the birds flitting among the trees had continued their singing. No one would have any notion what had happened to her ... and Aunt Sarah so near.

She was jerked to her feet and led off the trail, toward the river.

Fright was leaving her now and a raging anger was taking its place. The filthy rag in her mouth tasted horrible and was making her nauseous. She gagged and worked at it with her tongue. She managed to move the wad a bit, and hope flared. Maybe she could work it out and give a few lusty screams at least.

They were at the river and two of the Indians bent and pulled a bark canoe from under some brush. As it danced and bobbed in the water, a brave picked her up and tossed her unceremoniously into its bottom. Her chin hit with a dull thud and for a moment she thought she would faint. The braves climbed in behind her and took up the paddles, and with swift sure strokes, headed upriver.

Rachael's heart gave a leap. They would pass

grandpa's place. The cabin was only a short distance from the river and she must have this gag out of her mouth and be ready to scream when they drew near it. She turned her face from the Indian's view and began working her mouth.

After several minutes her ears and jaws hurt from the straining of her tongue, and one side of her face had gone numb. But she ignored it all. The rag was definitely being slowly pushed out of her mouth. She rested a moment, then gave one desperate thrust of her tongue and her mouth was free. She lay quiet, filling her lungs with fresh air.

She carefully watched the riverbank slide by, her eyes searching for a known landmark of some kind. But she recognized nothing and despair gripped her. They had already passed grandpa's place and she had missed it.

She would scream anyway, she decided. Someone might hear her. Raising her head as high as she could, scream after piercing scream came tearing from her throat. The brave at her head jumped and gave a short grunt, then a hard object came down on her head and she knew no more.

Adam lifted his head and listened intently. The scream had come from the river, and it sounded familiar. He broke into a light trot and soon saw the water gleaming through the trees. He slowed to a walk and moved more cautiously. He came to some tall brush and hurried to crouch behind it. Peering through the leaves, he had a full view of the river.

But it was empty.

Then faintly there came the soft slapping of oars on water. The sound became louder, and soon, hugging the riverbank, a canoe glided into view. Three Indians knelt in it, and on the bottom lay the limp form of a woman. The setting sun shone redly on raven black hair.

He went weak and his knees trembled. Elisha's woman. He had known it all along.

Now. How to rescue her. They were three, but he had a rifle. His best bet would be a surprise attack.

On his elbows, he wriggled through the brush and swore softly as the branches slapped and scratched his face. Finally, he heard the low murmur of rushing water and then he was crawling in gravel, the pebbles biting into his elbows. He gritted his teeth and inched along. Just a few more feet and he would reach what he sought.

A couple months back, during a thunderstorm, lightning had struck a large oak, splitting it in half. One half had stood erect, and the other had fallen out across the river. He would conceal himself amid the dead leaves of this half and get the drop on the red varmints as they rowed by.

The fallen half loomed in front of him, and in a short time he had buried himself deep in its limbs. He checked his rifle and waited.

Behind him, in a tall cedar, a blue jay startled him with its threatening caw. The damned bird would give him away sure. Indians read signs by the actions of birds and animals. They would know immediately that something disturbed the jay. He dipped a hand in the river, and his fingers searched the bottom for a rock. A tossed stone in the bird's direction might scare him away. But as he felt about, finding nothing small enough to throw, the jay fussed a couple more times, then flew away. Adam relaxed and drew his arm across his sweating face.

He turned his attention back to the river, then gripped the rifle tightly. The canoe was almost upon him. He eased back the hammer and curled his finger around the trigger. "Now," he thought, "you bastards just get a little closer."

Then suddenly, the jay was back, closer this time and making a raucous noise. The braves' heads jerked toward the bank and Adam could swear that they looked straight at him.

He swore under his breath, and then with a high-pitched yell sprang out of his cover and brought the rifle to his shoulder. For a fraction of a second the stunned braves stared at him. Then the one crouching beside Rachael was standing up and diving into the water.

But he was not in time to escape the bullet that came winging his way. His blood-curdling scream was cut short as his head disappeared into the river.

Adam dropped back down in his shelter, and with swift, sure fingers, tilted the powder horn over the rifle. He'd get at least one more of the varmints. Chances were good he'd get the other one, too, he thought, as he reached for the knife at his belt.

But when he peered through the branches again, the canoe was empty of Indians. He stood up and shaded his eyes against the sun. Several yards up the river, two black heads and four flashing arms were slicing wildly against the swift current.

He gave a satisfied grunt. "Lost your gut for my rifle, did you, you bastards."

He turned back to the canoe. The current was steadily drawing the light craft to the center of the stream. He'd have one hell of a time overtaking it if that happened. He dropped the rifle and scrambled his way to the end of the fallen tree and threw himself into the water. Its icy cold washed over him and he gasped.

Swimming with the current, he gained on the canoe steadily. But it was so quiet in there. Had they killed her?

He gathered his strength and gave a long lunge and grasped the side with his fingertips. He clung for a moment, catching his breath. "Now to get in the damned thing without tipping it," he muttered out loud.

He fastened his fingers on the opposite side of the vessel and pushed down as he drew first one leg and then the other inside. The canoe rocked crazily for a moment, then straightened itself and lay evenly on the water.

He squatted beside Rachael and quickly cut her bonds. His heart lurched. She was so pale. He turned her over carefully and laid his head on her breast. She was alive. The heartbeat was faint but steady.

He was laying her back down when he saw the trickle of blood running down through her hair. Gently he probed her scalp and his fingers found the long gash. "The bastard hit her with his tomahawk," he raged.

In near panic, he swore loud revenge on all red varmints as he grabbed up a paddle and drove it into the water. In a matter of minutes the canoe was scraping gravel and he was swooping Rachael into his arms and hurrying up the riverbank. He would pick up his rifle later.

He moved swiftly, almost running, and felt her

blood soaking into his shirt. "She will bleed to death, I know it," was a refrain running through his mind.

His fear nearly blinded him and he stumbled and lurched as he hurried on. He was halfway to the Jobe place when he met Nick Stone on the trail. The two large men, like strange dogs, glared at one another. Then alarm swept over Nick's face and he took a threatening step toward Adam.

"What have you done to her?" he demanded harshly.

Adam stared at the fear-stricken face bearing down on him. "By God, he's sleepin' with her too." For the space of a slow heartbeat, he thought to kill the man.

Abruptly angry, he snapped, "I didn't do anything to her. I took her away from three Indians."

Puzzled, Nick stared at the rage-filled face that glared at him. He hadn't said that much out of the way. Then it dawned on him. The woods' queer hunter was in love with Rachael. He wondered if they had met before.

Then Adam was thrusting her limp body toward Nick and saying brusquely, "Take her. I'm sick to death bothering with her."

Holding her carefully, Nick asked, "Do you know what's wrong with her?"

"One of the varmints tomahawked her in the head. She's bleedin' bad."

He turned and stalked back the way he had come. Nick stared after him, thinking, "It just about killed him to hand her over to me."

In long strides, he hurried to the cabin, spots of Rachael's blood making a trail in the dry dirt.

CHAPTER 8

Adam returned to the river, retrieved his rifle and stepped into the canoe. Angrily, he stared straight ahead as he dipped the paddle in and out of the water. "Damn the whore," he fumed. She was an ache that tore through him like something wild. He had almost stopped breathing back there when he thought she was dead.

He swung the canoe onto shore and tied it fast to a large rock. Climbing the hill that led to his quarters, he came to the conclusion that he'd better stay in camp until time for the hunt. "If I ever run into her again, I'll give 'Lisha cause to pump lead in me."

He heard his people before he saw them. Loud, drunken laughter floated on the still evening air, accompanied by the high, nervous squeals of the women. He sighed. Would he be able to endure them until time for the hunt?

Arriving at the clearing, he caught an excitement pervading the camp. Though dusk had just come on, already a huge fire had been built. Against its leaping flames, he watched the hunters milling about. The majority were already staggering and in a short time would be stretched out on the ground, oblivious to everything around them.

He leaned against a tree, debating whether or not to skirt the revelers and make his way to the cabin.

He didn't believe that he could put up with their drunkenness tonight.

For a moment he was surprised at his thoughts. Until lately such a thing would have never entered his mind. Always before he had been eager to join them at a moment's notice. He would drink his share of raw whiskey and use his share of the camp women. But the camp women were repulsive to him these days, and it seemed that he had lost his appetite for the liquid grain.

He pushed away from the tree and started to turn back into the forest. Then he stopped short, his eyes narrowing. There were three newcomers in camp. They stood in a small group talking to John. He moved back in the shadows and studied them.

Two of the men were nondescript, looking like a hundred other hunters. Their buckskins were worn and faded and the coonskin caps pushed back on their heads were dry and ragged. Adam dismissed them as unimportant and let his eyes study the third man.

The man was tall, thin and hawk-faced. The lines of dissipation running around his eyes and mouth lent a kind of attractiveness to him, and Adam disliked him immediately. His clothes were of the city and his neatness of dress, compared to the rough garb of the hunters, stood out like a drop of water in the dust.

He had a natural and friendly way about him, and as Adam watched, the camp women gathered about him, each vying for his attention. Two came close and stood on either side of him, and he placed an arm around their waists, not breaking his conversation with John. Adam's lips curled in contempt. "A ladies' man . . . a weakling," he decided.

John looked up and spotted him. "Hey, Adam, I want you to meet an old friend of mine. Me and him grew up together in Jamestown."

Annoyed at being discovered, Adam scowled and walked to meet them. The man pulled his right arm free of a clinging woman and offered his hand to Adam. But Adam ignored the proffered hand and looked at the stranger with cold eyes. After a moment, he asked curtly, "What's your handle, stranger?"

The man's piercing eyes stared back at him and for a time Adam thought that he wouldn't answer. Then finally he shrugged and dropped his hand. "They call me Jim Eagle." He paused a moment then added, "Like John says, we grew up together. He took to hunting and I . . . mostly gamble."

John knew by the signs that Adam didn't take to his friend and he spoke hesitantly when he interrupted to say, "I'd be obliged, Adam, if you'd take Jim and his friends on for the hunt."

It took Adam so long to answer, John was sure that he was going to refuse, and he wondered why. They needed extra men and he had seen his boss take on men that looked much worse than these.

The air was tense when Adam finally turned to Eagle and asked shortly, "You ever hunt before?"

John grew nervous when Jim's answer was also slow in coming. A sigh of relief escaped him when Jim answered, "I spent a couple of years at it one time. I carry my own weight around camp if that's what you're worried about."

After a short silence, Adam asked, "The law after you?"

Eagle's eyes went frosty. Adam read the indecision in them and hoped that the man would tell him to shove the hunt in his ass. That would give him the excuse to tell him to hit the trail. But then Eagle was shaking his head and saying quietly, "No. Not the law."

Adam debated asking him if an angry husband was on his tail, but glancing at the anxious look on John's face, he merely said, "I see."

Adam's suggestive tone did not escape Eagle, and angry, he was on the point of turning on his heel and leaving when Adam spoke again. "I need some new men. I'll try the three of you out."

They stared at one another for a short space, their eyes flashing a mutual dislike. Then Adam turned abruptly and walked away.

Eagle gave a short laugh. "He's not the friendliest cuss in the world, is he?"

"He is not that," John agreed, "but he's square. He won't shortchange you."

Rachael sat on the bottom step of the porch, stroking the two-inch scar above her left ear. A month had gone by since her encounter with the Indians and the scar still itched at times.

She mused on the fact that Adam Warden had saved her from them. It marked the third time he had saved her from some trouble or other, and she wondered if it meant anything significant.

Nick had given her what details he could about that day. "That hunter looked like death when I come on him and you. I think he's smitten with you, Rach," he had teased.

She had felt herself blushing and was thankful for the darkness of the bedroom. "Why is that so strange, Nick? You're smitten, aren't you?" she had teased back.

"I don't think it's strange that he would fall in love with you. Any man with eyes in his head would. But it strikes me kind of funny that wild man loving a woman like you."

She had leaned on an elbow and asked, "Why is it funny?"

"Oh, you know. Wasting his time on wishful thinking. He knows a woman like you ain't for the likes of him."

Silently she had wondered if Adam felt that way, too. She dismissed the thought as being unlikely. She had a feeling that Adam thought he was too good for her.

Nick had pulled her over on top of him then, chasing all other thoughts. It was the first time since her accident and they loved each other like a pair of animals. Still, when it was over and Nick lay deep in sleep at her side, her thoughts returned to Adam and she wondered what he was doing on his hilltop.

Elisha's loud, ringing voice called her back to the present and she looked his way. He and Nick were a short distance behind the barn, pulling stumps. By the light of the full moon, she watched the sturdy horses straining against the mighty roots that fought to keep their grip in the earth. Elisha was shouting encouragement to them and their muscles rippled in the effort that brought them almost to their knees.

"I'll be busy tomorrow," she mused.

Tomorrow, the first day of October, there would be a logrolling on the place. All summer whenever Nick and Elisha had a free moment, they felled trees, widening their acres. Dave and Rafe had lopped off the branches, and logs lay scattered all over the forest. In the morning, early, friends and neighbors would arrive with teams of horses and the logs would be dragged to the site where the new barn would be built next summer.

"Them logs has got to cure at least a year," Elisha had explained. "You put up a building with green timber, and within a year it'll be warped out of sight."

It was thanks to Rachael's money that the new barn was needed. When one of the homesteaders had decided to give up farming and leave the hills, she had purchased all his stock. With the additional cows, hogs and sheep, the old barn was filled to capacity. Elisha had grinned and remarked, "You're gonna make me a man of means, Rach."

She dreaded tomorrow. It would be her first time acting hostess for Elisha. She was nervous about it and had spoken of her fears to Elisha. "What will I do when all the cooking and eating is done? I just know I won't fit in with them. I won't even know what to talk about."

Elisha had laughed at her fretting. "They're like all other women, Rach. They'll sit around gossipin' . . . maybe sewin' quilt pieces or spinnin' thread. You can do all them things, so just get in there and do."

Before going off to the fields, he had patted her shoulder and added, "Anyhow, Ruby and your Aunt Sarah will be here. They'll carry you along."

She had felt some relief at his counseling. She did know how to spin thread . . . even knew how to weave it into material. Ruby had taught her.

Elisha, like all the other homesteaders, had a flax field. He had given Rachael the task of tending it, gathering it and preparing clothing from it. Sarah had taught her to sew, and the shift she now wore was of her making. She had even sewed a shirt for Elisha. It was far from perfect, but he had smiled and said it was just fine. Only Nick had seen his grin as he took a roll in one sleeve.

"At any rate," she thought, "I qualify enough with the needle to sew up plain dresses for the hill's poor children."

The poor would be here tomorrow also, she remembered. They came to all the affairs, knowing that a good hot meal would be served. But grandpa had said that they worked as hard as anyone else and were always made welcome. She had questioned him about these people. "Why is it, grandpa, that in this land of rich soil, we have poor people? Are they just plain lazy?"

He had wrinkled his brow in thought for awhile, and then said slowly, "Well no, Rach, I wouldn't say that they're plain out lazy. I think that the majority are just plain hard-luck prone. It's just as if every judgment they make is the wrong one."

Rachael nodded her head and he continued, "There are the dreamers of course. I think with them the realization of hopes and plans is nothing. I believe that it's all in the anticipation with some people. Almost always you'll find that it's the dreamer who's always movin' on."

Rachael had decided then that her grandfather was pretty wise for all his buffoonery.

She glanced across the yard at the table Nick had set up for tomorrow's occasion. It was a simple affair. Wide boards were laid across two huge tree stumps. Tomorrow they would groan with the weight of food placed upon them.

Nick had also, with the help of Dave and Rafe, dug a long trench and filled it with big chunks of green maple and hickory. Later tonight he would set it afire, and in the morning only hot glowing coals would remain. He had explained that he would then lay freshly cut slender poles across its width and the hill women would lay their great roasts of deer and bear upon them to cook.

It would be quite a feast, she knew. Besides the deer and bear, there would also be fish and pigeons and other small game. The meats would be crowded by vegetables of all kinds, plus cakes and pies and canned fruits and jellies.

A cool wind blew in from the forest, chilling her flesh. She gathered her shawl about her shoulders and hurried into the cabin.

The next day dawned bright and hot. "We've got us an Indian summer day," Elisha declared.

By midmorning, Rachael and the other women were wiping their faces and brows and pulling clinging clothes away from their bodies. Sarah had gone into the cabin and removed her underclothing, and as she moved about with swaying hips and bouncing breasts, the men ogled her openly. But Rachael noticed that she, herself, was viewed with sidelong surreptitious glances. No one was taking a chance on riling Elisha over his granddaughter.

White aromatic smoke swirled around the roasting meat, and the working men cast many glances at the sun and then at the pit. Finally at high noon, Ruby rang the bell mounted on top of a tall pole. By the time the teams were unhitched and tended, and the men had washed up at the river, the food was on the table.

It was a long leisurely meal with much laughter and good-natured fun-poking. Too seldom the homesteaders got together, and when they did, the gathering took on a party atmosphere.

The food disappeared at a rate Rachael couldn't believe, and when everyone's appetite had been sated, only scraps and bones remained. Hungry hounds hung around the table for those.

The men lounged in the shade in quiet talk, having a pipe before returning to the logs. The women busied themselves with clearing the table and washing dishes and pots. When Rachael tried to help, they insisted that she rest.

"You go sit down," an old woman ordered her. "You been flittin' around like a jaybird all day."

Rachael didn't argue overmuch. There was someone she wanted to visit with. Tidying her hair and removing her apron, she made her way to a solitary figure sitting some distance from the others. Elisha had pointed out the white-haired old gentleman as Adam's grandfather.

Silas watched her approach and thought to himself that the hills had never seen anything like her. Elisha had mentioned to him the spark that had quickened between their grandchildren and he could readily understand how untamed Adam would be drawn to this woman. Still he frowned. These hills could see bloodshed over this beauty. If Adam should want her bad enough, he would without hesitation take her. And with his nature, wild as the wolf he sometimes hunted, Adam would shoot the man who stood in his way.

But Adam had met his match in this proud beauty, he thought. Given half a chance this woman could handle him. She would do it in such a fashion that Adam would have no idea he was being managed.

He noted the visible nervousness about her when she stood uncertain before him, and he smiled at her encouragingly. She murmured, "Mr. Warden, I'm Rachael Jobe, Elisha's granddaughter."

Silas patted the ground beside him. "Sit down. I was hoping you would come and talk to me, child."

His kind wrinkled face made her feel instinctively that he was her friend and she smiled widely. Dropping down beside him, she said, "It's awfully hot, isn't it?"

"Yes, it is. Unusually hot for this time of the year. I'm afraid we're in for a bad heat storm."

Silas listened to her polite chatter . . . how well the crops had grown, how much she liked the hills and her new home. But he knew that Adam was utmost in her mind and that it was of him she wanted to talk. During a short pause, he said gently, "Elisha tells me that you have met my grandson, Adam."

Long lashes swept her cheeks as she murmured a low yes.

Was there a sound of hopelessness in that single word? Silas wondered. "He's a wild hellion, Rachael," he said quietly, "but there's good in him. His main problem is that he stays in the woods too long.

Goes off to the Indians too often. Sometimes he disappears, no one knows where, for months."

Rachael sat with lowered head, picking up dirt and letting it sift through her fingers. Silas looked at the bent head and wondered if he had spoken the wrong words. Then the fine eyes were giving him a long level look. "He's a hard, cold man, isn't he, Mr. Warden? A woman would be a fool to pin her hopes on him, wouldn't she?"

"Now that's where you're wrong, daughter," Silas was fast to answer. "It would depend on what kind of woman was interested in him. How much she loved him and was willing to sacrifice for him. She would have to be able to look beyond the face he shows to the world."

Silas paused for a moment, in deep thought. He sighed and continued, "There's a terrible force that pushes at Adam all the time. And since he's not the kind of man that one questions, no one can help him ... except maybe the right woman."

Rachael wondered hopefully if the old fellow knew what he was talking about. Her heart answered immediately, "Of course he does. He should know his own grandson." But in her head, words of realism were striving to get out. "The old man is prejudiced. He wants to see Adam in that light."

She sat forward and peered earnestly into his face. "Do you honestly think that a woman will come along some day and tame him a bit?"

Silas laid a gnarled hand on hers and his leathery face crinkled into a grin. "Honey, I honestly believe it, and what's more, I think that woman is already here."

Rachael felt herself blushing and was startled.

When was the last time she had done that? She turned her hand over and squeezed Silas's fingers. "Our secret?" she asked. He returned the pressure and nodded.

The men were returning to work and Silas rose slowly and stiffly to join them. Rachael was about to suggest he remain in the shade and rest, but realized in time that his feelings would be hurt if she hinted that he was unable to take his place with the other men.

He bent an elbow to her and smiled. She smiled back and laid her hand in the crook and together they walked toward the men. Rachael left him there, promising that she would visit him soon.

"He is lonesome," she thought. "I wonder if Adam ever goes to see him."

The women had gathered under a drooping willow by the river, hoping to catch a cool breeze off the water. Rachael joined them, and with her back propped against the tree's trunk, dozed off to the low murmur of her gossiping neighbors.

Sarah poked her and she jerked awake. The last log had been rolled into place, the hot sun had set and darkness was upon them. A huge bonfire was lighted and Nick brought out the whiskey keg. The men greeted its appearance with loud shouts and pushed and shoved around Nick. Tin cups were passed around and the men drank freely. It wasn't long before the single men were searching out Sarah.

As Sarah disappeared into the forest with one man or the other, Rachael watched the hill women for their reactions. When no one seemed to pay any attention to what her aunt was about, she was relieved. Evidently her aunt's way of life was accepted by everyone. "At least they pretend so in front of grandpa," she giggled inwardly.

Rafe and Dave tuned up their fiddle and banjo, and while they played, Elisha called the turns and everyone danced, hopping and stomping.

A hazy moon was quite high when the last of the whiskey was drunk and everyone was exhausted. Sleepy children were gathered up and good-byes were said.

Ruby decided to spend the night and the Jobe household lost no time in retiring. But Elisha's grunts and thumps did not resound throughout the cabin that night. He, like everyone else, was bone tired.

The next morning they awakened to the same stifling heat they had gone to bed to. Both Rachael and Ruby slipped out of bed before the men awakened. "It's too hot to fool around," Rachael laughed.

Ruby nodded her head in agreement. "It is for me anyway. It takes Elisha longer these days. I just can't imagine having him pump away for a half hour or longer in this heat."

As they prepared breakfast, Ruby talked of the days when Elisha was younger and of his stamina in bed. Rachael thought she sounded a little wishful.

They ate a lazy breakfast, slapping at the flies whose bites were worse than mosquito stings. "Them flies say that we're gonna have rain," Elisha announced. "In fact, from the size and color of them clouds forming in the north, I'd say we're gonna have one hell of a storm with it."

"I'd better get home before it starts," Ruby decided.

"I'll take you home by boat," Rachael offered.

As they clambered into the boat, a hot stiff wind

sprang up, driving the dark clouds before it. Ruby studied the skies, a worried frown creasing her forehead.

When Ruby was settled in the boat, Rachael pushed the craft away from shore and carefully climbed in. Picking up the paddle, she skillfully rowed it around low-hanging trees and jutting boulders. Downstream something splashed in the water and Ruby jumped nervously. Minutes later there came a thrashing sound as something fled through the forest. "A deer, I'll bet," Rachael declared.

But Ruby made no response. She now crouched in the bottom of the boat, cringing away every time a wind-tossed wave leaped at the fragile vessel. When they were halfway to her landing, the storm broke. The lightning was blinding, the thunder deafening and the water came in torrents.

Rachael dipped and pulled at the oars as fast as her strength would allow, and running through her mind were words of Nick's. "Don't ever be on the river in a thunderstorm, Rach. The water draws lightning and it will strike you sure."

Her mind a mixture of fright and confusion, she debated whether to continue on or to bank the craft until the storm was over. A jagged streak of lightning hit the water only feet in front of them and she decided. Swiftly she made for the shore.

With the help of the whimpering Ruby, she managed to turn the boat over and prop it against a big boulder. And in sodden clothes plastered to their skin, and hair that streamed water, they crawled beneath its protective cover and waited out the storm.

For over an hour the storm lashed at their dubious shelter while the wind threatened to carry it away. In the distance, over the crashing blasts of thunder, they could hear the dull roar of rushing water as the numerous gullies filled to overflowing. Ruby sat hunched, her arms around her knees, silently praying that they weren't in the path of one.

At last the drive of the rain slackened and soon only a fine drizzle remained. The thunder was a far rumble when the two women crept from under the boat. Silently they got the boat back into the water and climbed in.

The river had grown quite high and ran fast. But it posed no real danger and in a short time they were scraping ashore at Ruby's.

The air had grown cooler. The rain had swept away the false summer heat and it would be no more until next year. Rachael shivered in her wet clothing and Ruby said, "Come on up to the cabin and get out of those wet things. There's a dress there that I just finished making for you."

Following behind Ruby's brisk step, Rachael mused that Ruby was very good to her. "Almost like a mother."

Rachael headed back for the river, walking slowly in the mud. She had kicked off her wet moccasins in the boat and was sorry now that she had. The ground was quite cold and the downpour had brought many sharp stones to the surface of the path. Her mind intent on avoiding as many as possible, she did not see the figure that kept pace with her, off in the woods.

She was almost to the river when a man stepped out in front of her. She gasped and held her breath, then let it out slowly. Adam Warden stood there, looking mockingly at her. She gave him a timid smile. After all, he had saved her from possible death.

But the smile died on her lips when he spoke. "Well, whore, I see you're up and around. I guess that whack in the head didn't hurt you none."

His insolent tone and words were like a dash of cold water in her face. "There will never be a changing between us," she sighed. "He's an arrogant mule that has made up his mind and nothing will change it."

His eyes roamed over the new dress that Ruby had made too short in the hem and too long at the neck. Rachael knew that most of her breast was showing and a good part of her legs above the knee. "To hell with him," her mind cried silently. "Let him think whatever he wants to."

"I see old 'Lisha has put you in a sack dress," he sneered. "He always puts his women in them." He gave a sarcastic laugh and added, "I thought you'd get better treatment though."

Squeezing back the bitter tears, Rachael suffered in silence the painful contraction in her throat. She would never let him know how his words hurt.

Nonchalantly she leaned against a tree and rested her head on its rough bark. Looking at him from under lowered lids, she studied him coolly. And as she continued to gaze at him, she sensed rather than saw that an anger was building within him. Her apparent unconcern wasn't as he had planned. He took a step toward her and rasped out harshly, "I suppose the old fool thinks that if he takes away the whore clothing, no other man will look at you."

He paused and she knew that he waited for her to

refute him in some way. But she made no response and this time when he verbally abused her, anger was evident in his voice.

"Damned old idiot, doesn't he know you look more whorish in that rag than anything else you could wear?" he snarled.

She watched his breathing become heavy and saw desire building in his eyes. Elation sang through her blood as she answered him coolly and deliberately.

"The dress is my own choice. You see, it being such a simple affair, no time is wasted when desire comes over me. Can you not see, long-hunter, that nothing separates my skin from this 'sack.'"

She did not miss the swift tensing of his muscles as her words thrust out at him. Rage was consuming him and it was balm to her heart. But then, a flicker of fear ran through her as his fingers, hard as steel, fastened on her wrist. A quick jerk of his hand and she was held fast against his body.

He stared down a moment into her eyes, and then grated out, "Damn you, you beautiful whore. Don't you think I have eyes in my head?"

Then, so fast she could not catch her breath, he ripped the single garment to its hem and pushed her onto the ground. She clutched at the torn edges, trying to pull them together. But he squatted down beside her and grabbed her hands.

"Leave them bare," he snapped.

At the crisp crackle of his command, a stubborn defiance came over her face and she tried to scramble to her feet. Swearing under his breath, he slapped her sharply across the face. She went sprawling back onto the ground with tears smarting her eyes.

Blazing green eyes burned into steely blue ones,

clinging for unmeasured minutes. Then unexpectedly his expression was saying that he was sorry for his violent action. But when she would have sat up, his face became hard again and he warned her coolly, "I'm gonna have you one way or the other. If you want it the hard way, that's alright with me."

She knew it would be useless to fight him. Her puny strength would be nothing against the power of his hands. She sighed inwardly. She hadn't wanted it this way. She had dreamed that their first coming together would be warm and loving, and a willing giving of each other. Not a brutal attack on the dirt of the forest floor.

She relaxed, resigned, and nodded her head.

He stood up, his hands going to his belt. Then echoing through the hills came Elisha's voice.

"Hey, Rachael, where are you, girl?"

A strange look came over Adam's face. For some reason Elisha's call for Rachael brought back the memory of when Silas had used to call to him. How odd that Elisha's calling his whore should remind him of that.

He looked down at the beautiful body at his feet and was tempted to grab her up and run away with her. To hide her in some cave where only he could see her. But Elisha's voice came again, much closer, and he shrugged his shoulders.

"Well, Rachael, you've been saved for now, but my time will come."

She watched him stalk off and didn't know if she was sorry or glad that grandpa had chased him away.

Then she jumped to her feet and sprinted for the boat. She must get home and change her dress before grandpa and Nick saw it.

CHAPTER 9

A cold raw wind blew in one evening in the second week in November and the first snow came. The ice came with it, closing the creeks and freezing the river's edge.

It was soundless when it first began, great flakes sifting down slowly and hissing in fireplaces. Then it started in earnest and soon all the trails leading out of the hills would be locked tight until spring.

That same evening, Adam Warden sat before a small campfire, eating a meager supper. He had been alone in the wilderness for a month. A pair of green eyes and the unbearable company of his men had driven him there.

A solitary flake of snow hit his cheek and he looked up hopefully. It was a doubtful snow at first, melting almost before it hit the ground, and he swore in disappointment. He was eager to start the winter hunt.

But the air became colder and soon the earth was white. Excitement gripped him and he began to gather his gear. Stowing the bundle and rifle into the canoe, he stepped in behind it and picked up the paddle. With long sure strokes, he skimmed the top of the river, the current working with him.

Many times in the moonlight, he made out the bulky masses of beavers' dams. He marked their location in his memory. He and his party would travel this way as they worked toward the Ohio Valley.

He had chosen the valley this year because it was still practically virgin. The rivers and forests there had hardly been tapped. Old Bear had mentioned once that the streams teemed with beaver.

The ribbon of river gleamed in the light of the cold, white moon, and the lightweight vessel made good time. When the moon was fading against the brightness of the rising sun, Adam arrived at his destination. The snow had stopped when he rammed the boat ashore and fastened it securely to a tree.

Scrambling up the narrow path that led to the post, he judged the snow to be about six inches deep. A real good beginning, he thought.

He gained the clearing and in the distance he heard the rapid whack of a hammer. "Who's the damn fool who would build on such a day as this?" he muttered out loud.

When he stepped onto the single winding street of the village, he saw at once the source of the early-morning noise. The Reverend Tim Moser was perched on the peak of a low, weather-beaten building, patching the roof of the church. The tall, lanky preacher looked about frozen and swiped at his nose almost constantly.

Quite a controversy had taken place when the settlers decided that they needed a church. There had been heated arguments over what denomination the house of worship should be. Lutherans, Presbyterians and Baptists predominated, with a sprinkling of Methodists. After many bitter words that almost led to fist fights, it was decided that the new church would embrace all Protestant beliefs, and that they would call it the United Christian.

However, to this day, no one had learned the religion that Tim Moser claimed. He had ridden in one day shortly after the church was completed, a worn Bible in his hand and an equally worn mule between his legs.

The hillmen tended to look at him askance. It seemed that all his answers to their questions were elusive and they distrusted him. But the ladies wanted a preacher and the clamor they raised overrode the men's objections.

They threw together a one-room shack for him back of the church and promptly forgot about him. But the good women of the parish got together a bed and other necessary items and saw to it that food was brought to him every week.

His house of worship was filled every Sunday.

Adam had never been inside the church, but Silas attended all meetings, and his grandson now tipped his coonskin respectfully.

The barnlike post loomed in front of him and he pushed open the door. The single long room was lighted by two small windows, one on either end. He stood a moment, accustoming his eyes to the darkness, and sniffed at the mixture of odors that assailed his nose. Predominant over the smell of tobacco, kerosene, pelts and the sweet scent of sorghum was the overpowering stink of fermenting sauerkraut, aging in huge stone crocks.

On a long table spanning the length of the room was an assortment of various articles used by the settlers. There were iron kettles, pewter plates and cups, bone buttons, needles and thread and dozens of other trinkets.

Scattered among the gewgaws were shining squares of tin. These were passed off to the Indians as mirrors. Many fine pelts were traded for the small scraps that reflected their image.

At the farthest end of the table, rude clothing was piled. Drab homespuns, woolen underwear, caps, bonnets, and heavy stockings were placed in neat rows. A short stack of dull gray material took up one corner.

The storekeeper, a Scotsman, his bearing stern and his eyes wintry, bore down on Adam.

"What will ye be having, Adam Warden?" he asked, the burr strong in his voice.

Adam threw some money on the counter and muttered, "Some gunpowder and flint."

"Off on another hunt, be ye?"

Adam didn't answer, knowing that it wasn't required.

Skillfully the powder was measured and transferred into the pouch that hung at Adam's waist. He gathered up the flint and change, and nodding briefly at the Scot, left the store.

He made his way to Silas's cabin next. Even though months would often pass without him seeing the old man, he made it a practice to visit his grandfather before and after every hunt.

The sturdy door swung open and the spare figure of Silas filled the opening. The thin body was bent somewhat and he used a long stick to aid his steps. The first rays of the morning sun shone on his white head and a sharp pain jabbed at Adam's chest. "Why he's getting old," ran through his mind. Before long this fine old man would be no more. He would miss him dreadfully and would lose his one link to respectability.

He thought of their good times together and a lump formed in his throat. His hard eyes went soft as he gripped Silas's hand. "How have you been, grandpa?"

"I been alright, boy. Got a crick in my back is all. Touch of rheumatism, I guess."

He swung aside and let Adam enter. Inside, the cabin was almost identical to what it had been when Adam was a youngster. Everything neat and in its place. The same tangy scent of apples and drying tobacco filled the air. Adam breathed deep, recalling those days.

Silas hobbled to the hearth and took a chair beside him. "Gettin' ready to go out again, are you?"

"Yeah, it's that time of the year, grandpa."

"Ever since the snow began to fall last evenin' I've been expectin' you. I baked you an apple pie last night."

Adam smiled his thanks, afraid he wouldn't be able to speak. Apple pie was an old weakness of his and Silas always remembered.

The pie was cut and together they ate it, washing it down with cups of strong black coffee. Then pipes were filled and they sat in quiet talk, discussing where Adam would hunt and how long he would be gone.

A companionable silence fell between them and Adam stretched lazily and let his mind reach back into his childhood. The sound of Silas awkwardly clearing his throat broke his reverie and he looked at Silas, his eyes questioning.

The old man pulled at his beard a couple of times and finally began to speak. "A very small bird has told me that you have found a woman to your liking."

There was just a touch of mischievousness lurking in Silas's eyes and Adam felt his face growing warm. He shifted uncomfortably in his chair as he wondered how in the world Silas could have heard about Elisha's woman. Then the thought occurred to him that most likely his grandfather was referring to Little Flower. The long-hunters had been talking.

His mouth became an angry thin line and he snapped, "That's not true. Tell your bird he's singing up the wrong tree."

Silas nodded his head and Adam poured another cup of coffee, splashing the hot liquid over his hand in his annoyance.

Silas hid his grin, then spoke softly, "I have met the young woman in question. At Elisha's . . . when he had his logrollin'. We talked for quite awhile. I found her to be a complete lady."

Startled surprise swept across Adam's face. So it was Elisha's woman that he spoke of. He stood up and poked at the fire. She had taken the old man in. He resumed his seat and said sneeringly, "Any woman who would lie with 'Lisha Jobe couldn't be a lady."

Silas smiled inwardly, but said gravely, "I'd have to agree with you there, son. 'Lisha wouldn't know what to do with a lady in his bed."

Adam sent him a quizzical look and wondered if his grandfather was rambling in his mind. And later, when Silas asked if anyone had seen her in Elisha's bed, he snorted, "Aw hell, grandpa."

But Silas would not be put off so easily and pursued his line of reasoning. "I'm serious, Adam. I'm tryin' to put two and two together and come up with the right number. 'Lisha still makes his regular trips to see Ruby. She was at the logrollin', and she and 'Lisha were might chummy . . . right in front of the girl."

"That don't mean a thing with that old whorin' bastard," Adam growled. "He probably goes to Kate's place too."

He sat staring into the fire for a moment then looked at Silas. "Grandpa, you know there's no place for a woman in my plans. Why do you keep needlin' me about it?"

Silas sighed. He hated to bring up the old subject and make Adam angry just when he was leaving on a long trip of hardships that could possibly cause his death. Still he felt that his own time was short, and his wish above all others was that he could see Adam settled down before he died.

His voice was grave when he answered. "You know why I push you, Adam. The life you're leading is a purposeless existence and as long as I live I expect that I will harp on you to find a decent woman and marry her."

Adam's voice was sarcastic when he answered Silas with a question. "And you think that Elisha's woman is decent?"

His sarcasm didn't fool Silas. He studied the lean face and saw the wretched discontent in the eyes that stared moodily into the flames. A surge of sympathy for his grandson swept over him. Adam was hopelessly in love with Rachael Jobe and had no idea what to do about it.

It was on the point of his tongue to reveal Rachael's true identity even though he had promised Elisha not to interfere. In the end he consoled himself that if he knew women, Rachael was quite capable of doing her own matchmaking.

He nodded his head and said quietly, "She could very well be a decent woman. There are many factors involved in describing decency."

Adam snorted his disbelief and rose to his feet. Shrugging into his coat he remarked shortly, "I think you're gettin' touched in your old age."

Silas chuckled. "Could be you're right, son."

On the porch they gripped hands again and Silas's voice trembled a bit when he said, "God's speed, Adam."

"Take care of yourself, grandpa. Do you hear me?"

Silas nodded as his hand lingered on the muscular shoulder.

Adam decided to leave the canoe where it was. Overland would see him home faster. It would also be warmer than riding the windswept stretch of water. The tall pines and cedar made a wonderful barrier against the wind.

The forest was silent under its blanket of snow and only the crunching of his footsteps disturbed the quiet. His conversation with Silas crept into his mind and he grinned sheepishly and let it toy with his grandfather's expressed desire.

Could he adjust to being a family man, he wondered. Would he be able to provide for a wife and children? The big game had begun to move farther back into the wilderness, but a man could still make money from the beaver and other small animals that were in plentiful supply. And as for food, that was no problem. It was all around. Take the pigeons for instance. There were so many that sometimes the sky darkened from their numbers. Then there were the deer that roamed the forest in great herds. And if a man had a mind to, he could raise fifty bushels of wheat and corn to the acre.

A large buck with widely spread antlers crashed through the brush ahead of him and Adam came out of his dream world. He gave a soundless laugh at his foolish thoughts.

No great campfire greeted him this time as he stepped into the clearing. With the snow and cold, the hunters had moved into the large communal building that housed them. From inside came the bass rumble of men and an occasional high squeal of a woman.

For once the dogs caught his scent before sighting him and gave no outcry. He hurried to his own cabin before the men discovered his arrival. In privacy he could gather his traps and other necessary items in peace, and have a clearer mind to plot the finer details of the hunt.

When the sun was overhead, gear and traps were in readiness, placed in front of the door. He emptied the coffee pot, rinsed it out, then moved to the fireplace and shoveled ashes onto the glowing coals. He took a quick glance around the room and nodded his head. Everything was in order.

As he locked the door behind him, he noted that the air had become colder. Looking up, he studied the hazy ring around the sun and muttered to himself, "Another storm is on the way."

On his way to the shed that stabled the horses, he paused to pound on the hunters' door and to call out, "Come on, men. Time to get started."

A scramble sounded from within and the men came pouring out, bumping into each other in their eagerness.

"Hey, Adam," John greeted him. "When did you get in? We looked for you all last night."

"Got in a few hours ago. You men all packed?"

"Yeah, we're all set. We started gettin' ready when the first snow fell."

From the corner of his eye, Adam saw Eagle come through the door and amble toward him, fastening the front of his trousers as he walked. "Damned show-off bastard," he mumbled darkly to himself. His dislike of the gambler was as strong as it ever was.

Ignoring Eagle, he turned and continued on to the shed. The stallion tossed up his head and gave a whinny of welcome. Adam smiled, pleased. It was good to be missed.

Behind him the men hurried about, getting into one another's way and cursing good-humoredly about it. But amid all the confusion, the pack animals were finally ready. Their backs were piled high with provisions, gear, and bearskins for their beds.

The hunters stood waiting and Adam's eyes made a slow survey of them. Mentally he shook his head at their rough appearance, but smiled at the exuberance that gleamed in their eyes. With a new hunt before them, they were like children.

There was no excitement in the women's eyes however. Only a dull hopelessness gazed out of them. They knew that the next few months would be pure hell. They stood in a group to one side, ready to jump and do the bidding of any man. Adam ran his eyes over their worn-out bodies and gaunt faces and decided to stop at Bear's camp and pick up Flower. It would be impossible to take one of these poor creatures into his bed.

Looking up at the low, murky sky, Adam watched the dark gathering clouds for a moment and hoped that the new storm would hold off until they made camp for the night. He picked up his rifle that leaned against a tree and said, "Let's go, men," and turned into the forest.

The hunters, their step lively, followed him single file. John raised his voice in a bawdy song and the others joined in. The women plodded along behind, leading the pack animals, and the half-wild dogs ran barking through the woods.

They walked until darkness was almost upon them, and their luck held. No new snow had fallen yet. But the black clouds scudding across the sky warned that it could commence at any time. They climbed to the top of a hill and below was a small sheltered valley, an ideal spot for camp.

As usual, the first night out the men were short-tempered and quarrelsome. Months of soft living had turned them rusty and their movements were slow and awkward. But Adam dismissed their griping and cursing as unimportant, knowing that in a few days they would be back in the full swing of camp chores. Nevertheless, until then, he would keep an eye on them. They were not above pushing the work off onto the women.

It was not pity that prompted him to do this, but only that he wanted the camp to be made properly.

The women simply didn't have the strength to do some of the necessary work. He watched the broken-down hag who walked bent over with the load she strove to carry and recognized the pack as belonging to Jake and let out an angry roar. "Jake, you goddam lazy bastard, unpack that horse yourself. I'm not gonna have any sick females on this trip."

Bit by bit camp was made. The women busied themselves making supper over a glowing fire while the men took up their axes and went to cut cedar boughs that would be covered with the bearskins and slept on.

They were called to supper and ate a silent meal, too stiff and sore to even talk. Later they lit their pipes and listened to the howling wolves as they puffed contentedly.

The snow came, hissing as it hit the campfire. In an hour there was an additional inch on the ground. Adam stood up and stretched. "Pick your sentries, John," he ordered, "and the rest of you turn in."

As he crawled between the furs, Adam noted that Eagle had two women in his bed. "The slick bastard is makin' sure he keeps warm tonight," he muttered inwardly.

He had been surprised and somehow disappointed that Eagle had done his share of camp chores. Also he hadn't tried to push any of the work onto the women. It wasn't only the women who liked him, either. There was an easy friendliness about the man that drew the hunters to him also.

Eagle felt his piercing stare and leaned up on his elbows, gazed back a moment, then gave him a mocking smile. Adam scowled back, then turned his head away. His dog came to the furs and whined, and impatiently he lifted the corner of the cover. "Come on then, crawl in." The dog wagged his tail and wormed his way to the heat of his feet.

"Don't get too used to it, hound," he growled. "Little Flower will be in here tomorrow night."

The camp finally settled down. The last thump and groan was heard and Adam fell asleep to the roar of the northern wind and a pair of green eyes.

They were up the next dawn, shaking off the several inches of snow that had covered them while they slept. Stiff, cold and sore they stumbled around gathering gear and packing the horses. When the sky was turning pink in the east, the women had a breakfast of sorts laid out on a blanket.

The sun was climbing by the time they headed out again.

By late afternoon, they arrived at Bear's camp. Only squaws and children, along with a dozen or so mangy dogs, greeted them. Bear and the braves were out hunting, the chief's youngest wife informed Adam.

"You expect him back today?"

"He comes when the sun sets."

Out of the corner of his eye, Adam caught a movement in the forest and knew that Flower watched him. When her fringed skirt flashed out of sight, he smiled. She would be waiting in the teepee.

"We'll camp here tonight, men," he called out.

The hunters hadn't missed the little byplay between Adam and the girl, and sly winks passed between them. But Eagle hadn't smirked. His eyes had followed the rounded figure, hot desire shooting out of their depths. When one of the camp women laid a timid hand upon his arm, for the first time he was rude and roughly pushed her aside as he watched Adam follow the girl.

As the squaw had said, Bear and the braves returned to camp just as the sun was skimming the treetops. The old chief spotted Adam and greeted him warmly.

"You come to spend winter with Bear?" he wanted to know. "You make up your mind to marry my daughter?"

His question caught Adam by surprise and he wondered uneasily how best to answer the query. Bear was a proud man and would take it unkindly if he were to learn that his daughter was only wanted for the winter. Carefully, he chose his words.

"Actually we're on a hunt, Bear. Your camp lies in our path and I thought to stop and visit a time with you. Of course it is nice to see Flower again."

Bear frowned, his disappointment plain on his face. For awhile there was only the sound of the crackling fire and the supper sizzling upon it. Then the chief leaned over and laid a hand on Adam's knee.

"Bear been watching your white squaws. They weak. Never be able to take care of hunters all winter. I offer you some Indian women to help. Strong like men." He paused a moment, gave Adam a sidelong glance, and added, "Little Flower, she go too."

Adam repressed a sigh of relief. Evidently the chief wasn't going to give up having him for a son-in-law so easily. Gravely he thanked the old father and looked across the fire at Flower's happy, shining face.

He didn't join his men for the night meal, but accepted instead Bear's invitation to supper. Later, they sat long before the fire, talking and passing a pipe between them. Adam grew tired and thought of Flower waiting for him in the teepee. As he wondered how to politely interrupt the rambling of the Indian, he was suddenly interested in what the chief was saying.

"You go northwest about fifteen miles, you find old log cabin. Foolish white man build it some years ago. Him and family die this spring. Keep you and Flower warm."

Adam hid the smile that tugged at his lips. The old man didn't want his daughter sleeping on the ground.

"Thank you for telling me, Bear."

"Is nothing. You go to bed now. Squaws will be ready in the morning."

Adam found Flower waiting, warm and eager. But when he, as usual, sought only his own relief, tears of disappointment rolled down her cheeks. Remembering the look on Eagle's face, Adam debated sending her to him. The gambler would give her what she desired. He laughed aloud at the thought of Eagle's surprise when he found her to still be virgin. Then he remembered Bear. The little one would just have to ache.

True to the chief's word, four squaws waited in the cold dawn. The hunters stared at them with hungry eyes and made remarks to one another.

"How would you like to have that plump one between your legs?"

"Yeah. I'm sick to death of that bag of bones I have to ride every night."

The squaws overheard them and the older one muttered, "White men. It would never enter their minds that they have turned the white women into bags of bones."

Adam too heard the remarks passed between his men and a frown creased his forehead. Bear would be insulted if his squaws were mistreated. Gathering the men to one side, he cautioned them, "These women are going with us to be of help. They're not to be ridden day and night like your whores are."

A low murmur ran through the group and Adam sensed the anger his words had aroused and hurried to continue. "When we make camp tonight you men can draw for them. But, whoever wins one, he must use her only at night, and then within reason. If I see a squaw crawl out of bed, weak and drug out, that man loses her and she'll go on to another man."

Loud whoops greeted his announcement. When the shouting died down, Eagle strode forward and faced Adam. "What about the young one? Is she in the drawing?"

"No."

The hawk face grew dark with anger and his hand came to rest on the ugly knife stuck in his waist band. "Keeping her for yourself, I take it."

"For the time being."

"I suppose that means you'll keep her until you tire of her?"

"One would not soon tire of Little Flower."

"Then?"

"It is my affair."

Snapping his answer, Adam turned on his heel and walked away, feeling the smouldering eyes boring into his back. He knew for certain that he and the lean Eagle would have some battle one day.

Late that afternoon they found the dilapidated

cabin that Bear had spoken of. Adam pushed open the sagging door and entered, with Flower hard on his heels. The large single room was well constructed, but needed some repairs. The walls were of rough-hewn logs, the cracks in between filled with the red clay of the country. A huge fireplace took up most of one wall and a flagstone hearth reached at least four feet into the room.

"It's plain that man wasn't taking any chances on the place burnin' down," he remarked to Flower.

The few pieces of furniture had been crudely thrown together from rough planks, squat and ugly. "It will beat sitting and sleeping outside," Adam mused.

They discovered that the wood box still held wood and Flower soon had flames shooting up the chimney. The hound pushed into the cabin and curled up in front of the fire, sighing a contented sound. Adam roughed up his fur, then left to see to his men.

They too had a large fire going and were hunkered around it. The squaws were busy cutting cedar tips for the beds and the white women moved around camp preparing supper.

They were settled in now. This would be the permanent base from which they would hunt and trap. Tomorrow the men would raise the huge tent and call it home for the rest of the winter.

From his pocket, Adam took several pieces of folded paper and dropped them into his cap. He approached the men and called out, "Come on, men. Time to draw for your squaws."

Everyone scrambled to be first, and hopefully, to draw a piece of paper with a number on it. Adam was not surprised to see that Eagle was not among the hunters. The gambler would wait and take his chances on getting Flower.

Adam cheated in the drawing. He made sure his best four men picked paper with a number on it. It would be foolish to chance a man like Jake getting his hands on one of the squaws.

The four lucky men howled their glee and could hardly wait for the squaws to finish making the beds.

Later, the losing men stood around, scowling darkly as they watched the winners mount the plump bodies.

For Adam's supper, Flower made a stew from a deer shot on the trail, and he ate with a ravenous hunger. His appetite sated, he sat with stockinged feet stretched to the fire and relaxed enjoying the heat. As he puffed on a pipe, he watched Flower. Like all Indians, she was curious and slouched around the room poking and prying into corners and drawers.

He studied the shapely figure that already tended toward plumpness, and knew that after her first child, she would go to fat. She would become just another squaw, spiritless and dirty. Unbidden, a slender body took shape within the flames and he squeezed his eyes shut and forced his mind on other things.

His pipe went cold and he knocked it out on the hearth. Turning to Flower, he muttered, "Bank the fire and get to bed."

The bed was cold and damp and mentally he cursed Flower for not having warmed it. A white woman would have turned the covers back hours ago. Consequently, he was angry with Flower when she crawled into bed, and pushed her roughly away when she would have cuddled next to him.

He used her harshly, reaching his release in a short time. When she scooted up in the bed and lay her head on the pillow beside him, he lashed out at her, "If you're gonna cry all night, go sleep on the hearth."

Outside, he could hear the eager and noisy voices of his men. Bets were being called back and forth as the corn whiskey passed between them. Every year he promised a bonus to the man bringing in the most furs. And since the sum was substantial, there was always a high pitch of excited fervor in camp. Always before it had been so with him, but the old expectant feeling would not come and he tossed restlessly.

It was long after camp had settled down that he gave up trying to achieve a mindless relaxation. He sat up in bed, folded his arms around his bent knees and admitted to himself that Elisha's woman kept him awake. She was in his blood and he was on fire for her all the time.

Slowly, almost unaware of it, he was seriously considering the thought that had lurked in the back of his mind all along. Why not go and simply take her away from Elisha? After all she wasn't married to the old bastard.

Forgotten now that Elisha was his grandfather's closest friend, and forgotten for the moment that he considered her a whore, there was only the driving knowledge that he must have her at all costs.

His mind made up, he relaxed with an inner contentment. He would go after her tomorrow, he decided, and his eyelids drooped and he fell asleep to the sweet anticipation of taming her. A smile tugged

at his lips. It would be like trying to gentle one of
the wildcats that roamed the upper hills.

He was up before daybreak the next morning,
impatient to get started. He moved quietly about the
room, stuffing his pockets with jerked venison and
parched corn. As he shrugged into his coat, the
hound whined, ready to go with him. He shushed the
dog and looked anxiously at the sleeping Flower. He
didn't want her up, crying and badgering him with
questions. But the Indian girl slept on, and noise-
lessly he inched open the door, then carefully
closed it behind him.

Before leaving, he stopped and watched the men
struggling with the tent. Their curses rang out on the
air and sweat poured down their faces. Anchoring
it into the frozen ground was proving almost
impossible.

He glanced at the squaws bustling around, and
decided that they seemed fresh enough. Satisfied that
everything was going as he had planned, he signaled
John to his side.

"I'm gonna be gone for a few days, John, so keep
an eye on the men. Keep them busy and they'll stay
out of trouble."

Adam glanced across the camp to where Eagle sat
before the fire lacing his moccasins. He looked up
and caught Adam's gaze and some seconds passed
before either man spoke. Finally Eagle said gruffly,
"Good morning."

Adam walked over, and hunkering down beside
him, said quietly, "I'm going to be gone for awhile.
I'd like for you to move in with Flower . . . look out
for her. Keep the other men away."

Eagle stared at him, his narrow eyes alert for

deceit or trickery. "And sleep on the floor, I suppose?" he sneered.

"Only if she tells you to."

Eagle stared another moment, then nodded his head. "I'll move in, but don't be surprised if she throws rocks at you when you return."

This time Adam took a horse on the journey. He was in a hurry.

CHAPTER 10

Elisha and Nick enjoyed the sound of the howling blizzard as they sat safe and warm before the open fire. But it made Rachael nervous and uneasy and at first she paced the floor. But gradually she became accustomed to nature's icy blast and settled herself at the spinning wheel.

She had insisted that Elisha buy some sheep, and complaining loudly, he had made a ten-mile trip and purchased six ewes and a ram from a sheep herder. He had arrived home angry and tired. The sheep had not herded as cattle would, and had run every which way all over the countryside.

As they milled around the yard, their constant baaing mingled with the hound's barking raised an ear-splitting racket. Elisha had plopped down on the porch and snapped angrily, "It's your job to take care of the smelly things. I won't go near the dumb things again."

She had wrinkled her nose. "Whew, they do smell."

Nick built a pen and shelter for them several yards from the cabin, and in time she had grown used to their offensive odor and became attached to them. And in the process of tending them, she had found that aside from their wool, there was an added benefit in raising them. There was a rich oil in their wool and Nick showed her how the Indian women used it on their skin.

It was quite simple. One merely rubbed her hands over the sheep's back and then transferred the clinging substance to her face. She had found, as Nick had promised, it worked wonderfully well.

After a week of the falling snow, Elisha grew edgy and restless and paced between the two windows. When finally a morning dawned clear with no more flakes filling the air, he announced, "I'm gonna go see how Ruby is makin' out."

As he left the cabin, muffled to the ears and with snowshoes on his feet, Rachael felt a pang of uneasiness. What if the blizzard should come on again? Many a man had become turned around in a snowstorm and had frozen to death. She ran to the door and called after him, "Grandpa, you be careful, you hear me?"

He grinned back at her and waved.

Around noon the sky began to darken and as Rachael watched anxiously, a wind sprang up and great flakes came tumbling to the ground. In a short time even the barn was blocked from view. Rachael lost count of the trips she made to the window searching the deserted trail for some sign of Elisha.

Her mind veered away from the thought of him falling on the trail and maybe breaking a leg . . . and the idea of attacking wolves. She glanced at Nick sitting beside the fire. He was worried too she knew, even though he was putting on a big front to fool her. But his tone and repetition of words showed the fear that gripped his mind.

In the late afternoon she sat down beside Nick. "Why don't you notify the law, Nick?"

He looked at her in surprise. "Notify the law, Rach? We don't have any real law here in the hills, honey. We only have what you'd call 'hill justice.' When a man commits a crime, we hold court and then the elders decide the seriousness of it and pass judgment."

She gazed back at him a moment then asked sharply, "What do you do in a case like this, just ignore it?"

"Of course not, honey. If he's not home soon, I'll gather up the men and go looking for him."

Rachael shook her head, not satisfied. "Why do you wait? Why not go now?"

Patting her tense shoulders, Nick explained. "First, 'Lisha is most likely bedded down with Ruby waiting out the storm. He'd be madder than hell if we came marching up there interrupting him. And second, with this heavy snow falling, it would cover our tracks so fast we wouldn't be able to tell what part of the forest we had covered. We could walk in circles for hours."

She jerked away from him and stood up. "I'll go myself."

Nick sighed resignedly. With many misgivings and against his better judgment, he nodded. "Alright, Rachael, I'll go take a look. But don't you leave the cabin, no matter what."

She helped him into his coat and placed the coonskin on his head. And standing in the open doorway, watching him disappear into the whiteness and gathering dark, a sharp pain shot through her breast. "Am I to lose them both?" her mind cried out.

She tried to keep herself busy—she spun some yarn, tried to read. But her mind was on the two men out in the storm. She looked at the clock for the dozenth time. Nick had been gone for two hours and it was totally dark outside. A heaviness hung over her as she went and sat before the fire. Surely they should have been home by now.

Over the howl of the wind she could hear the animals in the barn raising a ruckus, hungry and wanting to be milked. Occasionally she could hear the sheep bleating, and debated if she should try to get to them. But the long drawn-out yowl of a timber wolf made her shiver and change her mind. It wouldn't hurt them to go hungry just once.

The mantle clock stopped ticking and she looked up at it. It was Elisha's custom to wind it every evening right after supper. She stood up and took the key from the mantle and inserted it into the matching grooves of the clock. She turned it twice and the cabin door banged open.

She spun around and the keys dropped from her nervous fingers. Adam stood in the open door, the snow blowing and swirling around him.

For a long moment they faced each other, the silence tense between them. Finally Rachael spoke. "What are you doing here, long-hunter, did you lose something?"

He studied her coolly, then snapped, "Get your heavy clothes packed."

Her eyes went wide and she demanded, "Why should I, I'm not going anywhere."

In two strides he was across the room and gripping her wrist. Twisting it cruelly, he spoke low and threateningly. "I gave you an order, bitch. Go pack your clothes. You're coming with me."

Angrily she jerked loose, shouting, "Like hell I am."

His open hand shot out and landed sharply across

her face. She staggered back and was brought up against the wall.

"You're gonna learn not to cross me, woman," he growled, "Now get busy."

She glared back at him, knowing it would be useless to resist him. And with her face smarting and beginning to welt, she lifted her head proudly and walked into her bedroom. Through hard, slitted eyes, Adam watched her go and his heart was heavy that he had struck her.

She was soon back, her clothes rolled in a bundle and her coat across her arm. "I suppose it would be asking too much to leave gr . . . Elisha a note?"

"Go ahead. Write him whatever you want to. He won't find us in this storm anyway."

Her thoughts were a turmoil as she dipped the scratchy quill into the homemade ink. What would Nick think and do? Would grandpa ever read the note? And how should she word it, in case this wild man should want to read it? At last she wrote,

> Adam Warden came for me this afternoon. I don't know when I'll see you.
>
> Love, Rachael.

As she had feared, he jerked the note from her hand and read it. Then he laughed, a low taunting sound. "You'll see him when I'm finished with you."

When they stepped outside, darkness had fallen. Rachael gave a startled jerk when Adam's hand grasped her elbow firmly and guided her to a stand of cedars back of the cabin. Then he was scooping her up and sitting her astride a horse. She clutched at the saddle horn as she felt him swing up behind her.

At a low word, the horse tossed his head nervously, then moved out in the face of the storm. Rachael gave a ragged sigh and sank into an ache of desolation. When would she ever learn about grandpa?

After riding for several hours, Rachael became conscious of her extreme fatigue. The trail was uneven and straight up and her back ached from leaning against it. She hoped that the horse knew where it was going in the blinding snow.

She had long since given in to her outraged pride and had turned her face into the warmth of Adam's chest. His steady heartbeat beneath her cheek had become a lulling rhythm. The wind had died down and apart from the squeaking saddle, there was no other sound in the forest.

The snow had stopped and the skies cleared when they came to a river. It was deep and swift and the horse had to be urged several times before he would enter it. On the other side, they came to a pine grove about a hundred yards from the stream. Adam halted the horse and stiffly stepped down. He tethered the animal to a tree, then ordered sharply, "Get down. We'll camp here."

Attempting to dismount, she almost fell out of the saddle, then surprisingly, Adam was there, quick to help her. And when accidentally he touched her icy fingers, a stirring of pity went through him and he hurried to make a fire.

Between two large trees, he scooped away the snow until the ground showed through. Then from beneath ground-hugging branches he brought dried

leaves and twigs and carefully stacked them in a pile.
Pulling his flint from his pocket, he soon had flames
reaching for the sky. Dragging the saddle from the
horse, he brought it to the fire and bade her sit down.

As she gratefully stretched feet and hands to its
warmth, Adam brought the horse in close and
rubbed him dry with a piece of blanket.

Later, as Adam moved around making camp, he
avoided her eyes and Rachael took to studying him.
The cold had turned the scar an angry red and it
glaringly stood out against the brown of his skin.
Even so, she couldn't remember ever seeing a more
handsome man. "What a pity he is so cold and
unfeeling."

Once when he came to the fire and let drop
several rocks into the hot coals, she thought for a
moment that he was going to speak. But he merely
scowled at her and walked away to make their bed of
cedar boughs.

Chewing a piece of jerked venison he had handed
her earlier, she watched him turn from the finished
bedroll and cover the horse with a woolen blanket.
His acts of kindness to the animal surprised her.
There was nothing about his outward appearance
that suggested any softness in him.

She saw him stalking back to the fire and watched
him gather the heated rocks into a blanket. Then
without looking at her he rose and said shortly,
"Come on. It's time to turn in."

For a second she thought to refuse. But even as
she hesitated, she knew it would be a futile action.
He would only pick her up and throw her into bed.
When she stood beside him, he motioned to her

boots. "Take them off. You'll feel the heat of the rocks better."

When she had crawled between the furs, he added, "When you're warm, take off the rest of your clothes."

Again her mind rebelled, but again she shrugged her shoulders. Why fight him? He would only win in the end.

When her clothing was a neat pile at her head, he removed his moccasins and joined her. For a moment the furs jerked back and forth as he removed his clothing, and then he was lying motionless beside her. Moments passed and his body heat flowed out and enveloped her. Her anger slowly melted away and she relaxed.

Then she stirred for a more comfortable position and her thigh came against his. She heard the fast intake of his breath and suddenly he was leaning over her, his mouth groping for hers with an eager hunger. His hands began to range over her body and she sensed his desperate need through them. She moaned low in her own desire and with a strange utterance, he drew her into his arms.

Her arms crept around his neck and she pressed herself into him, needing the feel of his weight flattening out her breasts. He laid her back and swiftly straddled her waist and eased himself upward. But her hands grabbed his hips, stopping him. "Not that way, Adam," she whispered, pulling his head down to her own and forcing his body into the hollow of her hips. "This way."

He pulled away for a moment, his eyes probing hers doubtfully. Seeing the indecision in his face, she pulled his head down again and softly covered his lips with her own. She felt a matching tremor pass through his body as she caught his tongue and drew it gently between her teeth. When she began to suck it rhythmically, his breathing became fast and ragged and she placed a hand on either hip, urging him to raise his body.

For a moment he hung suspended above her and she again watched his wavering indecision. Slowly she brought her legs up around his waist, and reaching down, she expertly guided him into her.

As he came thrusting against her, over the sigh of her contentment there drifted faintly the howl of a wolf, and as she raised her body to meet his mighty drives, she heard the report of a rifle. But the rising ecstasy that was shaking them overshadowed any thought as to why.

The first time was disappointing, for with a few great shoves he had moaned and collapsed upon her. But the others following exceeded all her other experiences. His hard thrusting body was what she had always wanted. His desire had seemed unlimited at first, but finally he was sated and she now lay warm in his arm, contented just to have the feel of him.

Long after breathing had calmed, Rachael lay quietly, watching the campfire flames through the evergreens. She mused on what the years ahead would bring to her. Would Adam tire of her and discard her, or would he fall truly in love with her and keep her always. She sighed softly and nestled closer to him. In his sleep his arms tightened about her and she smiled.

Dawn swept across the hills and Rachael opened her eyes and reached a searching hand for Adam. But she lay alone. For a moment she panicked, then the sound of an axe relaxed her. Later, as she watched him build up the fire, she thought of what they had shared and wished him back in the bed.

She leaned up on her elbows, and disregarding the cold, let the furs drop to her waist. "Good morning, long-hunter," she called out.

He looked over at her, his eyes fastening on her bare breasts. He tore his eyes away and looked into her face. She shivered and smiled a lazy, suggestive invitation.

He stalked over to the bed and squatted down. His answering smile was a slow exasperating tilt of his lips and she wanted to slap his face. And when he sneered, "What's the matter, whore, didn't you get enough?" her hand did come up.

But he caught her wrist and as she struggled against him, he added, "I'm about drained. I don't know how old 'Lisha keeps up with you."

For a heartbreaking moment she lay motionless. Then feeling his sardonic gaze upon her, pride came to her rescue and she retorted sharply, "There's Nick, too."

She jerked loose and in one graceful movement she was on her feet. But fast as a cat he was beside her, forcing her back between the covers. "My way this time," he muttered, grasping her jaw.

He had won. He had succeeded in degrading her. Choking on her tears, she watched him disappear into the forest.

In her anger Rachael had not seen the pained expression that flashed in Adam's eyes as she deliberately referred to Nick. She had given him cause to hate two men now.

In his helpless fury, Adam struck out at a tree,

whispering, "Whore, whore." But most of his rage was directed at himself. As usual he had said and done all the wrong things. He had committed a despicable act treating her like one of the camp women.

"But damn it," he swore inwardly, "is she any better than they? If I know Elisha Jobe, she's done plenty of things with that old raunchy bastard."

But he could not bear to think about that and forced himself to return to camp.

Rachael wiped away her tears with the back of her hands and reached for her clothes. But the neat pile was not where she had left them. What is he up to now, she wondered. But when she was about to demand from him where they were, she saw her riding habit and underwear propped beside the fire. She shook her head. There was no figuring this man.

A short time later, he tossed the warmed clothing to her and said shortly, "Time to get up."

Pulling the clothes into bed with her, she scrambled into them, then hurried to the fire. Adam ignored her presence and kept busy with the camp chores. She noted how easily and relaxed he moved. He was thoroughly at home in the wilderness and she realized that it would take a hardy woman to be a fit mate for him. She wondered if she would be able to live up to his expectations.

Her stomach rumbled and she debated asking him for some breakfast. No doubt his Indian women could go for days merely chewing on a piece of bark, she sneered to herself. But the emptiness inside her growled again and she decided that she didn't care what Adam thought. Sarcastically she inquired, "Are we going to have any breakfast?"

He was concentrating on rolling their bed into a bundle and took his time in pointing to a small bag lying next to the fire. "There's parched corn in there."

As she chewed on the hard grains, she made an attempt at conversation, but gave up when she only met with grunts and nods of his head.

Once again they were in the saddle. But this time Rachael sat erect. There was no snow or wind to excuse her snuggling up to him as she had last night.

The countryside became wilder with each mile they traveled. Later in the day they rode into Indian territory and began passing parties of braves. She noticed Adam's ready speech in their own language and the deference paid him by them. The stolid stare of one young brave, a necklace of bear claws adorning his bronzed neck, filled her with forboding and she shrank closer to Adam. But when she heard his dry chuckle, she jerked away.

Just before darkness fell, they happened onto a cave, wide enough and tall enough to accommodate the horse also. Rachael barely had time enough to eat her share of the venison before Adam was hustling her off to bed.

This time she encouraged him in no way, but left all moves up to him. Never again would she leave herself open for another insult from him. Nevertheless, his caressing hands and lips brought her body responding to him in a wild abandon. It seemed that he would never tire and she was utterly exhausted when finally he slept at her side.

But the next morning his face once again wore

the same cold, hard look. She could not understand him. He had taken her so eagerly, so tenderly, his every action speaking of love. She sighed. It was something she would have to accept, she reluctantly decided.

Late that afternoon Adam halted the horse and remarked, "We're home."

Shielding her eyes against the setting sun, Rachael looked across an open space and finally made out the shape of the big tent with a score or more rough-looking people milling around in front of it. Dispirited, her shoulders slumped. She would have to live with these people, all crowded together under one roof. There would be no privacy, and in the end there would be no pride.

But Adam seemed to sense her dismay and pointed beyond the tent. "Our place is over there."

Her eyes followed his pointing finger and she spotted the low cabin, almost obscured by the tall pines surrounding it. A column of blue smoke curled up against the sky and she could hardly wait to get inside. The little place looked like a palace to her.

A dog barked and there arose a chorus of yips and yelps, not at all friendly. Then the camp people looked their way and with welcoming cries started toward them. But Adam waved them back, calling out, "I'll be with you in a minute."

He reined in at the cabin door, and as he helped Rachael to dismount, her eyes took in the small moccasin prints that led in and out of the cabin. Were they not to be alone after all, she wondered. Maybe he meant her to share him with his squaw. It would be like him to do such a thing.

But when Adam pushed open the door, her

pulse quickened a bit. A man sat with the Indian woman before the fire. On closer inspection she saw that the squaw was no woman but a mere girl of no more than twelve or thirteen years.

But when the girl jumped to her feet exclaiming excitedly, "Adam, you're back," there was no doubt whose squaw she was.

Repulsed, Rachael drew away from Adam and he knew it. From the corner of her eye, she had the satisfaction of seeing him blush.

The man unwound his long length from the chair, and giving Adam a stinging look, spoke sneeringly. "Back to claim your property, I see."

"Maybe. Why, don't you like her?"

"Would it make any difference?"

"Yes. If you like her, you can have her."

A small distressed cry escaped the girl and Eagle's flinty gaze went over Adam's face, searching for the lie that must be there. "How come?"

Adam pulled Rachael into the center of the room and drawled, "I've a new one that pleases me better."

Rachael and Eagle gasped in unison. And while Eagle's glad cry of "Rachael!" rang out, she stood as though turned to stone.

Her past had come back to laugh at her. For the hawk-faced man striding toward her was the first man ever to arouse passion in her. And as Adam took a step toward them, his fist balled, she could only stare at Eagle, her eyes silently pleading.

Eagle folded his arms around her trembling body and held her close. Then smoothing back the hair from her forehead, he murmured, "Rachael, honey, how did you ever turn up here?"

She hugged his waist and whispered, "Please don't

give me away, Jim." Aloud, she answered, "It's a long story. Someday I'll tell you about it."

"Your friends all miss you and wish you were back."

Nervously she glanced up at him and caught the teasing gleam in his eyes. Relieved, she answered quietly, "Whatever happens, Jim, I won't be going back to Jamestown."

A jealous rage ate at Adam and his fists hurt from clenching them. Angrily he caught Eagle by the shoulder and spun him away from Rachael. "I see you've already tasted this whore's wares."

The two tall men stood facing each other, each measuring the other's worth. In the silence, tense with the hatred between them, Eagle spoke. "Who, besides you, calls her a whore?" When Adam only glared back at him, Eagle added, "You damn fool, you don't even know what you've got. What a pure waste."

Between clenched teeth, Adam snarled, "Take your squaw and get out."

A moment longer they stared at one another, knowing that someday they would battle it out. Then Eagle turned to Rachael and said quietly, "If you ever need me, Rachael, I'll be at the tent."

She nodded dumbly and watched him leave.

Turning around, she saw the girl sidle up to Adam and in a fawning manner, coax, "Let Eagle have the white woman. She weak. Not take care of you like Flower."

He caught Rachael's amused smile and became flustered. Frowning at the young squaw, he ordered coldly, "Go with Eagle. He'll give you what you want."

Dismissed so completely, the girl's shoulders drooped and she began gathering her belongings. But as she walked to the door, she darted a look at Rachael that was full of malicious intent.

Rachael threw her a mocking smile, but she could tell that the girl had a vindictive mind and that she hadn't seen the last of her. She turned to remark to Adam about this and his hand came across her face, sending her reeling. He stalked after her demanding, "How many men have you slept with, whore?"

An anger so strong she shook with it swept over Rachael. She was up to her teeth with this man's arrogance and brutality. Almost without realizing it, suddenly she was springing at him, her nails ripping across his face. So unexpected was her assault, her weight bore him to the floor, and in his surprise, she had been able to straddle his waist and now pummeled his face with her hard little fists.

Not wanting to strike her again, and sorry that he had already, Adam finally managed to grasp the slender wrists and hold them still. Staring up into the eyes that were now yellow in her fury, he wanted to shout his joy at her spunk. "What a woman. What a mate for a man," he thought.

But then the picture of Jim Eagle holding her so familiarly swam before his eyes, and in his jealous torment he leaped to his feet, bringing her with him. And when she began kicking out at him, her booted toes striking him painfully, his anger grew and he twisted her wrists until she knelt before him. "You don't ever learn, do you, woman," he panted.

She glared up at him and read his intent. Scorn shot out of her eyes and she warned him lowly, "This time I'll die first."

He glared back at her, his eyes telling him how desirable she was in her anger. He wanted to take her into his arms and love her as he had last night. But only cold contempt looked back at him, and angrily then, he wanted to hurt her. To see tears in her eyes. But he knew that she would not cry, no matter what, and he flung her from him, yelling, "Go to hell," and stormed out the door.

A gust of wind blew down the chimney, scattering ashes on the hearth. Rachael rose to her feet to sweep them back. She took one step, tripped on a bedroll carelessly thrown to the floor, and lay there, hard sobs racking her body.

When she had cried herself out, she rose to her feet and sat down in front of the fire. Gradually she warmed and relaxed. Rising from her cramped position, she found the sun had set and she looked around for some candles. On a crude table she found one still quite long. Lighting it with a splinter, she carried it with her as she made an inspection of her new home. Her eyes took in the accumulated dirt, and in a short time she was her usual bustling, efficient self.

She didn't know that Adam had returned and jumped when he spoke behind her. "It don't look like much, does it?"

"Who's to know yet. Your squaw wasn't the best housekeeper in the world."

He denied so vehemently that Flower was his squaw, Rachael looked at him in surprise. "You're not trying to tell me you haven't had anything to do with that girl?"

"Not like with you. Only like . . . you know."

"I see. And does she like that?"

"How in the hell do I know? I didn't ask her."

"You wouldn't use me like that, long-hunter."

"You step out of line and see if I don't."

"You go to hell."

Startled, his black eyes bored into her. Then darkly, he warned, "You'd better watch that sharp tongue of yours, lady."

Amused, she watched his stiff back as he wheeled and sat down by the fire. Intuition told her that he would not be so ready to strike her from now on.

A weight was lifted from her and she renewed her cleaning with fresh energy. Several times Adam had to draw back as trash and rags flew past his head and into the fire. Once when she broke into song, Adam rocked gently, knowing a contentment entirely new to him.

Later, when she called him to supper, it was all he could do not to repress a pleased smile. The table wore a cloth she had unearthed from some drawer, and the plates were sparkling clean. She had placed scrubbed flatwear alongside them as though they were sterling. Adam was used to the eating utensils being held in a jar and everyone helping himself. In a colorful Indian bowl, she had placed some hastily cut pine branches along with some orange bittersweet. Sitting in front of it was a platter of thick, spicy stew. And to the side, a plate of hot biscuits and a pot of steaming coffee ready to be poured into tin cups.

The food was the most tasteful Adam had ever eaten, and he was so pleased with her, he felt foolish. To cover this feeling, he spoke no word of praise. But the amount he consumed was silent testimony.

After supper he sat before the fire smoking his

pipe while Rachael washed the dishes and swept the floor again. When she was finished, she rummaged in a drawer for a moment, then brought out clean bed linens. She stripped the bed, fluffed up the feather mattress, then remade it, leaving the covers turned back to warm.

She glanced around the room, found it to her satisfaction, then removed the towel from around her waist and went and sat beside Adam.

Secretly, through lowered lids, he watched her, his eyes drinking in her beauty as though it were fine wine. Beneath the shift she wore, he knew every curve and valley, and once when she stretched, her breasts thrusting against the material, his loins tingled and he looked longingly toward the bed. But it was much too early he knew. He would only get one of her looks if he suggested going to bed so early.

Moodily he puffed on his pipe thinking what an odd pair they made. She, soft and delicate, and he, like a piece of hard rawhide. He was a damn fool to think that she would ever want him . . . as a person, that was. He had known from the beginning that her body desired him, but he felt that otherwise she felt only repulsion for him.

At first it hadn't mattered what she felt. But now possessing her wasn't enough. He needed and craved her love. He wanted her woman's gentleness . . . to talk to her. To tell her of the thoughts he sometimes had. And too, he wanted this tense wariness that floated between them to be gone. Her hard cold acceptance of him in the daylight and the wild lovemaking at night were drawing his nerves taut.

Beside him, Rachael's thoughts ran in the same vein, and separately they suffered.

Adam finally broke the silence. "Have you ever noticed how at evening a melancholy settles over the hills?"

Rachael looked at him, curiously surprised that he had these finer feelings. She thought a minute then replied, "Don't you think it's more tranquility rather than melancholy?"

Adam mused on her words and was surprised to find that she was right. Formerly the evenings had brought him only sober reflections. Reflections that left him pensive. But now, sharing the darkness with her, he realized the difference. A tranquil peace did prevail in the room.

A log burned through and fell to the grate. Rachael looked up and met his questioning gaze. And in bed, between warm fresh linens, they loved one another long into the night.

CHAPTER 11

After battling the blizzard for two hours, Nick found Elisha at Ruby's, as he had expected.

"I figured you'd know I stayed because of the storm," Elisha explained.

"I did, but there was no convincing Rachael. Come on, we'd best start home. She's like a crazy woman."

Elisha swore at women's damned-fool notions but nevertheless tugged on his boots and shrugged into his coat.

Ruby stood at the window watching them soon disappear into the whiteness. They moved as fast as possible, taking advantage of the fast-fading daylight hours. Nick's footprints were still faintly discernible, and they made good time following them. But dark had fallen by the time they arrived at the cabin.

It struck them as strange that no candles were lit and that Rachael hadn't opened the door as soon as they began stamping the snow from their boots. With a sudden fear and urgency, Nick banged open the door.

The cabin was empty as he had known it would be. The leaping flames in the fireplace seemed to mock him and the simmering meat on the crane seemed to whisper, "She's gone, she's gone."

He immediately thought that she had gone out to

search for Elisha; then the sheet of paper on the table caught his eye.

When Elisha entered the cabin, Nick stood as if in a trance, the note dangling from his fingers. Elisha took it from him and swore loudly at its contents.

"What does it mean, 'Lisha?"

"Just what it says, old friend. The damn wolf has come and took her. He's had his eye on her ever since she arrived."

"I'll kill him, so help me God, I'll kill him."

Everything happened so fast after that, Elisha could hardly grasp what was going on. His long rifle in one hand and a lantern in the other, Nick was going back into the storm. Finally Elisha grasped his intent and called after him, "Wait for it to stop snowing, Nick. The snow will cover their tracks. Anyway, Adam won't harm her."

If Nick heard him, he gave no sign as he bent down to examine the moccasin prints. He discovered that they weren't too old, for only scant drifts were beginning to cover them. When he jumped to his feet and headed into the forest, Elisha yelled after him, "At least take the dogs. They'll help you keep his trail."

Elisha stood in the swirling snow and watched his friend and dogs disappear from sight. A chill unrelated to the weather rippled through him, and he repressed the urge to call Nick back again.

The tracks led Nick to the edge of the forest. He groaned aloud when the prints stopped and horse hooves now trailed out. The dogs let out a howl and he urged, "Come on, boys, let's get him."

For the first couple of miles he was able to run along with them. But the storm increased its fury and the wind blowing against him gradually slowed him down. His feet became leaden and long strands of hair lay frozen against his cheeks. Searching the forest through this curtain, he began to imagine that he saw shapes moving in and out of the trees.

"I've got to get hold of myself," he muttered.

His weariness was bone deep when he came to the river. It was wide with swiftly running water, and the ice along the sides had been broken where the horse had entered it.

For the first time his courage faltered. Could he survive swimming the icy water? Then the thought of Rachael with the long-hunter sent him walking along the bank, looking for the narrowest part of the stream.

About a half-mile downstream, he came to where the river made a bend through solid granite; it was no more than fifty feet wide. He stood a moment gazing at the opposite shore, then with a shuddering sigh, waded into the freezing water. His breath came out in a gasp as he immediately went into water up to his waist. Higher and higher it rose until it reached his armpits. He was completely numb now and hardly heard the piteous whining of the dogs as they swam beside him.

Almost at the end of his endurance, he was finally across and crawling up the riverbank. He noticed vaguely that the snow had ceased, and in the light of the soft white moon that was just beginning to disentangle itself from the treetops, he fell forward and lay unable to move.

High in a tall cedar, a whippoorwill proclaimed

his lonesomeness and farther down the river his mate answered him. In the dim land between sleep and wakefulness, Nick was aware of the hounds creeping close to his side, seeking the warmth of his body.

And moving like shadows against the forest background were the wary forms of wolves.

Nick's first acceptance of reality came with the growl of an animal and a full moon shining in his eyes. Until then, he had hung in a suspended state of cold and pain.

In his delirium, his mind had rambled back through life as he tossed restlessly on the frozen snow. In his dreamworld he relived his struggle to catch up with Rachael and Adam Warden. Then he had uttered happy sounds as once again he sat with his mother on the wide veranda of their Virginia plantation. And later his chest had heaved, and he had cried out as he stood beside the open grave of that mother.

But subconsciously, survival had clung to a small part of his brain. "I must keep my body moving. I must keep the blood flowing," was a determination running through his mind.

At one point in his rambling, he had sensed a warmth stealing over his body and had heard clearly his mother call to him. "Don't fall asleep, Nickulas. You must stay awake, son. There is much danger for you in sleep."

It was then he had fully awakened to the snarl of a wolf. Slowly and painfully he struggled to one knee, his frozen buckskins crackling. Through ice-laden lashes he peered into the shadowed forest.

Twin points of red glared back at him from every direction.

"Dear Lord, they're everywhere," he whispered.

Frantic, his eyes searched the torn-up snow for his rifle. There was no sign of it. But a few yards from where he knelt, he saw the broken bodies of the faithful hounds. They had fought valiantly for his life.

Fighting against the sleep that hammered at him, he flexed frozen fingers and stiffly swung his arms. He must get the blood to circulating. If he could only get to his feet he might be able to climb one of the large cedars a short distance away.

Finally his fingers were tingling and the excruciating pain was pulling his brain back to an almost normal alertness. His eyes never wavered from the wolf pack that now moved in slowly as he inched himself up until he stood straight. But his frozen legs wouldn't move. He groaned aloud his frustration and tried to stamp his feet.

The wolves were closer now and he could easily make out the rough gray shapes and gaping jaws. The leader advanced in a stiff-legged movement and from the corner of his eyes Nick saw the others begin to circle. His only escape now lay in the icy river which would certainly kill him.

He resigned himself to the fact that it would be but a matter of time. Rachael's face floated before him and when the animal sprang for his throat, she was the only thing he regretted leaving behind.

But in mid-air, the beast yelped and fell to the ground, and the report of a rifle rang through the forest. Yipping and snarling, the others wheeled, streaked off, their piercing howls gradually fading.

Slowly and in great relief, Nick twisted his body and looked in the direction of the shot. For a moment he feared he had slipped back into delirium. In the soft glow of the winter moon, a tall slender woman stood a few feet behind him, a rifle cradled in her arms and gunpowder smoke swirling about her. Silky black hair was gathered on top of her head, showing in relief a quiet, sad beauty. Her widely spaced brown eyes gazed at him steadily.

"Are you hurt?" she asked softly.

"Not by the wolves, ma'am, but I'm damn near frozen to death."

For the first time she noticed his wet clothing and with a pitying sound hurried to him. "Oh dear, can't you move?"

"No, ma'am . . . just my arms a little."

She knelt quickly and with strong fingers began to firmly knead his legs and thighs. Gradually a prickling and stinging sensation ran through his body and he bit back the yells that tore at his throat.

Seeing his pained expression, she scrambled to her feet and placed his arm across her narrow shoulders. "You can walk now if you'll just concentrate on it," she coaxed. "My place is only a short piece down the river."

Step by agonizing step, they finally arrived at her door and Nick sighed in relief. He knew that his vast size had hung heavy on her delicate body.

But once inside, before the glowing heat of the fireplace, real pain set in. It was so all-consuming, he felt no embarrassment when she stripped him bare of clothing and urged him into the deep featherbed.

She then moved swiftly to the fireplace and fed

wood into it until the flames leaped high. And as he lay shivering, and his teeth chattering, she stepped out of her own clothing and moved toward the bed.

"Her body is more beautiful than Rachael's," was his last conscious thought as she climbed in beside him and took him into her arms.

Once during the night, he half aroused and smiled contentedly. The holding of each other had reversed. She now lay in his arms. He felt the smooth satin of her stomach against his and thrilled to the thrust of a silky leg between his own. He raised a hand to stroke her and midway fell back to sleep.

Nick awoke the next morning to the aroma of frying bacon. He lay alone and for a moment he wondered if he had dreamed the whole thing. But he decided that the feel of her had been too real. He was convinced that she had shared his bed.

He turned his head and watched her graceful movements as she moved between table and fire, and when she went and pushed aside a drape at a small window, he was again struck by her serene beauty in the sun's light. "She is like a queen," he mused.

She seemed to sense his gaze, for she turned and approached the bed. "How are you feeling this morning?"

A feeling of excitement came over him as he watched the movement of her legs against the material of her dress. He recalled with a thrill the feel of them entwined with his own and felt his face grow warm. "My feet . . . my feet are kinda sore," he stammered and felt like a schoolboy.

She leaned over him and laid a cool hand on his brow. His gaze fastened boldly on the curve of her well-rounded breasts and she blushed faintly.

Straightening up, she remarked coolly, "I see you're improving Mr . . . ?"

"The name is Nick, ma'am. Nick Stone." When he would have said more, a voice from the other end of the room called out, "Is breakfast ready yet?"

Startled, Nick jerked his head toward the sound and peered at the outline of a body deep beneath the covers on a narrow cot. Regarding him with twinkling eyes, the woman said, "Don't look so glum, Mr. Stone. It's only my son, Benji."

Surprise flashed across Nick's face and she smiled again. "You are surprised, Mr. Stone? Why shouldn't I have a son? I'm old enough."

Any reply he might have made was cut off by the appearance of a youngster about nine years old. He was a handsome lad, resembling his mother. She pulled him forward. "Benji, meet Mr. Stone. I saved him from the wolves last night."

The boy offered his hand, open curiosity in his eyes. "Did the wolves really attack you, Mr. Stone?"

"They sure did, button. Your maw saved my life."

Benji glanced at his mother, pride shining in his eyes. Then back to Nick he asked, "Was you scared?"

"I was scared and no mistake."

"The wolves got my paw two years back." His face took on a look of sadness. "I guess he was scared too."

"So she's a widow," Nick mused and wondered at the excitement this news brought him. He glanced at her but the smooth calm face revealed nothing.

"I'm sorry to hear that, button. It must have been a hard blow to you."

"It sure was at first. But me and maw keep ourselves busy and it's not so bad anymore."

"All my friends call me Nick. Why don't you?"

"I'd like that... Nick."

Nick's eyes took on a teasing twinkle. "What do they call your maw?"

"They call her Nora. Nora Hadely."

Across the room, he smiled at her and said softly, "I'm happy to know you, Nora Hadely."

Although his mother did not answer, merely nodded her head, Benji knew that she liked the big ugly man lying in her bed. He studied the strong face outlined by the snowy white of the pillow and decided that he too liked Nick Stone.

For the next five days, Nick's frostbitten feet kept him mostly in bed. He managed to hobble to the table for meals and to a chair flanking the fireplace.

He now slept in Benji's narrow bed, the boy having moved in with his mother. Settling into the peaceful life of the Hadelys', he began to know a contentment he hadn't known for a long time. Nora's quiet ways brought a sereneness to the little cabin that he had never known before.

At night when the candles were snuffed and only the faint glow of the fire shone in the room, he would lie staring up at the rafters as he listened to her even breathing a few feet away. And in guilt, as he desired her, a small face nagged at his memory. He had loved Rachael so, and yet, he wanted this woman as he had never wanted another.

Strangely enough, he did not think of Nora in the lustful way he had with Rachael. Rachael's wild young beauty had called to him, and his equally wild nature had responded. But thinking back, he realized now that their lovemaking had generally left him only exhausted. There was never quite a feeling of satisfaction . . . a peaceful calm.

Idly he wondered how much Nora's young son contributed to this new feeling. He was a likable lad, a boy any man would be proud to call son. Benji liked him, he could tell. He was always near him, hanging onto his every word. He hadn't been around a man for two years and it was plain that he hungered for the companionship of another male.

He thought of Nora living so long without a man and wondered if she missed the arms of her husband. Suddenly a rush of jealousy swept through him, causing him to clench his fists. The thought of another man holding her, loving her, tore at his very insides.

The time came when the swelling was gone from Nick's feet and he could once again pull on his moccasins. Gradually he took over most of Benji's chores, leaving the lad time to hunt and to set traps along the river that rushed past the cabin.

It was the first time Benji ran his traps that Nick and Nora found themselves alone for a length of time.

They sat in front of the fire contentedly eating corn that Nora had popped. The room was quiet and peaceful with the late sun throwing a shaft of light through the small window. Nora rose to lay another stick on the fire and Nick watched the curve of her hip as she bent over. Suddenly he blurted out, "Nora, do you still miss your husband?"

For a moment her body froze in position, then

with a long sigh, she straightened up. "I loved Zeth very much. He was a good husband and a loving father." She stood a moment as in deep thought, then added, "But time is healing."

She turned from the fire and gave him a long look. When he read the message in her eyes, he was on his feet and sweeping her close. His voice hoarse with his desperate need, he begged, "Nora, love me . . . love me right now."

Her slender hand came up to caress his cheek, then pulled his face down in surrender. His lips claimed hers urgently, and with fingers that trembled, he began to unbutton her blouse.

As he stroked the soft satin flesh, he felt her heat rise, strong, to match his own. She whispered softly, "Let me bolt the door."

When she came to the bed and saw his bareness, she blushed. He smiled, swung his feet to the floor and reached to disrobe her. When she stood bare and shy before him, his breath shuddered and he pulled her to him and buried his head between her breasts. Softly he kissed the milky white mounds, closing his lips for a moment over each rosy tip. Then pulling her onto the bed he let his lips wander over her body until she moaned her desire.

Surprised, he realized that this was a new experience for Nora and shook with the knowledge of what he could teach her. Gently he took her hand and laid it on his hardness. She gasped and hesitated. He folded her fingers around him and urged them up and down. Then ever so slowly, on her own, she began to stroke him. His breathing became hard and fast and he edged upon the bed. "Kiss me, Nora," he groaned lowly.

She reached to pull his head down and he pushed her back murmuring, "Not that way, honey. The way I did you."

She gazed at him out of desire-ridden eyes, then inched her way down alongside him and he sighed raggedly as her soft, warm mouth came down and covered him.

When the pain of the rapturous moment became more than he could stand, he gathered her beneath him and thrust deep within her.

When at last he rolled over onto his back, he had achieved complete fulfillment.

Nora leaned on an elbow and trailed her fingers down his body. He watched her in lazy relaxation, then asked softly, "This is all new to you, isn't it, Nora?"

She nodded and asked shyly, "Is it . . . is it wrong, Nick?"

He gave a low laugh and pulled her close. "Nothing is wrong in love, Nora." He waited a moment, then asked, "You do love me, don't you?"

"Oh, yes, Nick. I love you so much I couldn't have borne it if you hadn't loved back."

"Show me again," he whispered and began to stroke her back.

They sat long before the fire that evening. In quiet talk they discussed their future together. He had known from the start that she was the kind of woman that one offered marriage to. And surprisingly, he not only wanted to marry her, he also wanted to be father to her son.

Many times lately his thoughts had been drawn back to the home of his childhood. He had not been there for many years and a homesickness for the place came over him often. About once a year he received a short note from the cousin who ran the plantation for him and a few years back he had written that the murder charges against Nick had been dropped.

He had been forced into a foolish duel of honor, and when he had killed his man, the outlawed practice had sent him into the wilderness to escape the law. Only once had he slipped back, and that was to attend his mother's funeral.

But at the time of his cousin's letter, urging him to return, he had been enjoying his way of life and had answered that maybe later he would come back.

"It's all different now," he thought. He would soon have a family to support. In his mind he could see Nora sitting at the head of his table and running the large household of slaves.

Into a short silence, he spoke. "Nora, how would you like to leave the wilderness and go live in Virginia?"

She looked at him questioningly. "What would we do in Virginia?"

"I have a place there. A plantation. You would live like a lady."

A small sound of pleasure escaped her and she came and sat on his lap. "Tell me about it. Do you have slaves? Are there Indians?" Her words came tumbling out.

Holding her close, he went back through the years recalling and relating events almost forgotten. He talked long into the night, enthusiasm gripping him.

Later, lying alone in bed, he thought of Rachael and her youthful gusto for life. He earnestly hoped that she would find happiness with wild Adam Warden. They were young and of the same piece of cloth and could have long years of happiness together.

And last, he remembered his long-time friend. "It's gonna be hell saying good-bye to Elisha," he thought.

CHAPTER 12

The next day dawned clear and cold with an icy wind blowing out of the north. Rachael awakened first and sat up in bed. She glanced at Adam's half-covered body and remembered the delight it had brought her last night.

She became aware of the stealthy cold creeping in through the cracks and snuggled back into the covers. The place had to be better weatherproofed before another day, she decided.

She turned her head and saw that Adam was awake and watching her. She gazed back, trying to read what lay in the back of his moody eyes. As she watched, they darkened with a look she knew well.

He raised on an elbow and pushed the covers to her waist. The chill of the room moved across her breast, causing the nipples to stand erect. She heard his breath catch and felt his lips come over them.

Gently she stroked his head and arched her body to him. Then above her rising passion, she heard the door slowly creak open. Her eyes flew open and she saw Jake standing a few feet from the bed, peering at them intently. In his hand he carried a shovelful of live coals. His eyes glued to Adam's mouth at her breast, he snickered, "Adam told me to come over this morning and start a fire."

Angrily embarrassed, she poked Adam, trying to push him away and at the same time struggling to cover her nakedness. But Adam only muttered his annoyance and pushed away the covers again. And when he pushed a knee between her legs, forcing them apart, she hissed in his ear, "Jake is here. He'll watch us."

Adam's answer as he moved into her was a grunted, "Let him."

Enraged, she whispered, "No," and Adam whispered back, "Yes."

As his hands came under her buttocks, holding her tight against his drives, she pulled the covers over their heads and eagerly clasped his hips. Dimly she heard Jake's knowing cackle and yearned to choke him.

Later, after Jake had the fire burning high, Adam arose and tossed her robe on the bed. She jerked it under the covers and struggled into it. He chuckled at her modesty and she whizzed a pillow at his head. Grinning, he caught it and tossed it back. She glared at him and he pulled her from the bed and shoved her toward the fire.

Jake giggled and proffered her a pan. "I got some hot water here if you want to wash up."

She looked into his leering face, and then quite deliberately she flicked open her robe. As Jake stared, his mouth hanging open, Adam roared, "Rachael, what in the hell are you doing?"

She had seen Adam mad at her, but never like this. For a frightening moment she thought that he would beat her. But instead, he suddenly wheeled on Jake and back-handed him across the face. "You son-of-a-bitch, get your eyes back in your head."

Casting Adam a glowering look, Jake shuffled out of the cabin, swiping at his bleeding lips. Adam spun around and glared at her. At first she became nervous and felt guilty. Then she remembered why she had done it and glared back at him. "What's the difference if I show him or you do?" she demanded.

"I didn't show him anything. I had you covered."

"Oh, yes, you had me covered alright."

"You know what I mean. You ever pull that trick again and I'll give you such a beating you won't be able to sit down for a month."

"Just don't you try to pull your trick again," she shot back at him.

They stared fiercely at one another for a moment, then Adam walked away from her.

Rachael smiled a secret smile as she prepared a breakfast of salt pork and gravy along with hot biscuits. "He's jealous," her heart sang.

When the meal was finished and the cabin straightened, Rachael wondered what she was to do with the rest of the day. In fact, how was she to spend her time all winter? Adam would be going out on a hunt any day now and she dreaded the long, lonesome days ahead.

Adam was lacing his boots, preparing to leave, and as though he sensed her thoughts, he looked up and said, "I'm goin' over to the tent. You can get dressed and come with me if you want to. That is, if you think you can behave yourself."

At first she thought he joked about her behaving, but one look in his steely blue eyes showed that he was dead serious. She ignored his remark and quickly slipped into a one-piece garment that fell to her knees. Tightly knotting a colorful sash around her waist, she tugged at the dress until the low neckline showed the swelling of her breasts.

As she ran a brush through her hair, she saw

Adam's eyes narrow in anger and she was sure that he was sorry he had asked her to come with him. Pulling on her coat, she said sweetly, "I'm ready."

For a moment she thought he would refuse to take her after all. But then he turned to the door, muttering gruffly, "Come on."

Adam lifted the tent flap and they walked in. The hunters and women stood around in various states of undress, gaping at them. Adam frowned and they became conscious of their nakedness, and it was comical to watch them scrambling into their clothes.

The women drew off to one side and pity welled in Rachael as she gazed at them. They were a dejected group if ever she saw one.

A nervous titter ran through the room and someone called out, "Introduce us to your lady, boss."

Rachael felt Adam's hand come possessively on her arm. "This is Rachael, men," he said, a hint of pride underlying his words.

She braced herself for the sneers and sly grins, and was surprised to hear only pleasant utterances of welcome. Only Jake snickered, and threatening looks from the others quickly squelched it in his throat.

Rachael's eyes scanned the winter quarters and she wondered how the women could stand the cold, dreary canvas shelter. Her survey was stopped at a corner secluded by a hanging blanket and she was curious about it. But when a quick glance revealed Eagle and Flower missing, she understood. Eagle would want his privacy.

The room had sprung into noisy life, the men all talking at once and bringing Adam into it. Someone helped Rachael off with her coat and she was conscious of hungry looks cast her way. Across the room she saw Adam's face grow dark and she knew he was angry about it.

A worn-out relic of a woman moved toward Rachael, holding out a cup of coffee. Rachael looked at Adam and he nodded his head. She smiled her thanks as she took the cup and the woman bobbed her head shyly and melted back with the others.

When they made no effort to talk to her, Rachael joined them and sat down on an upended keg. A few of them smiled timidly at her and the others dropped their heads and nervously played with their fingers.

But only at first were they ill at ease with her. As she continued to talk to them in an easy chatter they began to relax and talk along with her.

Over in the sheltered nook, the blanket moved and Eagle emerged with Flower at his heels. Catching sight of Rachael, Flower's smug smile turned to a dark sullen scowl. When Eagle hurried to Rachael's side and lifted her hand to his lips, two pairs of eyes darted angry glares their way.

The room grew tense as everyone's eyes swung to Adam, awaiting his outburst. But the expected roar did not come. Instead, Adam's face took on a cunning insolence and he crossed the room to Flower. The girl's face lit up and her face was wreathed in smiles. And as Adam led her to the blocked-off corner, the look she shot at Rachael was full of smug satisfaction.

As everyone stared at the insult thrown in Rachael's face, Eagle felt her stiffen and he leaned over and whispered, "Don't let it show, Rach. He won't do nothing with the squaw. He's just crazy jealous right now. Keep on talking like it don't bother you."

For the next half hour her gay lilting voice could be heard as she entertained and captured the hearts of the wild bunch.

She was to be awarded for her effort. For later, when the pair joined the laughing group, the disappointment on Flower's face said plainly that nothing had happened. And better yet, Adam had the grace to look sheepish as everyone stared at him, some showing clearly their disapproval.

From the corner of her eye, Rachael saw the woman of the coffee lash out and kick the Indian girl when she walked past.

Eagle looked at Rachael, and with a big grin on his face, winked slyly. But Adam had caught the little interchange and his face grew dark. Without a word, he jerked Rachael to her feet and pushed her toward the tent flap. The low objecting murmur of the hunters followed them outside. His fingers bit into her arm and she stumbled against his fast stride.

They were some distance from the tent when one of the women came hurrying to place Rachael's coat around her shoulders.

Immediately when they were inside the cabin, Adam flung her across the room. She spun and reeled and came to stop against a chair. Stalking after her, he snarled, "What in the hell did you think you were doing, playing up to that bastard?"

She stared back at him, examining the rage in his face, then quietly, "You are impossible."

Her cool self-control only maddened him more and his questions came pouring out. "How many times have you lain with him? When do you plan to again? Don't think I didn't see the look he gave you."

He stopped short. Tears were running unchecked down her cheeks. Suddenly he wanted to take her into his arms and ask her forgiveness. But even as the thought came, his arms went slack at his side and the wall between them grew taller.

Rachael heard the soft brush of his buckskins and the click of the door. She looked up and found herself alone.

CHAPTER 13

Elisha awoke in the early morning with a feeling that a great sadness would fall on him before the day was over.

He rolled over on his back and gave a forced laugh. "I'm gettin' worse than a fanciful old woman."

He was too much alone he realized and was in danger of contracting cabin fever. For some time now he had thought seriously of bringing Ruby to his cabin permanently. His hound came and nudged him and as he scratched the dog's ears absent-mindedly, he muttered, "The place is too lonesome with Nick and Rachael gone."

As he often did in the mornings, he lay and thought of his friend and granddaughter. Something had happened to Nick, he was sure. Either he had become lost in the storm and frozen to death, or he had caught up with Adam and the wolf had killed him. He was sure that only death could have kept him from returning with Rachael.

He sighed deeply. What about Rachael? Was she alright? Was that rakehell treating her well or was she living like some squaw, forced to sleep outdoors and do heavy camp chores?

He felt his anger mounting and cursed the white world outside that kept him from going after her himself. Stiffly he rose from the bed and stumped over to the fireplace. When the ashes had been raked aside and wood fed to the red coals beneath it, he pulled on his homespuns and turned his hand to breakfast.

The sun broke through the window as he mixed up biscuits and fried salt pork. When the coffee had finished perking, he called the dog and gave him half the meat and bread.

After three cups of coffee, he struggled into his heavy coat and made his way to the barn. He worked slowly, killing time, as he fed and watered the animals and chickens and milked the cow. Then grumbling, he made the trip to the sheep pen to tend to Rachael's "pets."

By the time he carried in wood and straightened up the cabin (a chore he never neglected because Rachael liked it neat) it was lunchtime.

For this meal he ate whatever was handy. Today it was breakfast leftovers, washed down with glasses of buttermilk.

Then the long afternoon stretched ahead of him, the time he dreaded the most. It was these long idle hours that had led him to the idea of having Ruby with him all the time. He sat down before the fire and drowsed in the rocker as his mind wandered back over the years to the good times. The hound sighed contentedly and stretched out at his feet.

Dimly, Elisha counted four bongs as the mantle clock struck. Time to get to the barn again. He started to rise then stopped when he heard footsteps on the porch. Then suddenly the door was flung open, and startled, his eyes flew wide as they rested on the tall figure silhouetted against the setting sun.

He had a vague notion he was dreaming as he half arose, shushing the dog's deep growl. "Nick?" he questioned, then eagerly, "Is it you, old man?"

Before his words were hardly out, he was being

crushed in a bear hug that could only happen in reality. They were like two great boys, banging at each other in joy and embarrassment.

"Where in the hell have you been all winter?" Elisha demanded. "I thought the wolves had got you." Then peering over Nick's shoulder, he asked hesitantly, "Did you . . . did you find Rachael?"

Nick shook his head sadly. "I failed you, 'Lisha. I'll tell you all about it later. Right now I want you to meet somebody." He turned to the door and called out, "Nora, will you and the boy come in now?"

Elisha stared. Other than his dead wife, he had never seen a woman so completely female. When Nick proudly made the introductions, she clasped his hands warmly. "I am honored to meet you, Elisha Jobe," she smiled. "I have listened to Nick talk about you all winter. I am truly sorry to be separating two such good friends."

Elisha gave an uncertain laugh. "What are you talkin' about, Nora? We ain't gonna separate, not me and Nick." He turned to Nick, "Ain't that right, Nick?"

Nick realized it was going to be worse than he had expected. But unwavering, he met Elisha's eyes and carefully explained. "She means, Elisha, that me and her are gonna get married."

He waited for his long-time friend to grasp his words and their meaning. Then quietly he continued, "I love her, 'Lisha. I'm tired of living from day to day, going nowhere. You above everyone else know what a useless existence I have led in the past."

Elisha was stunned and it showed. Nick getting married. It was hard to visualize the rough hillman married to this dainty woman.

He looked uncertain, and then embarrassed somehow. Finally he nodded his head agreeably. "You don't have to justify yourself with me, Nick. Nora is a beautiful woman and I'd probably do the same thing in your shoes."

Nick sighed a relieved sound. "Thanks, 'Lisha. I knew you'd understand."

"Fact of the matter, Nick, I'm glad you got yourself a good woman. It's hard to be alone when you get to my age." He paused a moment then added reflectively, "I've been thinkin' about bringin' Ruby down here to my place, but now I've got a better idea. I'll move up to her place and you and your new family can stay here. How does that strike you?"

Nick removed his coat and then helped Nora off with hers. Then patting the chair next to him, said, " 'Lisha, sit down please. I have more to tell you and I don't know how to begin."

"Just spit it out, Nick," Elisha encouraged as he sat down.

Nick studied him a moment, then nodded his head. He and Elisha had never talked of the past except to say where they had come from and that Nick's parents were dead and that Elisha's wife had passed away and that he had a son and daughter. That was all that had been necessary between them.

So now, Nick went back to his younger days, telling of the plantation and his reason for leaving it. "But I can go back now," he ended. "I feel that I owe it to my future wife and son to give them a comfortable home."

Elisha remembered his premonition of sadness and thought to himself, "This is it. Nothing could be sadder than losing an old and trusted friend."

He dug his pipe from his pocket and took a long

time filling and lighting it. After drawing on it noisily for some time, he finally said, "What can I say, Nick? I'll miss you like hell. For awhile it'll seem all over again, like a part of me is missin'. But you got the right idea. It would be a pure waste to keep a woman like Nora in the wilderness when you got something better to give her."

He glanced at Nick and was surprised to see a hint of indecision in the raw-boned face. His heart lightened. Nick would remember often the hills and the wild good times they had shared. He knocked the dead ashes from his pipe and said, "Now tell me what you can about Rachael."

While Nick related his run-in with the wolves and Nora saving him, Nora moved about preparing supper. In a short time she called them to eat and as they arose, Nick laid his hand on Elisha's shoulder. "Don't worry about Rach, 'Lisha. You know that little spitfire. She'll come out on top."

"Yeah, I guess you're right. But I can't help worrying about her. Lord knows what conditions she's livin' under."

They ate the tasty meal and Elisha was surprised and disappointed when Nick announced that they'd be pushing on. "I want to make the post tonight and get our provisions and then tomorrow morning we can get an early start."

Elisha watched them out of sight, then listened to the hoofbeats fade away. "Good-bye, old friend," he whispered softly. "God be with you in everything you do."

He went to bed early, determined that he would go for Ruby the first thing tomorrow morning.

CHAPTER 14

Adam didn't return to the cabin until the sun was a red ball in the west. On a string, he had strung a dozen pan-sized trout.

"So that's where he's been," Rachael mused.

He laid the fish on the table and with an air of authority, snapped, "Clean and cook these for supper."

Rachael's face flushed and she jerked erect. So he was still on his high horse. Lifting her chin defiantly, she retorted, "Have your squaw take care of them."

The only sound in the room was the snapping of the fire as he moved toward her. And even though a tremor of fear ran through her as he lifted his hand, she stood her ground, her eyes daring him. She was determined not to be cowed by him and turn into the likes of the poor women in the tent.

She heard the distant laughter of the wild bunch and for a split second she wanted to bolt and run to them. But suddenly Adam's hand snaked out and imprisoned her wrists. "I gave you an order," he grated out.

"To hell with your order," she yelled back.

Slowly he twisted her arm back, until she was powerless. Step by step he walked her to the table. The long speckled fish seemed to stare at her out of round dead eyes. "Are you going to clean them?" he demanded.

Dumbly, she nodded.

He released her and stepped back, a faint smile of satisfaction curving his lips. It was high time she learned that he was boss.

Rachael rubbed her throbbing arm, her narrowed eyes shooting fire at him. Then before Adam could comprehend what she was up to, she had moved out of the circle of candlelight, and fast as light, the fish was in her hand and slapped up against his face.

He stood a moment, too stunned to move. Then with a roar he was around the table after her. But as she retreated before him, the flames from the fireplace shone on the broad blade of his hunting knife clasped in her hand. He had tossed it on the table along with the fish.

"Touch me again, you bastard, and I'll cut your heart out," she panted. "I'll do it if I have to wait until you're asleep."

Adam stared at her, unable to believe his eyes. Her tearless, tortured eyes gazed back at him, telling him it was true. He made a feeble gesture. "You would kill me?"

"Try me," she spoke in a grave voice.

He hadn't counted on her defying him to such lengths. He had thought his greater strength would bend her to his will. Once again he was impressed with her mettle and courage, but as before, strove to hide his admiration.

Nevertheless it was maddening to have this slip of a girl outdo him every time. Surprise had cooled his anger, and in a calm state, he could never lay a hand on her. But still, he argued with himself, she must not know that she had licked him.

He bent over and picked the fish up from the floor and said coolly, "Have it your own way. Flower will be honored to cook them for me. She'll warm my bed tonight, too."

The door slammed and Rachael sank into a chair, emotionally drained. "So he has gone back to his squaw," she thought and wondered if he intended to bring Flower back to the cabin.

She brought her clenched fist down on the table. "If he does, so help me I'll go to Jim."

Adam did not return that night. Rachael ate a lonely supper and spent a lonely night in the big bed. But the next morning, early, her spirits were lifted. From the safety of the covers she watched Jake build a roaring fire, and then carry in a good supply of wood. She snuggled contentedly between the covers and smiled. "He hasn't forgotten me completely."

For the next half hour loud laughter and talk came from the neighborhood of the tent. Then after a sharp calling to the dogs, all noise dwindled and died away as the hunters disappeared into the forest. The hunt had begun.

When the cabin was thoroughly warm, Rachael rose and made her breakfast on last night's reheated supper. She straightened the cabin and planned the evening meal, wondering if Adam would be there to eat it.

Last, she dressed and made her way to the tent.

Inside the canvas shelter, two candles shed a dim light, making the room and its inhabitants appear more squalid and wretched than they were. The women were gathered around a huge, rusty iron kettle set in the middle of the floor. The flickering flames inside it fed on a pitiful amount of wood. Rachael's eyes followed the wispy spiral of smoke up to the peak of the canvas where it disappeared through a hole.

The doubtful heat coming from its bowl barely reached five feet in any direction, and Rachael marveled that the women weren't all sick. The thin, ragged clothing they wore were poor protection against the steady flow of icy cold permeating from the frozen dirt floor. As they stamped their feet to keep warm, Rachael mentally cursed the hunters for treating them so callously.

"They'll never last the winter under these conditions," she thought angrily.

Annie, a small woman and the one who had defended her the day before, was the first to discover Rachael's presence. A smile of welcome came over the thin face and she hurried to greet her. Then the other women gathered around, all talking at once.

Rachael was relieved to see that Flower was not among them. The Indian girl was the last person she wanted to see today. She looked toward the cloistered corner and Annie sniffed. "That lazy bitch is still asleep. We could hear her after Eagle all night. I never saw a one so crazy to have a man atween her legs."

Rachael's heart leaped. Adam hadn't shared Flower's bed after all.

She held her hands over the meager fire, then turned to Annie, "Why don't you put more wood on the fire?"

Annie made a weary gesture toward the small pile of wood next to the kettle. "It took us women two hours to chop that stack. The sap is frozen now, you know, and the damn axe bounced so in our hands, it hurt all the way up to our shoulders." She laughed bitterly. "We try to keep most of it for the men at night. They like it warm."

Rachael's voice was trembling in anger when she asked, "Do you mean to tell me that those big men make you women chop the wood?"

Annie gave a nervous laugh. "They'd beat hell out of us if we didn't."

The others grunted agreement.

As Rachael ranted and raved against the injustice of it, she did not notice that the women's chatter had died down. When she found herself starting all the conversation, she became aware of the uneasiness on the camp followers' faces.

Finally, bluntly, she asked, "Annie, should I go back to the cabin? You and your friends don't seem to want me here."

"Oh, no, miss, we love havin' you here," Annie exclaimed. "But we just remembered that last night Adam told us he didn't want you around the likes of us. He can be mean when he's riled."

Rachael could only stare at Annie. How could Adam talk so cruelly to these poor women? He was much too arrogant and it was high time someone clipped that rooster's feathers, she decided.

"Annie, I could care less what Adam Warden says. I choose my friends, not him."

She saw them exchange a look that said plainly they didn't believe she could do as she claimed. In true fact, she didn't feel as brave as she sounded. His dark scowling face swam in front of her and for a moment she was tempted to return to the cabin and not start a battle that in all likelihood she would lose.

Annie sensed Rachael's hesitation and laid a hand on her arm. "We'll understand, Rachael, if you want to leave. We know things ain't right between you and Adam and we wouldn't want to make them worse." The others nodded their heads vigorously and even the squaws grunted sympathetically.

Rachael gazed at the downtrodden women and knew that she had a friend in every one of them. She wanted to laugh hysterically. Proud Rachael Jobe was coming down in the world. A short time ago she wouldn't have even looked at these creatures, much less call them friends.

So be it then. If they were to be her closest friends, then they would be her allies also. Together they would teach the men of this camp to treat them as human beings, if not with respect.

Her mind made up, she spoke rapidly. "Annie, don't you gals worry about me. Right now let's try to make this place a little warmer."

In unison they asked, "How can we women do that?"

Rachael's eyes moved over the faces that crowded around her. Hope fought with doubt in their tired eyes and she became more determined to help them.

"I don't know yet. Let me think a moment."

She recalled that Elisha had shoveled the first snow up around the cabin. "It will block out the wind," he had explained. So why wouldn't it work as well here?

But the dirt floor was another matter. It would take the strength of the men to weatherize that and she would tackle the hunters on that problem. But hopefully at a time when Adam wasn't around, she added mentally.

The women stood waiting and she smiled at them encouragingly. "Alright, girls, put on your heaviest coats ... no, better yet, wear the men's extra coats. I'm sure they're warmer. We're going outside and shovel snow."

Bewilderment spread across their faces and they looked at one another. She knew that her statement didn't make sense to them, and not wanting to answer a dozen questions at once, she spoke before they could. "We're going to bank snow around the tent."

Their eyes lit up as they remembered a father doing the same thing a long time ago.

Once the women overcame their fear of rummaging in the men's gear, they laughed and poked good-natured fun at one another in clothes much too big for them. They even became so brave as to pull on fur-lined moccasins belonging to the men.

Outside, they bent their backs to the shoveling and it was lunchtime when they had finished. Snow was now piled at least three feet deep all around the sides.

When they went back inside, the room was decidedly warmer and they were able to discard their coats. Rachael piled wood generously on the low fire and they gathered in a circle around the leaping flames. Annie passed out dried venison and poured cups of strong black coffee. And as they munched contentedly, they talked.

"Rachael, you're awfully lucky that Adam won't let the other men use you," Annie said. "You wouldn't stay pretty very long iffen he did."

Rachael was surprised at the wistful note in her voice. She hadn't realized that the women cared who they slept with. Grandpa had led her to believe that their kind accepted their way of life as a natural way, never complaining. He had said they were conditioned to this from early childhood. That they had seen their mothers before them blindly obeying orders and that in their hard, simple life, men ruled supreme.

She put down her empty coffee cup and gazed at Annie. "Do you women mind being passed around?"

"God's mercy, yes," one thin woman exclaimed. "It wears a body out. Nights when they've been drinkin' is terrible."

"That's the God's truth," Annie interrupted. "They're nights when we don't get to close our eyes."

"Why do you put up with it?" Rachael demanded angrily. "I'd kill the bastards."

"We have to take their ornery ways, Rachael. We got nowhere else to go," Annie explained. "Nobody else wants us. The long-hunter only takes us because he can't get anyone else."

"Alright then," Rachael spoke excitedly. "That's your ace in the hole. He can't get anyone else so make him treat you decent."

"If we complain they just knock us down," someone said, and the squaws grunted in agreement.

"If you joined together and stuck to your guns, you'd win out," Rachael urged. "You know men. They can't go very long without their loving."

"Yeah, we noticed that about Adam last night," Annie giggled. "He sure was hurtin'."

"He sure was," another agreed. "We thought for sure he'd hotfoot it back to you before the night was out."

"That red bitch over there in the corner sure wanted him, but Adam didn't even look at her," Annie smirked.

Rachael felt her body go warm and she yearned for night to come . . . and Adam to share it with her.

They joked back and forth, discussing this man and that, and Rachael was surprised to learn that some of the women had favorites. The glimmering of an idea took shape in her mind. But after a moment she discarded it. She was overreaching her imagination, she decided.

Then unexpectedly the sun was setting. Rachael arose to her feet exclaiming, "I've got to get home and get supper started."

The others, alarm in their faces, hurried up with her. "If supper ain't ready when the men get here, all hell will break loose," Annie worried.

The fire had burned low and like frightened sheep they scurried around feeding wood to the kettle and burrowing in sacks for the evening meal.

Rachael stared at them. They had forgotten her advice already. Was it a hopeless idea on her part? She opened her mouth to remind them, then heard the men's voices coming up behind camp. A tight silence descended on the women and they looked at one another fearfully.

Rachael slipped into her coat. She hated to leave them to fend for themselves. They were so inadequate. But she was anxious to have supper started in case Adam showed up. She stood uncertain at the tent flap, her conscience nagging at her. Then Annie broke the silence.

"Go on home, Rachael. I'm sure your man will be along. And don't worry about us. We're used to their meanness."

"But, Annie, I want this meanness to stop. I want you girls to stand up to them. If they hit you, so what, they've done it before. You're fighting for a cause and that is never easy. Better they kill you than to continue as you are."

Hope and a faint determination shone in their faces. She had started a small fire, now if only they would feed it a little. But before she left, she added, "If things get too bad, hotfoot it to my place. I dare any of them to come in there."

She was halfway to the cabin when she heard steps crunching behind her. She knew it must be Adam, and though her heart sang, she forced herself not to look back. But when a long shadow reached and walked alongside her own, she looked sideways at the owner.

It was her intention to ignore him, but she could not rid herself of the joy his presence brought her, and looking up through her lashes, she said quietly, "How was the hunt?"

"We done real good."

"I'm glad for you."

"What's for supper?"

The hunger in his eyes however was not for food, and Rachael hid a smile as she answered, "Bear steak and potatoes."

As she busied herself at the fireplace turning the steaks, and then setting the table, Adam watched her every move through half-closed eyes. Rachael was conscious of his close study and her blood tingled and she was anxious for the time when they would retire to the big bed.

The steaming food was on the table and she called to him that supper was ready. But they had only begun to eat when a loud clamor arose from the tent. Adam paid no attention to the noise, only remarking, "Sounds like the sluts are catchin' hell."

But Rachael's stomach was tied in knots and she glared at him as he continued to shovel food into his mouth.

When the angry curses of male voices and high squeals of frightened women drew closer to the cabin, Adam swore under his breath. "What in the hell are they comin' over here for?" he muttered, rising to his feet.

He jerked open the door and was immediately thrust aside as bloody and beaten women surged past him. Rachael jumped to her feet, the chair going over backwards.

"Annie, in heaven's name, what has happened?"

Any reply Annie might have made died in her throat. The irate hunters were coming to a halt in front of the door, howling their rage and shaking their fists. "Send them sluts out here, Adam," they demanded. "We're gonna beat the livin' hell out of them."

Adam stepped aside, but Rachael sprang into the vacated opening. Her eyes flashing and her body trembling, her words rang out. "It seems to me you've already done that. They aren't coming out and I dare any of you to set foot in this cabin."

The bewhiskered crew stared at her, their mouths hanging open. Then they looked at Adam, waiting for him to slap her down.

She planted her fists on her hips and waited. If these browbeaten women were ever to take a stand against the men's tyranny, it would be up to her to show them the way. The thought crossed her mind that she would most likely get knocked around in the process.

Behind her, Annie was gasping out curses between her sobs and Rachael wanted to shout, "Shut up." But Adam seemed oblivious to the racket and continued to stare at her, an uncertain confusion in his eyes. He knew that the men expected him to beat her, but all he could think of was taking her to bed. Then strangely, he was irritated at the men for forcing him into this position.

But he turned his anger on her. "You're making a hell of a show of yourself," he snapped. "If you'd stayed home where you belong none of this would have happened."

"I'm glad I went. It's shameful the way these women are treated."

"Those women are just sluts, why do you care how they're treated?"

"I care because they're human beings. And did it ever occur to you that you and your friends have made them what they are?"

She saw his face darken and tensed herself for what was surely to come. But surprisingly he still talked . . . almost reasoned with her. "They've got to go back with the men. That's why they're here . . . to take care of the men's needs."

Once again Rachael's previous idea nagged at her. Did she dare put voice to it? A small voice whispered, "There will never be a more opportune time."

She pushed back her shoulders and directed her words to the angry, milling hunters. "They'll go back when each of you men has chosen one woman and promises to stick to her. There will be no more swapping them around." As they stared at her in disbelief, she took a deep breath and added, "And another thing, there's to be a floor laid in the tent and warm clothes provided for the women."

Adam stared at her incredulously. She was going too far and he felt a swift rush of embarrassment that his men should witness such a thing.

"Woman," he shouted, "you're crazy. We've never done that. The women are always shared."

"Then it's high time you stop."

"I'll see you in hell first."

"Good, I'd like that fine."

Unconsciously Adam clenched his fists as he glared back at her. Then, his voice dangerously quiet, he said, "So be it," and slammed the door behind him.

The small cabin trembled and Rachael pressed her forehead against the quivering door. "Gone again," her heart cried silently. "Surely he will go to Flower this time."

CHAPTER 15

When the last angry footstep died away, Rachael turned and looked at the women. Their faces displayed a mixture of gladness and concern. Gladness for themselves and concern that they had been the cause of added trouble between Rachael and her man.

Forcing a smile on her lips, Rachael spoke, "Well, ladies, we've won the first round."

"Oh, Rachael, we're so sorry that we chased Adam away," Annie cried.

Rachael patted the bony fingers lying on her arm and assured her that she and the others weren't to blame. "Adam did it himself, the ornery bastard."

"What do you think they'll do now, burn the cabin down?" one of the women asked.

"I don't think they'd go that far," Rachael laughed. "They'll get drunk and abuse the squaws tonight. Then tomorrow morning they'll be sick, and along toward evening they'll start thinking on my words."

Annie gazed at her with eager eyes. "Do you think they'll do as you asked, Rachael?"

"I have a sneaking hunch that they will. It's a long winter, you know."

"That's true," someone agreed, then added, "and them raunchy devils want their pleasurin' every night."

"Yeah, two and three times a night," a woman

said bitterly. "Take crazy Jake for instance, that loony wants to ride all night."

"Let's forget about them for now," Rachael suggested. "Did you girls get to eat any supper?"

There was a chorus of noes.

"Not a bite," Annie added. As soon as they came in and seen we had been wearing their duds, they started in beatin' on us."

"Alright, we'll finish Adam's supper then. If that's not enough we'll cook some more."

When everyone's stomach was full, they tidied up the cabin and brought in wood and water for the night. Then, with the door barred, they gathered around the fire and began to lay their plans.

Part of Rachael's plan was to make the women as attractive as possible. "Ladies," she began, "we'll start tomorrow by bathing and washing hair. And from hereafter I want you to do this at least once a week."

"That will take some doing, Rachael," Annie said doubtfully.

"If we get a floor in there and enough wood to burn, you're going to be surprised at how warm the tent will be."

In a short time, the women, unused to heat, became drowsy and their heads began to nod. Rachael glanced at the only bed, and always fastidious, shunned the idea of sleeping next to an unclean body. Not wanting to hurt feelings, she said matter-of-factly, "When you girls go to bed tonight, if you lie crosswise, you'll be more comfortable."

She cringed inwardly as they, yawning loudly, piled into the bed without removing any clothing. As they exclaimed over the warmth and softness of the mattress, she thought dryly, "I've got to introduce them to nightgowns."

Rachael rolled herself into the furs that she and Adam had used on the trail. Snuggling down, she caught his scent and cried herself to sleep.

Rachael awoke the next morning to a cold cabin. Jake hadn't come to make a fire. She lay a moment gazing at the icicles hanging past the window. The cold glitter reflecting off them made her shiver. "I wonder if I could start a fire," she mused.

But over in the corner, the covers stirred and Annie scurried across the floor and began poking in the ashes. Feeling Rachael's eyes upon her, she turned and smiled. "I'll have a fire goin' in a minute, Rachael. I banked it real good last night."

To Rachael's surprise, beneath the cold ashes and charred wood, red coals glowed. Feeding small pieces of wood to it, Annie soon had a roaring fire shooting up the chimney.

"Did you hear anything from the tent this morning?" Rachael asked her.

"Just a few cuss words," Annie grinned. "They sounded pretty grumpy."

"Good. I hope they grump all day."

After breakfast was finished, they started lugging pails of snow into the cabin and melting it on the hearth. As the water was heated and poured into a wooden tub, each woman in turn climbed in and washed away the grime and dirt from her body and hair.

They were so pitifully thin, Rachael hated to look at them. "They'll stay here until they get some meat on their bodies," she vowed silently.

She was pleasantly surprised at how well they looked with scrubbed faces and clean hair and couldn't get over Annie having blonde hair beneath the dirt. The pride they took in their new appearance more than made up for Adam's absence.

Wrapped in blankets, they sat before the fire waiting for their laundered clothing to dry. Later as they patched and mended worn dresses and petticoats, Rachael taught them how to brush and dress their hair.

In the early afternoon, dressed and ready for inspection, the women stood before Rachael. She smiled. She had succeeded in her endeavor. They looked respectable, and a man wasn't so apt to beat a woman who looked clean and decent. She smiled secretly at the countless trips made to the small mirror hanging on the wall.

Around dusk, just when the bubbling deer stew was sending mouth-watering aromas throughout the cabin, a low knocking sounded on the door. The women stopped their chatter and glued their eyes to the door.

Rachael rose and moved away from the fire. "Who is it?" she called out.

"It's us, miss," came a gruff voice.

"What do you want?"

"We come to choose us a woman."

Rachael waited a minute, then asked, "What did you do about the floor?"

She listened to their low mumbling and soft swearing. It wasn't going to be so easy for the big men, she grinned inwardly.

Then, cajoling, came the same voice. "We plan to do that tomorrow."

"In one day? I doubt it, that's a big tent. I don't think you could do it properly in one week."

"Naw, you're wrong, miss. We can do it in a couple of hours."

"A couple of hours? What do you plan on using?"

"Why cedar boughs, of course."

Rachael allowed a smile to play over her lips and the women behind her looked at one another uneasily. Annie touched her arm and whispered, "Cedar boughs are no good, Rachael. In a day's time they will be trampled into the dirt and become a hindrance to walk on."

From outside came, "Well, what about it, miss? Can we start pickin' our women?"

Rachael heard the quick intake of breath behind her and turned to wink encouragingly. She was enjoying the situation. "I'm sorry, men," she called out, "but the women vote against cedar boughs. They want poles laid on the ground . . . nice and tight together."

The women, fearful, waited for the explosion that was bound to come. Surely Rachael had gone too far this time.

There was silence outside and Rachael grinned at Annie, picturing the men's faces as her demands hit them. The loud shouts of rage were not long in coming. "A wood floor?" someone shouted. "Who in the hell do them whores think they are?"

Rachael's grin broadened into a wide smile as they continued to rave and threaten. "You wait until we tell Adam about this, missy. He'll come over here and beat the life out of you, while we take care of them other bitches."

Finally their angry voices died away as they

stomped back to the tent. Annie, her voice quivering, whimpered, "Do you think they'll come back and beat us?"

"They'll get a blast of buckshot if they try to open that door," Rachael answered soberly.

She moved back to the fire and sat down. The fight had gone out of her and her heart was heavy. She was convinced now that Adam had gone back to Flower. "Otherwise he would have been out there with the others, shouting his head off," she told herself bitterly.

The next morning early, they were awakened to the ringing sound of axes. "Is it possible?" Annie whispered.

Rachael sat up in the bedroll, her eyes bright. "Girls, I think we've licked them."

All day the chopping continued and the women watched from the small window. In the beginning the men's faces looked like thunderclouds as they dragged long straight poles into the tent, but as the day wore on, a change took place in their behavior. Loud, good-humored laughter spilled out of their mouths as they joked and ragged one another. Meanwhile the women chattered incessantly about the floor and the difference it would make in their comfort.

That evening as they sat together, Rachael took the opportunity to give them some advice. "Girls, I'd like to give you a hint on how to keep the progress you have made." They were listening to her attentively and she continued.

"You know those men are nothing more than grown-up boys. Handled correctly, a woman can do most anything with them. If you want them to justly value your person, you must work at it."

"Oh, we're more than willing to treat them right," Annie exclaimed. "Just tell us what to do, Rachael."

"Well, the number one item is to keep yourselves clean and attractive. And equally important, keep your home comfortable. Keep the tent as clean as you possibly can. Wash the blankets every week, keep the dishes washed and put away, and most important"—she stopped and gave a small laugh—"have the aroma of something good cooking in the pot."

They joined in her laughter and one of them said eagerly, "We can do that. Is there anything else?"

"Try always to be pleasant, but don't take any guff from them. The moment they raise a hand to you, come hightailing to me."

"By God, we'll do it," Annie's bony fist banged down on her knee. "To tell you the truth, I'm kinda anxious to get started."

"I'm excited about it, too," Rachael smiled. "If this works out, I want you women to band together and demand a place of your own when you get back to summer quarters."

Annie's eyes grew round with the thought of a home of her own. "By God, we'll do it. There ain't no reason in the world they can't build for us. They don't do nothin' all summer but drink and pester us women."

"Will you be there to help us, Rachael?" a woman asked.

Rachael bent forward and shoved a piece of burning wood closer to the coals. That was a good question; she wondered if Adam would send her back to Elisha when the hunt was over. As things stood now, she expected him to send her packing any day. She looked up at the waiting group and smiled faintly. "I have no idea."

On the third day, around noon, the knocking on the door was repeated. This time Rachael opened it to the hunters. Unshaven and disheveled, the men stood uncertainly, with weak grins on their faces. Then the leader spoke hesitantly, "We're . . . we're happy to report, miss, the floor is finished."

Surveying them with a critical eye, Rachael asked, "Have you come for the woman of your choice then?"

"Well I . . . I guess you could put it that way. We're not particular which woman though."

Sighing to herself, Rachael wondered if these men would ever change a great deal. "At any rate," she consoled herself, "each woman will only have to contend with one of the louts."

She didn't try to conceal her dislike of them as she said coolly, "If that's the case, we'll let the women choose the man she wants."

Amid the doubtful muttering of the hunters, Rachael called out, "Come on, girls. Come pick one of these handsome men for your very own."

The men glared at her, fully understanding her intended barb. Then they grinned sheepishly as they fingered their whiskered faces.

Giggling like a group of schoolgirls, the new-born women came forward and the men, their eyes round in wonder, gaped at the strangers. When Annie marched up to a man two times her size and claimed him, the big burly person stared down at her, then smiled foolishly, very pleased.

The others surged forward, eager to be picked by one of the sweet-scented ladies. But the hill's rejects were enjoying their moment of triumph and were slow in choosing. With a freedom new to them, they laughed and flirted with the wild bunch. And the hunters, never having had this happen to them before, were enjoying it fully. Soon they too were finding glib tongues and compliments flowed through the air.

Finally they were paired off. The unchosen ones, such as Jake, stood to one side mumbling darkly to one another. "If nothing else," Rachael mused, "I've saved the women from those polecats."

Chattering and laughing, the women hurried to gather their meager belongings. Rachael had shared her rice powder and bath salts with them, and they carefully wrapped them in pieces of homespun.

Annie, not quite believing their good fortune, stood rubbing her chin thoughtfully. "Rachael, would you go back with us and take a look at the floor . . . and maybe give the men a last warning?"

Rachael smiled. "You know," she confessed, "I had that in mind all the time."

Laughing together, they joined the others.

The floor was sturdy and tight, well laid together. Without being told, Rachael knew that Adam had had a hand in its proper construction.

As the women exclaimed over the floor as if it were gleaming hardwood, Rachael caught sight of Adam. He sat next to the fire kettle, and as she passed him, she looked at him through lowered lashes. His eyes piercing as a wolf's caught and held her gaze. She caught and held her breath at the raw, fierce look in them. Only the emergence of Eagle from the sheltered nook saved her from bolting the tent. Adam hadn't gone back to Flower after all.

As usual, Eagle greeted her warmly and with respect. "How are you, Jim?" she smiled.

"Fit as a fiddle." A mischievous glint came in his eyes and he teased, "And how are you?"

Her eyes crinkled back at him. "Never been better." She paused a moment then asked, "What do you think of my girls now?"

"I can't get over it, Rach. But how long do you think they're gonna look like this . . . living with these hounds?"

Rachael was aware that Eagle was baiting Adam and decided to play along with him. "I'm hoping," she began, "that some of them still have a spark of decency left in them and will treat the women well. But, then, of course, there are those that were spewed out of hell and there's no way of reaching them."

Adam's exploding snort came from behind them and they both chuckled at his rage.

Annie tugged at her elbow. "What do you think, Rachael? Ain't it nice and warm in here now?"

"I think it's fine, honey. Now all you have to do is make your man behave and treat you right."

"I know," Annie answered doubtfully. "Already he wants me to lie with him right here in front of everybody, just like before."

Rachael caught the mocking sneer on Adam's face and heard his low mocking laugh. Anger ripped through her and she hissed, "Dirty rotten animals."

Annie nodded in agreement. "We forgot about that, didn't we, Rachael?"

"Yes. But we can remedy it."

She climbed upon a keg and clapped her hands for attention. The women gathered around her and the men stared, wondering what the wildcat wanted next.

"You know," she began reflectively, "the women forgot to tell you one more little request. Each womans wants her own little nook. One like Eagle provided for Flower. I'm sure you men would want your white women to have the same consideration."

The dark rumble that had started when she first began to speak choked off in mid-stream. Of course their women deserved as good as a red squaw, they mumbled to one another. And as they hurried for blankets and began good-humoredly to mark off sections, Adam regarded Rachael sharply. "You're a smart bitch, aren't you?"

Her heart leaped. There was unmistakable pride underlining his hateful remark. She looked at him coolly and smiled sweetly. "Why, Adam, are you just now noticing that?"

She saw his angry jerk and heard him swear under his breath. Then she turned her back on him and watched the women bustling about.

They moved in and out of the cubicles, laying down pallets. She noted that Annie seemed eager and she wondered if the little woman loved the man she had chosen. She sighed. There was no reason for her to stay here any longer. Everyone was preoccupied and she was out of place amidst the hot anticipation that hung in the air. She called to the women.

"I'm going now. I'll see you all tomorrow."

They flocked around her, their eyes giving thanks.

Then she turned to leave and Eagle spoke quietly, "Wait, Rach. I'll walk you home."

In the awkward pause while everyone's head swiveled to Adam, she and Eagle stood regarding each other. There was an undisguised question in Eagle's eyes and Rachael looked away from it.

She recalled his desire for her in the past. Many times he had paid for an entire night of her company while Beaulah turned away the rest of her clientele. For a moment she was tempted to take his silent bid. She would let him make love to her, then ask him to take her out of this wilderness. Take her away from this arrogant man who was making her life so miserable.

But the decision was taken out of her hands. Without comment, Adam rose from his seat, grasped her arm and opened the flap. As they moved down the snow-trampled path, she felt his rage burning through the trembling fingers that still gripped her.

They arrived at the cabin and Rachael debated if she should let him come in or not. And as she was thinking to herself there was nothing she could do if he wanted to come in, he shoved his hands into his pockets, hunched his shoulders and walked away.

She experienced a quick flush of confusion and insult. Fumbling, she opened the door and let the latch fall. Frustrated tears ran down her cheeks and when she realized that the fire had died down and the room had grown cold, she cried in earnest.

CHAPTER 16

A full week went by and still Adam stayed away. Rachael had seen him, been in his company, but no word passed between them.

Each day, in the early afternoon, she made her way to the tent and waited eagerly for the sunset when the hunters would return. Adam's lithe-limbed body always led the way. He had the free grace of an Indian and she delighted in watching him.

Each man's first act on arriving was to bend down a slim sapling, tie his catch to its tip and spring it high. This kept the furs out of reach of the dogs and other marauding animals until they could eat their supper. After filling their bellies with supper and a couple of swigs at the whiskey keg, they would clean and stretch the hides.

If it wasn't snowing or the weather below freezing, the women cooked out of doors. This kept the clutter out of the tent which they now kept religiously clean. The sizzle of broiling meat on the red coals, and the aroma of coffee steaming from a battered and blackened pot marked the nicest time of the day for Rachael.

But when the hunters were called to eat, it was disgusting the way they fell upon the food. They ate in such a manner they resembled animals rather than humans as they wolfed down the food. Rachael and the other women were always relieved when they were finished and went outside to clean their catch.

As they gutted and skinned, they vied with one another over the size and amount of their pelts. They boasted of the size of this beaver and the length of that weasel. Adam called it swapping lies.

Later, sitting before the fire, their feet almost in the ashes, they would sometimes sing bawdy songs. But more often the bottle made the rounds, and one by one they searched out their women and sought the beds.

Then Adam would rise, stretch, and wait for Rachael to leave. Every night he marched silently beside her, escorting her home. When she would lift the latch and open the door, he would wordlessly turn and leave. She had pondered on his baffling behavior until only the sensation of anger remained. Lying alone in bed, she cursed him, muttering, "Who in the blue blazes does he think he is?"

One morning Rachael awakened early, gray dawn still showing through the window. She drowsed in and out of consciousness until the noise of the hunters awakened her fully. Rushing to the window, she was in time to see Adam leaning against a tree, staring at the cabin. For a moment her heart softened toward him. He looked so lonesome, she thought.

But remembering his cold and stubborn attitude, she rehardened herself. "I will not make the first move." He must come to her on his own. In fact, she decided suddenly, from now on she was going to stay away from the tent when he was there. She would visit the women in the daytime. Annie would see to it that she got food.

When the hunters had gone, she dressed and banked the fire. After that one dreadful night of returning home to a cold cabin, she had vowed it would never happen again.

Crazy Jake, of all people, had taught her how to do it. It was at that time that she also learned that Jake carried a strong hatred of Adam.

After spending a cold and uncomfortable time that dreary night, she had seen Jake the next morning limping around camp. Almost frozen, she repressed her fear of him and called out her problem. As he built her a fire, he explained why he had been left behind. He had stepped on a trap spike that had penetrated his moccasin and slashed his foot. Adam had sworn at his carelessness and Jake was still smarting from his biting words.

"I'll fix the bastard," he threatened. "I'll go down and tell 'Lisha where you are."

Curious, Rachael asked, "Did you ever tell Adam that I'm Elisha's granddaughter?"

"Nope. Ain't gonna tell any of the wild bunch."

"I'm glad that you didn't, but why didn't you?"

"Cause if Adam knew, he wouldn't have stole you. I mean for him to get his ass in real trouble. Then we'll see how much he kicks Jake around."

She had laughed and thought to herself, "You may be loose in the head, Jake, but you're slicker than hell."

Two weeks later, Jake was dying. Gangrene had set in the festering wound and his foot and leg were swollen all out of proportion. In his delirium he ranted and raved, mostly at Adam, and only the gentle touch of Rachael's hand could calm him.

It was a relief to all when one gray morning a

wolf howled his lonely note and Jake breathed his last.

It took the hunters close to a week to dig a shallow grave through the frozen ground. Meanwhile, the camp women had washed his dirt-encrusted body as best they could and dressed him in clean clothes. Then rolling him into a piece of canvas, he was ready to be laid to rest.

There had been no Bible among the hunters and Annie fussed that even if Jake was an ornery cuss, there should be some words read over him. So as they all stood silently around the open grave, Rachael quietly said a prayer, remembered from her Sunday school days.

Rachael sighed and pushed the thought of Jake away. Giving one last look at the fire, she donned her coat.

She found the women busy, cleaning the tent. The pride they took in the rude shelter was almost pathetic and she vowed that if it were in her power, each woman would have a home of her own someday.

Unnoticed, she watched them a moment. From their appearance, they were being treated well, she thought. They had gained weight and a healthy color now flushed their cheeks. Even the squaws had become prideful of their appearance and every time the white women bathed, they did likewise.

However, the young squaw, Flower, was going the opposite way. The deep shadows that always lay beneath the black eyes intensified the hunger that looked out of their depths. Eagle had long since ceased trying to satisfy her constant craving and allowed the unattached men to visit her. And though she pretended to be indignant and insulted, she nevertheless invited the hunters in when they scratched at her curtain.

The women noticed her and greeted her arrival with pleasure. "How come you're here so early, Rachael?" Annie asked.

"I've decided to stay home in the evenings. I thought I'd give Mr. Warden something to think about."

"That's good thinking," a tall dark-haired woman declared. "Let him wonder what you're up to."

"Yeah, and not only that," Annie chimed in, "let's have Eagle disappear for awhile every evening. I know he'll go along with it. He dearly loves to aggravate Adam."

Rachael laughed. "You know, Annie, you're a conniving little thing. I couldn't have thought of anything better."

Together they plotted and giggled. Before they realized it the hour was approaching for the men's return.

While Rachael pulled on her coat, Annie hurried to put food into a cloth. "Here's your supper, honey. When you come here tomorrow, we'll report to you how Adam acted."

That night she kept vigil at the darkened window until the last man had entered the tent. She giggled when that last man was Eagle. She had watched him earlier melt into the blackness of the forest and for a moment thought that Adam would follow him. He had jerked erect and made as if to rise, but then settled back and glowered at the cabin. Behind the cover of the drape, she smiled happily.

"Suffer, you arrogant bastard. You think you're so high and mighty."

The next morning, sitting around a crude pole table the men had knocked together, the women told Rachael, with amusement, of Adam's behavior.

"It was so funny, Rach," Annie began, "I thought I'd bust a gut. When he first come in he looked startled at not seeing you here. Then after awhile I seen him lookin' around as if he thought you was hidin' from him. Then he started glarin' at Eagle's corner. Eagle was in there, but by himself. I swear that Adam thought you was in there with him."

"Yeah," another woman took up the tale. "When Eagle came out later, Adam gave a big sigh of relief."

"That's right," Annie continued. "And after that, every time the tent flap opened, he'd jerk up his head and look to see who come in."

"And remember," someone else said, "when we was outside and Eagle left like Annie told him to, how Adam's face looked like a thundercloud?"

"Oh, he was mad alright," Annie laughed. "But that proud galoot didn't ask one word about you."

Rachael sighed. "He wouldn't. He's the proudest man that ever walked the face of the earth. He's got it in his head, you know, that I'm Elisha Jobe's whore."

"But, Rachael, ain't you?" Annie queried.

"No, Annie, I'm not. It's a funny story and some-day I'll tell it to you."

"All the hunters think that he took you right out of 'Lisha's bed," one of the women volunteered.

"Well he didn't. But I wouldn't put it past him to do such thing. Anyhow, he thinks I'm a loose woman and it's burning his behind that he's fallen in love with me."

"Oh we can tell he's crazy about you," they all agreed. "The men know it, too," Annie added. "They say that you've got him pussy-whipped. That you're the only thing he's got on his mind."

"He's got a poor way of showing it," Rachael retorted. "I want him so much I hurt. But evidently he's getting along just fine."

They laughed at her sally, then one of the squaws grunted, "Him hurt too. Every night, big bulge in buckskins."

Rollicking laughter followed the red woman's comment.

Before Rachael left, it was decided that Eagle would continue to leave the camp each night. "We'll bring him to his knees," Annie declared, walking Rachael to the tent flap.

But night followed night and Adam made no move toward the cabin. Almost in despair, Rachael debated giving in and going to him.

Then one late afternoon, after a day of cloudy skies, a snowfall began that lasted for four days. The white stuff piled and drifted almost to the top of the cabin window.

There was no activity around camp that night and Rachael lit a candle and settled down in front of the fire. She sighed, dreading another long evening. Many times she glanced at the clock as the hours dragged on. "If only the hands would move a little faster," she fussed. In sleep she could rest her mind for a while and with luck keep it free of Adam.

Then, over the din of the howling wind, a knock sounded at the door. She stopped her rocking and listened intently. "Maybe it was only the cracking of a frozen tree," she muttered to herself.

But after a moment, it came again, a decided rapping of knuckles. She hurried to the door, then paused. Maybe it was some stranger. But hope and curiosity made her lift the latch and edge the door open a crack.

In the swirling, dancing snow, Adam stood before her.

She felt herself go weak with gladness and for a moment she couldn't speak. Then she saw anger gathering in his eyes and she hurriedly swung open the door, stammering, "Come . . . come in."

He stalked past her and silently removed his coat. Then as he used to, he went and sat down in his favorite chair and stretched his feet to the fire. Rachael stood undecided a moment, then followed after him, taking a chair a few feet from his.

After several minutes of silence, Adam cleared his throat and said gruffly, "I saw that Eagle wasn't comin' over and I figured that somebody ought to be with you in this blizzard."

"Thank you," Rachael murmured and hid a smile.

Silence built again and she made no effort to break it. She had made up her mind that in no way would she help him to converse.

Then she jumped as Adam looked at her and blurted out, "Why do you torture me like this? Whoring around with Eagle. Shaming me in front of my men."

The feeling of elation was still with her, even as she wanted to slap his hateful mouth. She realized that jealousy made him speak so, but still she was becoming a little tired of always listening to his false accusations.

"Are you sure that the men think I'm lying with Eagle," she retorted hotly, "or is it only in your own dirty mind the thought lies?"

Her question opened his eyes wide. His voice rose truculently, yet hopefully. "Do you deny that he's been beddin' you these past nights?"

She stared back at him, her green eyes blazing. "I'm not denying anything to you. You don't own me regardless of what you may think. I've told you before, I'm nobody's woman."

His chair went over backwards as he grabbed her shoulder, making her cry out. "Goddam you, whore. You're my woman, now get to bed."

She struggled against his strength and felt her dress ripping as she tore free. She stood glaring at him, one shoulder and breast bare. His eyes darkened in the old remembered way and he swept her into his arms.

They were like two starving animals, unable to get enough of one another. They loved away the night hours, sometimes slowly and gently, then in a furious movement that left them spent and shaken. And without Adam realizing it, Rachael had led him onto paths that were all new and thrilling to him.

When the eastern sky turned a blurry pink, they fell asleep.

Rachael awoke in the early afternoon and heard the snow still whispering on the roof. She discovered a white mist shifting through the cracks in the wall and forming a film on the covers. She moved closer to the warmth of Adam's body and fell back to sleep.

They both awakened fully in the late afternoon,

ravenously hungry. It was while they sat eating that Rachael noted sadly that their closeness of the night had disappeared with the day. When she tried to talk to Adam, he was unresponsive. He was back in the old mold of glowering at her, or totally ignoring her presence. After a time she responded in the same way.

As the next three days dragged on, Rachael became pale and drawn and Adam's face took on a new leanness. When at last the snow ceased and they were able to dig out, it was a great relief to them both.

When the men pulled on snowshoes and took to the woods again, Rachael hurried to the tent. The women were a harried-looking group, and after staring at each other a moment, they laughed together in a companionable understanding.

"Wasn't it awful?" Annie gasped out. "Havin' a bunch of men underfoot that long could drive a woman crazy."

"One more day and I couldn't have borne it," Rachael agreed.

"You do look peaked, Rachael," Annie worried. "Did that devil give you a hard time?"

"He's a contrary one. He's like living with two different men. There's the bedtime Adam who won't leave me alone, then the daytime Adam who leaves me alone too much. Sometimes I think that he hates me."

"Ah no, Rachael, I'm sure you're wrong," they reassured her. "It's just being snowbound that bothered him. You know how men are, they like to be doing."

Rachael shook her head. "It's more than that. I'm

sure he hates me because he desires me. He calls me a whore at least once a day."

"Ah, honey, I'm sorry to hear that," Annie sympathized. "I'd hoped that you'd got that ironed out with him."

Rachael didn't answer. Her mind was on the day that Adam had drunk too much. He had started early in the morning and it seemed that with each swallow of the raw whiskey he became more insulting and more determined that she admit to being Elisha's whore. When she refused to answer him, he began shouting obscene questions at her, demanding that she answer. Finally when she would not even acknowledge his presence, he turned into a stranger.

Without warning, he ripped off her clothes and threw her onto the bed. There he had taken her brutally and angrily. He had kept at her most of the day, treating her as the lowest prostitute. She had fought him at first, tearing and scratching like a wildcat. But in the end he had bent her to his will.

The following day she could tell that he was sorry and ashamed of his actions. For once he tried to strike up a conversation . . . even went so far as to say that her roast was "good eatin'."

But his repentance hadn't stopped him from claiming her when they retired that evening. But this time he was very gentle, willing his body to relay his apology.

She wondered now if this would ever happen again. She had no assurance that it wouldn't. He, like the other hunters, drank every day, and it could become a daily occurrence.

She could not bear it, she knew. Not only would her body suffer, it would also crush her mind.

Reluctantly she faced the fact that she had to get away from him. If she remained the rest of the winter, she would end up hating him. But if she could get away from him and return to her grandfather, she might later, in the summer, meet him in a more civilized environment and somehow come to an understanding.

After an hour or so of idle chatter, Rachael returned to the cabin to take care of tasks that had been impossible with Adam around. She was in the middle of setting the supper table when she heard the crunch of Adam's footsteps.

Determined to start the evening on a friendly basis, she smiled at him warmly when he entered. But he ignored her welcome and ordered brusquely, "Put away the dishes. We're eatin' at the tent tonight. John shot a deer."

His short, sharp manner was not unusual but she had the uneasy feeling that anger edged his words. And later in the tent she noticed a decided coolness between him and Eagle. Wearily, she wondered what new thing had happened between them.

They had been there but a short time when Eagle approached them, smiling at Rachael. "Can I get you anything, Rachael? Maybe a cup of coffee?"

She felt Adam stiffen, and glancing at him sideways, saw the twitching muscle in his jaw, warning of a building anger. Nervously, she answered, "No, thanks, Jim. I'll wait until after I've eaten."

Eagle nodded pleasantly and walked away.

Rachael could never fully remember the events that happened next. It came about too swiftly for her to clearly comprehend. She had vaguely noticed Flower crawling from behind the screening blanket as she talked to Eagle. Then as he walked away, without warning, the girl was upon her, knocking her over backwards. Her head banged onto the hard floor, and the people, shocked into silence, swam before her eyes. Then Flower's fingers were tangled in her hair, tugging and ripping.

She fought the dizzy sickness that gripped her and reached for the young squaw's face. But before she could make contact, Eagle had leaped over a bench and caught a long black braid in his hand. Jerking Flower to her feet, he rapidly slapped her face, making her head jerk with the motion. Then grasping her by the shoulder, he sent her spinning into the table.

Confusion followed. The women squealed and caught at the platters of food as the table crashed to the floor and the men milled around trying not to look at Adam. It should have been he who intervened for his woman.

Eagle knelt beside Rachael and lifted her up. And as she shook her head, clearing her vision, she saw Adam's hand descending and grasping Eagle's shoulder.

Catlike, Eagle was on his feet, his body slightly bent, his eyes eager and watchful. Rachael's muffled cry went unheeded and the tent became deathly still. Then suddenly Adam gave out a roar, his fist lashing at Eagle's jaw. "You two-bit gambler, who told you to defend my woman?"

Eagle scrambled to his feet, his hands clenched. "She's no woman of yours, you crazy wild man. If she was, you'd have drug that red slut off her. You saw that she was stunned and couldn't help herself."

Adam gave a forced laugh. "She was foxin' you." Then darkly, added, "Flower probably had cause."

A look of disgust swept over Eagle's face and with an impatient grunt his fist shot out, landing square on Adam's chin. Adam staggered, caught at a chair, missed and fell to the floor. Eagle lunged after him, tripped on the pole floor and fell sprawling.

Adam leaped to his feet, his face drawn in lines of hate. When his men would have stepped between them, he motioned them back. "Let the bastard up," he panted. "I'll fight him to the death if that's what he wants."

Eagle looked up and for the first time saw the long hunting knife lying comfortably in Adam's hand. He had heard of the skill the hunter possessed with the killing blade and a chill went over him. And as he stared at the wicked gleam of it, life became very sweet.

Carefully he arose, his eyes never wavering from the clasped weapon. There was no doubt in his mind that Adam would try to kill him. Jealousy of Rachael was eating him up.

The hunters parted silently, making room for them. Slowly Eagle unsheathed his knife and carefully they began circling, each man alert to find the weak spot in the other man's defense. Adam slashed out first, the long blade missing Eagle's stomach by inches as he jerked back. Rachael saw the flash of steel and screamed a muted sound.

Warily the two men watched each other as once again they bent and circled. Eagle tried to get under Adam's guard and failed. A moment later Adam slashed swiftly and Eagle's shirt was rent from shoulder to elbow. Eagle's return jab pricked Adam's arm and blood stained his shirt. He smelled the sweet, sickening odor and pushed on, seeking to get under the gambler's guard. But Eagle weaved and dodged, keeping out of reach.

There was blood on the floor now, almost black by the candlelight. Both men bled. Eagle had been cut in Adam's second lunge. Sweat streamed from their faces, but they fought on, each man determined that the other die. Rachael shivered and whispered, "Neither one can take much more."

She stood up. They had to be stopped before one of them died. She took a step in their direction and a solid blackness descended on her. She felt herself falling and heard Annie scream, "Adam, Rachael has fainted."

There was a noise and Rachael's eyes flew open. She lay in the cabin, in her own bed. Across the room, her eyes sought Adam's. "What happened? Is everyone alright?"

Adam put down the poker he had been absentmindedly holding and answered shortly, "Nothing happened. Your gambler friend is still alive if that's what you mean."

He heard her whispered "Thank God" and bounded across the floor, grabbing her shoulder. "Does he mean so much to you?"

"Only as a friend," she quavered, frightened at the look in his eyes.

Roughly he thrust her away. "Do you expect me to believe that?"

"It is true," she began, but he fiercely interrupted. "I don't want to hear your lies. You want Eagle and he wants you. Get your things together, you and him are leaving here tomorrow morning." He turned on his heel and slammed out of the cabin.

Rachael stared at the closed door with mixed emotions. Anger that he hadn't believed her and anguish that she was losing him.

He didn't return that night and Rachael cried herself to sleep.

She was up early the next morning, in time to hear the hunters leave the tent with their usual grumbling and loud noises. But for the first time, she did not watch for Adam. "What is the use," she sighed.

When Eagle and the women arrived a short time later, she was dressed and waiting. The women were distressed at her leaving and Annie was crying, "Rachael, will we ever see you again?"

She hugged the little woman's shoulder. "Annie, I don't know. I certainly hope so."

"Adam is nothin' but a dumb fool," Annie sniffled.

Rachael gave her one last squeeze and moved away. As a last act of kindness to Adam, she raked ashes over the glowing coals. Then donning her coat and tying a scarf around her head, she was ready. She embraced each woman and cautioned each to keep after her man. "Make sure they continue to treat you well."

With tears burning her throat, she hurried from the cabin. Just outside the door stood Adam's stallion, saddled and waiting. Surprised, she turned to Eagle. "I can't believe that he gave us his horse."

"Only until we get to Devil's Ridge. We're to leave him there." He helped her to mount and swung up behind her.

They rode for some time without speaking. The sun climbed higher and the wind came out of the south, turning the snow soft. There was the smell of spring in the air, and at one point, Rachael was sure that she saw the red flash of a robin's breast high in a tall pine.

She sensed that Eagle was in a thoughtful mood and dreaded when he would speak his mind. When she felt his arms tighten around her, she became tense. "Well, Rach," he began, "where shall we go?"

"To my grandfather's on Devil's Ridge."

"Your grandfather? I didn't know you had one."

"None of the hunters know it. Adam stole me from him."

"The hell you say." Shaking his head, he added, "That wild man beats anything I ever saw."

Rachael nodded dumbly, hoping he wouldn't discuss the "wild man" in great detail. But his next sentence sent her heart to singing and she hung on to his every word.

"He's crazy about you, you know that, Rach. He looked like a whipped dog this morning. If I didn't hate him so, I'd feel sorry for him."

She was barely aware of sitting in Eagle's arms, barely aware that he continued to talk. Her mind was busy digesting his first words. She chewed them over and over and the flavor was sweet.

Her thoughts went flying ahead to spring and Adam's return. "By all that's holy," she vowed, "the next time I see him we're going to have a long talk. He's going to listen to me . . . if I have to hit him with a stick of wood."

She heard Eagle say, ". . . Jamestown," and pulled herself back to the present. "I'm sorry, Jim, but I didn't hear that last part."

He looked down at her radiant face and disappointment flashed in his eyes. Forcing a small laugh, he said, "I don't remember what I was talking about."

Each night they slept in their separate bedrolls and on the third morning arrived at Elisha's.

CHAPTER 17

Ruby had been with Elisha for a month now. He had grown used to seeing her move about the cabin, and rather liked it. He enjoyed watching her plump, shapely figure as she cooked his meals or cleaned his home, but mostly he enjoyed being able to call out to her at any time, "Hey, Ruby, what about a little kissin'." She was always obliging, dropping whatever she might be doing at the time. With her, his comfort came before anything else.

Elisha didn't allow Rafe to lie with Ruby anymore. He hadn't known before how harshly his oldest grandson used her. One day when Rafe prepared to leave, Elisha had growled, "You're too rough, boy. You go to Kate's from now on."

But Dave still came. At least once a week, sometimes more often. And watching his grandson mount his mistress one day, Elisha became aroused and joined them for some "kissin'." After that, Ruby grew used to being shared between them occasionally.

Life in the cabin ran smoothly. The wind blew in from the south these days, and the snowdrifts were shrinking. At last, winter was giving a hint of releasing its icy grip.

One morning as Elisha and Ruby sat at the breakfast table, Grizzly moved to the door, cocked his head attentively, then started a slow wag of his tail. "Dave must be comin'," Elisha allowed.

But from outside came a throaty, "Hey, grandpa, are you home?"

Elisha jumped to his feet, the chair skidding across the floor. "By God, it's Rachael." He squeezed her in his arms. "I about gave you up, honey."

"Ah, grandpa, so did I."

"Let's have a look at you." He stepped back and studied her. He saw that the wild life had agreed with her as far as her health went. But he didn't like the pained, shadowed eyes and he barked his question. "How did that wolf treat you, Rach?"

"About as you'd expect. Can we talk about it later, grandpa?"

As Elisha nodded his head, she turned back to the door and motioned. When the tall man stood in the opening, she said, "This is Jim Eagle, grandpa. He brought me down from winter camp."

While Elisha shook Eagle's proffered hand, Ruby clasped Rachael to her large, warm breasts and they both cried a bit, woman-wise to the heartache a loved man could subject them to.

Rachael reached for the bowl of potatoes for the third time. Elisha watched and grinned. "You ain't been eatin' high on the hog, have you, girl?"

She gave a derisive grunt. "Grandpa, I've eaten so much venison, don't be surprised if I grow antlers. I used to have dreams of potatoes and milk and especially eggs."

"Ruby will have a good breakfast of ham and eggs for you tomorrow morning, and Jim, too."

Eagle spoke. "Not for me, Elisha. I'll be movin' on as soon as I'm finished eatin'."

Elisha looked at him in surprise and disappointment. He liked the quiet, ugly man and had hoped that Rachael did, too, that she had gotten over her fascination with Adam Warden.

Eagle stared down at his plate, his body held stiff as though waiting for something . . . perhaps for some word.

"You're welcome to stay as long as you want, Eagle," Elisha said quietly.

He watched Eagle's glance fly to Rachael, silently asking, almost begging. But Rachael gazed back, silently denying.

Eagle sighed and pulled his eyes away. "Thanks, Elisha, but I'd better be movin' on."

Mutely, Elisha echoed Eagle's sigh. The silent exchange between the pair had informed him that Rachael was still of the same mind. "She's still hellbent for Adam."

Out on the porch, Eagle stood facing Rachael, his face pale above his coat collar. He wanted to ask her again to come with him but knew it would be a wasted request. Instead, he cupped her face in his hands and slowly kissed her. "If ever you need me, Rach, you'll find me in one of the gambling parlors in Jamestown."

She nodded, and with a finger he traced away the single tear that ran down her cheek. Softly, he whispered, "Bye," and climbed into the saddle.

She watched him disappear into the forest and choked back fresh tears. "Oh, Jim, I wish I could have returned your love."

She remained on the porch for awhile, thinking about love. It seemed to be such a fleeting thing sometimes. She had been sure that Nick loved her, and yet he had married another woman. Perhaps grandpa was right after all. Maybe the only true, lasting love was the kind that a person had for his parents and children. Maybe the kind that existed between male and female was only a lusting for each other.

But then again, that couldn't be true either. Nick had lusted for her and still married another. There had to be a difference between love and lust. She leaned on the porch railing and breathed deep of the piney air. Come spring, maybe she would find some answers. She lifted the latch. Grandpa was waiting with a hundred questions on his lips.

Rachael skipped lightly over the time spent with Adam, saying only that they fought like a pair of animals, that he was a hard-headed bastard, but that she still intended to have him.

And because Elisha didn't want to hear this, he queried hopefully, "Did anything go on between you and Eagle?"

Rachael jumped to her feet, wanting to shout her impatience. She was so tired of being asked that. She retorted sharply, "No, nothing went on. There could have been but I wasn't interested."

"Now don't go gettin' yourself into a huff," Elisha placated. "I could see that he had a feelin' for you and I thought maybe...."

"Well, I don't."

Ruby sat through all the talk, quietly listening. Now she asked, "Have you made any plans, honey? Would you like for me to move back to my place?"

Rachael hurried to the kindly woman and sat beside her. "Ruby, I wouldn't for the world have you move from here. You're finally where you belong.

My scampy old grandfather should have brought you here years ago." She paused a moment in thought, then continued, "As for my plans, they aren't completed yet. But for starters, I'm taking up housekeeping in Adam's cabin tomorrow."

Elisha looked doubtful. And although Ruby shook her head at him, he ignored her silent caution and spoke his mind. "That might not be a good starter. How are you going to manage away up there by yourself? There ain't another place around here for miles. It's too far for me to travel every day."

"I won't need somebody every day. All I want is for Dave and Rafe to go up there with me and get me settled in. See that I have enough wood and that the place is weathertight. Anyhow, spring will soon be here and Adam should be returning then."

Elisha made a grunting sound. "What if he sends you packin' when he gets back? He might not want you."

Rachael tossed her head. "He'll want me," she said confidently.

"Don't pay any attention to him, honey," Ruby smiled. "We'll be up there at least once a week to see how you're gettin' along."

"Thank you, Ruby. I was hoping you would."

The next day dawned clear and sunny. The horses' hooves sank into soft mud as they made their way up the mountain. Two pack horses loaded with provisions and household gifts from Ruby plodded along behind Rachael and her cousins.

They reached Adam's clearing around noon. Rachael pulled off the trail and reined in the mare while the cousins rode on. She wanted to take a good look at her future home. It was a sturdy little place, nestled among the towering pines and oak. A well-built chimney rose above a roof that was whole and tight. She had the feeling that inside she would find it equally well constructed.

Some distance to the right of the cabin, a long, crude building canted crazily. She frowned. "That must be where Annie and the others lived."

The wind whispered and rustled through the trees and she felt that they welcomed her. As she urged the horse on, she hoped that Adam would welcome her when he returned.

Dave and Rafe were unloading the horses when she rode up. When Dave lifted down the last bag, he turned to her and asked, "Where are we gonna put the mare? There's an old shed back there in the trees, but the snow has caved in the roof. It wouldn't be no protection for her. The wolves could jump right in."

Until now, Rachael hadn't come up with a good idea of how to get the women their own home. Now she smiled wickedly. What better way than to turn the hunters' quarters into a stable. Pointing to the rickety building, she said, "Put her in there."

Dave looked doubtful but shrugged his shoulders. "Adam is gonna be madder than hell, finding it turned into a barn."

"He'll get over it," she retorted.

Inside the cabin Rachael was surprised to find that there were two rooms. It hadn't looked that big from outside. And in the main room, in a corner, a ladder led to a partially floored loft. If she stood beside the large, fieldstone fireplace, she could see into it. "An ideal spot for children someday," she mused.

Pleased, she discovered that each room had two windows and was light and airy. Also, the little bedroom had its own small fireplace. She smiled and commented inwardly, "My hunter likes his comfort I see."

A homemade bed consisting of four cedar poles attached to the floor and strung with strips of deerhide stood in one corner. On the woven hide support was a straw tick. She thought of the feather mattress and linens that Ruby had insisted she bring, and was glad. There probably wasn't a sheet nor pillowcase in the cabin.

A row of shelves hung on a supporting wall and Adam's clothes were neatly stacked there. Right beside the door hung a good-sized mirror, and beneath it was a wide ledge holding a comb and brush and a fresh candle. A rocker beside the hearth completed the furnishings.

The large room was sparsely furnished also. At one end sat a long table, a bench on either side. A dry sink sat under a window and two rockers flanked the hearth. In here the fireplace took up most of one wall. On its mantle was a clock needing to be set and wound. Directly over it hung a huge elk head. She wrinkled her nose at the musty odor that came from closed buildings and itched to start cleaning.

Her cousins returned from stabling the horse and Dave brought in wood and built a fire. Rafe went outside to check the sun in order to set the clock. He returned, saying that the sun was directly overhead.

"I'll put the hands on twelve, Rach, and don't forget to wind it every day."

She nodded, anxious for them to leave. But they were enjoying her company and the clock struck three before they rode down the mountain. She stood on the porch waving to them and they called back that they'd return in a couple of days to see how she was making out.

She closed the door and rolled up her sleeves. She had found a broom in a corner and now she attacked the floors with a fury.

A couple hours later her stomach growled, alerting her that it was empty. But she had finished her cleaning. She paused a moment to look at the results. "It is almost perfect," she exclaimed.

Only one thing was missing. Adam.

CHAPTER 18

Adam felt like running away the morning Rachael left. But he knew his men were watching and somehow he went through the same motions he had made all the other mornings. But he avoided Eagle. If the man spoke one word to him, he would put a hunting knife through his heart.

He had slept little last night, rolled in a blanket on the bumpy floor. He could have gone to Flower's pallet for Eagle had not gone near her since the fight. But his thoughts had been of Rachael and the idea of the red girl repelled him.

Time and time again he had started to rise and make his way to the cabin. He would tell her that he was licked and would she please stay with him. But each time, pride pushed him back onto the floor, swearing harshly, "No, by God, I won't beg a whore. I will not love her." But inwardly he had groaned, knowing that he could not help himself.

Returning from the hunt at dusk, his eyes sought the cabin, looking for the dim candlelight that had always filled the window. But this time it stared back, vacant-eyed.

All day he had told himself that maybe she hadn't gone. That maybe out of pure orneriness she had remained. If only when he opened the door he would find her there, soft and yielding. The door swung open to emptiness. There was only her faint perfumed scent remaining. His slow survey took in the cozy room that had truly meant home to him. She had left it neat and tidy, and when he discovered the banked fire, he struck out at the wall and groaned her name.

Always before, Adam had been the first to spring his kill into the trees and the first to wash and change his bloody clothing. But nowadays his pelts were thrown beneath some tree and not remembered until late night, and often not until the next morning when the men were on their way out again.

He grew used to awakening with a dry mouth and a throat that felt on fire. His unshaven whiskers turned into a curly beard and his hair grew past his shoulders. Somehow Annie managed to coax him into clean clothes once a week. When she was questioned about this, she answered, "I do it for Rachael. She would feel bad if she knew he was walking around looking so seedy."

Adam pushed the burning chunks of wood closer together and sat hunkered, watching them burst into flames. He could hear pigeons overhead in the cedars scratching and fluttering about, upset by his presence. Sometimes there were so many their weight would break the limbs of the trees.

The night wind moaned through the trees and in the distance he heard his hound baying. "Got himself a coon," he thought. He settled back against a tree and listened to the dog's sound while his mind mulled on other things.

It had been a relief when patches of brown grass began to show through the snow. It was the first of March and soon the hunters would gather up their pelts and head back to the post and summer camp. He would send them on alone, he decided. In the absence of their watchful eyes, he could stop his pretense of not caring and could break down and howl if he wanted to.

He would, of course, have to deliver Flower and the squaws back to Bear. After that he had no clear plans. "There's little sense in plannin' when a man has no future," he mumbled to himself.

He heard the men leave the tent, noisily laughing and talking. In the darkness he made out the swaying lights of the lanterns as they worked their pelts. His own had been finished hours ago. He had gradually gotten back into his old pattern and seldom ever drank anymore. Annie had pointed out that when he was drunk was when he had treated Rachael so badly.

The hound's long-drawn yowl was fading away and an atmosphere of loneliness settled around him. With a sigh of resignation, he rose to his feet and made his way back to camp.

"Hey, Adam," someone hailed him, "we can start packin' for home soon, don't you think?"

"Any time you feel like it. We've had a good catch this winter and a few days one way or the other won't matter much."

"Annie and the other women, they've been fussin' about gettin' back to summer quarters," Annie's big man growled.

Adam grunted. Since when did the men start caring about what the women wanted? Silently he cursed Rachael for turning his wild bunch into ordinary hillmen. "The next thing I know they'll be takin' up farmin'."

* * *

The women all talked at once, the excitement in their voices building to a high pitch. Standing unnoticed, Adam watched and listened. "I wish Rachael was going to be there with us," Annie was saying. "I don't know if we can get the men to build our cabins without her help."

"We're just gonna have to stand up to them and demand it," some woman remarked. "Just like Rachael used to do to Adam."

"But she's got so much spirit," another chimed in. "I don't know if any of us can do it."

Adam recalled Rachael's spirit and would have given anything to have her back there again, yelling in his face and demanding her own way.

Then a woman was saying, "Annie, you've got spirit, we'll let you do the talking. Anyhow, you've got more reason than the rest of us. Your baby will be born in a few months and you'll need a place of your own."

Adam's head came up with a jerk. He peered closely at Annie's small body and saw that she was indeed with child. He wondered if the father knew and shook his head ruefully. Everything was getting out of hand.

He could see how things were developing. Before long his oldest and best hunters would become fathers and would no longer go on the long hunts. But after pondering it more carefully, he had to admit that settling down would probably add years to their lives. He remembered it hadn't been too long ago when he had worried what was to become of them.

"Anyhow," he assured himself, "there are always

new ones coming along to replace anybody that wants to quit the rough life." His spirits lifted and he slipped unseen through the tent flap. Behind him the women finished their packing.

The next morning he watched them leave with mixed feelings: relief to be away from their prying eyes and a sadness that he would never again go on long hunts with some of them. His best men had been woman-tamed. He sighed and turned to the Indian women huddled together. He would soon have them back with their own people.

But Flower had other ideas. She sidled up to him and laid a possessive hand on his arm. "Send the red sluts back to my father," she wheedled, "and me and you will stay here in the cabin."

He bent a stinging glance on her and she quickly moved her hand. Coldly impersonal, he said, "Come on, Bear will be waiting for us."

Leading the way with Flower's glowering stare stabbing him in the back, Adam walked swiftly. Once he stopped and looked back at the cabin and campsite. The empty cabin seemed to call to him, urging that he remember the joy as well as the heartache he had experienced under its roof. He moved his glance to where the tent had been but only the platform of poles attested to the fact that the tent had once been there. Last night's heavy rain had washed away all signs of habitation. Even the shapes of the many campfires had been beaten into the ground.

He stayed in Bear's camp only long enough to share the chief's lunch and to smoke a pipe. He sensed the old man's disappointment that Flower was staying behind and their conversation was a little strained. But when he arose to leave, Bear nevertheless shook his hand and wished him God's speed.

He had no idea where he would go. He only knew that he must put as many miles as possible between him and Rachael. Maybe he would go farther into the Ohio Valley. Find a spot unknown to the white man.

He had gone some distance into the forest when one of the squaws who had wintered with them stepped out into his path. She stared woodenly at him for a moment then spoke gravely, "You go to Elisha Jobe and take your white squaw. She not what you think. She a fine woman."

Adam smiled pityingly at her serious countenance. "She has even fooled you, White Dove."

The squaw studied him a moment, her expression puzzled. Then, "She no fool White Dove. Rachael good inside."

He moved his shoulders in a disparaging shrug. "Even if what you say is true, she wouldn't want no part of me. I'm just a rough hunter that don't know how to treat a woman like her."

"Why you not act like your heart tells you? I watch you all the time. You no act the way you feel."

Adam lowered his head against the truth of her words. He had always acted the fool with Rachael. He wondered if the squaw really knew what she talked about. He was at the point now where he clutched at any hope.

"White Dove," he began tentatively, "I want to ask you something and I want you to tell me the truth. Do you truly think that I have a chance with her?"

White Dove hesitated. Should she break Rachael's confidence? The white woman had been good to her . . . had taught her pride in herself. But if somebody didn't point out the way for them, these two foolish white people would never get together. Finally she nodded solemnly.

"You got big chance if you treat her right. She proud woman. Won't be treated like whore or Indian woman. You go to Elisha Jobe and take her."

A welling hope built within Adam as the squaw spoke. Her words echoed what was in his own mind, only he had been too stubborn to listen to them. For more assurance he recalled words of Silas. "The red people are very wise in the ways of human nature. They have a built-in knowledge that escapes the white man . . . a power of seeing things as they really are."

He grabbed the fat squaw and hugged her. "By God, White Dove, I'm gonna take a chance on your hunch. I love that woman and I don't give a damn if she is 'Lisha's whore."

White Dove watched him hurry away, a slightly contemptuous smile curving her lips. "Damn fool, white man. He get the biggest surprise in his life."

Adam walked the winding trail in the face of a slashing rain. The woods were sodden and silent. Around noon he came to the swollen river and stood a moment, watching it hurry along as though anxious to escape an enemy. He scanned it anxiously. Would he be able to ford it? But remembering that Rachael was only a few miles on the other side, he cautiously stepped in, holding his rifle high.

The stream was not a great deal colder than the

rain that pelted down, and once on shore again, he ran awhile, the fast pumping of his blood warming him.

It was late in the afternoon when the Jobe buildings came in view. Warily he squatted behind a large cedar and studied the cabin. Maybe Rachael would step outside and he could take her without confronting Elisha.

But the squaw's words nudged his conscience and he admitted that it would be an underhanded act. He would face the old bear in his den.

Only a lazy spiral of smoke drifting from the chimney denoted a presence in the cabin as he rehearsed what he would say to Elisha . . . and Rachael. Drawing a deep breath, he rose from his cramped position and strode purposefully toward the wide rough door.

Stepping upon the porch, he hesitated a moment. What if the old bastard came to the door with his rifle? "What the hell," he grunted and rapped loudly.

From inside he heard heavy footsteps clomping across the floor and his blood raced, eager to do battle with the man that sheltered his woman. The door swung open and grizzly-haired Elisha stood staring suspiciously at him. After a moment he stepped aside and growled, "Come on in, Warden."

But Adam stood resolutely on the porch. He hadn't come on a friendly visit and he wouldn't pretend that he did. He cleared his throat loudly, then blurted out, "I'll stay right here, Elisha. When you learn why I come, you won't be so ready to welcome me in your home."

"Is that so? Did you come here to shoot me or to beat me up?"

Adam saw the teasing twinkle in Elisha's eyes and lashed out, "I come to take your woman away from you."

Elisha struggled to hide the mirth that threatened to escape his throat. Finally he was able to feign surprise, and frowning darkly, he demanded loudly, "What in the hell do you want with Ruby?"

Ruby appeared at Elisha's side and Adam stared at her owlishly. "I don't mean her," he stammered. "I mean the young one, Rachael."

"Oh, Rachael," Elisha nodded in understanding. "You mean my granddaughter."

The look that swept over Adam's face was worth all the anger and worry the long-hunter had caused him. He whooped and laughed and slapped his thighs. "You damn wolf cub," he gasped out, "it's been a long time comin', but you've finally had one put over on you."

Then the laughter left Elisha's face. His eyes frosty, he advanced on Adam. "Who in the hell do you think you are accusing my granddaughter of being a whore? I ought to gut shoot you where you stand. Only the thought of Silas holds my hand."

Adam had backstepped as Elisha stalked him and now his foot came over the edge of the porch and he was sitting down in the mud, heavily. He stared up at Elisha, a despairing look in his eyes and the older man's face softened a bit. "Damn wild hellion," he snorted, "you don't know any better."

Adam scrambled to his feet and Elisha said in a calmer voice, "She ain't here. She stopped long enough to let me know she was alright and then moved on."

Disappointment gleamed in Adam's eyes and he

asked sharply, "Was she with a man called Eagle?"

"That's the name Rachael gave him."

"Did they say where they were goin'?"

"Rachael only said that she was going where she belonged."

Adam tried to read Elisha's expression. Was the old devil trying to tell him something? He stared at Elisha another moment, then nodded his head and walked abruptly away.

Elisha watched the erect figure disappear into the forest and chuckled drily, "Chew on that for awhile, Bucko," and closed the door.

CHAPTER 19

Rachael awoke to a bitter spring rain. Another long, dreary day, she sighed. For the most part her days had passed swiftly enough. She had found a loom gathering dust in the hunters' quarters. After Dave had cleaned it up and moved it into the cabin, she used it daily. She had woven yards of material and sewed it into curtains for the windows and covers for the bed and table.

Ruby had taught her how to dye the cloth with certain barks and berries. The bark from the sassafras had turned the curtains into a pinkish orange, while the pokeberry had made a splash of dark blue in the bedroom. And when she mixed bark and berries together, the tablecloth became a deep purple. And to finish the decor, she and Ruby had torn the remaining cloth into strips and crocheted colorful rugs for both rooms.

In between the busy projects, she waited for the hunters' return. The snow was practically gone now, with only a few snowbanks remaining. The falling rain would soon melt those. And only yesterday she had seen a robin.

Up until the first signs of spring, she had enjoyed the hushed solitude of her mountain as she waited Adam's return. Most times she had been sure he would return. But once in awhile a little demon voice would whisper, "He's with Flower and never gives you a thought." This conclusion would chill the enthusiasm of her daydreaming and she would be in a dark mood for the rest of the day.

As each day passed with no sign of the hunters, more and more she gave up the idea of a reunion with Adam. She was slowly succumbing to the idea that the hunters might stay away for months yet. Even a year. She knew that they often did this.

Lying in bed and watching the rain spatter against the window, she gave serious thought to her future. She couldn't stay perched on this hill alone for the rest of her life.

She tried to imagine a life in the hills without Adam. She could think of no way and reluctantly she let her mind wander back to Jamestown. She had enough money to live there in style now. But it would be a lonely existence she knew. She would be remembered and never be accepted into the town's better society. Anyhow, she hated the idea of going back to the crowded, dirty city. She loved the hills with their pure air and simple people.

She sighed deeply and sat up in bed and rested her head on her bent knees. Then faintly into the misery of her thoughts, she heard the muted sound of voices and laughter. Springing from the bed, she rushed to the window, exclaiming, "They're back."

Anxiously her eyes ran down the line of men and women. Her spirits dropped. Adam was not with them. She turned from the window and began to dress. She must put on a brave front and greet them. She smiled crookedly. "I'll have to explain the horse in their quarters too."

She walked outside and Annie was the first to spot her. Wildly waving an arm, she ran in an ungainly gait toward Rachael. Rachael gaped. "She's expecting," she thought happily and ran to meet her.

Hugging each other, they murmured their happiness. Annie wiped away her tears and panted out, "I never dreamed that you'd be here, Rachael. I'm so glad you are."

"I probably shouldn't be and I guess I'd better leave. I see his 'Highness' didn't come back with you."

"He'll be along later, I'm sure," Annie hastened to assure her. "He had to take the squaws back to Bear."

"And Flower? What about her, was he going to leave her too?"

"I honestly think that he will. He didn't go near her after you left."

Hope flared for a moment then slowly died. Adam was so unpredictable. That he hadn't been with Flower didn't necessarily mean a thing. He could very well have her under some tree this very minute.

Annie saw the suffering in her eyes and said softly, "Don't hurt so, Rachael. He'll be back. He ain't gonna forget you in a hurry."

Rachael smiled at her small friend, still unconvinced. Then looking pointedly at Annie's protruding stomach, she teased, "I see you've been a busy girl."

Annie, pleased, blushed and said proudly, "Can you imagine me being a mother?"

And surprisingly enough, Rachael could imagine it. Annie, with her compassionate heart, would make a fine mother. She smiled. "I think it's wonderful, Annie." Their arms around each other's waists, they went to greet the others.

Rachael was relieved when the men greeted her warmly. She had imagined they would still be miffed at her for changing the attitudes of their women. There was something different about the men, and as she studied them, it took her awhile to realize that they looked like other men now. The old wolfish faces that had glared at her before were now replaced with pleasant-looking countenances. With the exception of a few bearded men, the others were clean-shaven. And all of them, like the women, were clean.

The women gathered around, all talking steadily. From the corner of her eye, Rachael saw the men become restless and begin to move toward their quarters. She gnawed at her lip a moment and then hurried after them.

Exchanging quick glances, the women stared after her and watched her put out a hand and stop John. They watched him bend and listen to her and then his face grew dark. He straightened his back and let out a roar like a bear.

"You got your horse in our quarters? Where in the blue blazes are we supposed to live?"

The women hurried to them in time to hear Rachael say, "I figured you men could camp out and the women could sleep in Adam's cabin with me until you each could build your own place."

By this time the other hunters had become curious and had joined John. At her words, they all let out a roar.

"Are you daft, woman?" someone shouted. "Each of us build a cabin? For what?"

Rachael was angry now and the fingernails of her clenched fists cut into her palms as she shouted back, "For the women's comfort, that's what. They work damned hard for you men and they deserve a place of their own."

"No," John stolidly declared. "We ain't gonna go to all that trouble. We'll just pitch the tent again."

"Very well, you can shift for yourselves then. The women are staying with me."

The men looked at her sharply, alarm showing in some of their faces. They were remembering the last time this hellcat had kept their women from them. They hadn't liked taking care of themselves, and besides, it was different now. They had become accustomed to having their own private woman do for them and they liked it.

Annie's big man looked at her and growled, "Is that the way you feel, Annie?"

Annie gave him a quick nervous glance and started to answer. But Rachael rushed in ahead of her. "Annie above the others wants and needs a place of her own. She'll be having her baby in just a few months."

Simultaneously the men's eyes bugged and turned to Annie. She blushed and looked down.

As Rachael had suspected, the men hadn't known. "How very typical of them," she thought disgustedly. "Can't even see what's under their noses."

Her eyes fell on Annie's man, and seeing the pride building on his face, Rachael hurried to press her argument. "Now one big room filled with noisy hunters is no place for a baby to be born and live in. It will need quiet and peace as will the mother. The way I see it, if Annie can have a baby, so can the other women. Doesn't it make sense to go ahead and build your place now and when your own little ones come along they'll have a home of their own."

The clouds disappeared as if by magic and their faces were fired with excitement. They gathered around the expectant father, slapping him on the back and making obscene remarks. Rachael smiled resignedly. She mustn't expect too much from these half-wild men. She would just feel grateful that the women were getting their most earnest wish.

By noon the big tent was once again erected and Adam's people settled in. After a fast meal, the forest began to ring with the sound of axes. They had started on Annie's cabin.

CHAPTER 20

Adam pulled his coat collar higher against the rain that had slowed to a drizzle and climbed the last hill to summer camp. He moved slowly, planning. His anger at Rachael for going on with Eagle had left him. There remained only a determination to find her and make a plea for her love. A life without her would be no life at all. He would rest one night at the cabin and tomorrow morning he would start for Jamestown.

Night had fallen but there was still a half-light when he stepped into the clearing. The first thing he saw was the tent rising on the skyline. He wondered idly if the old shack had fallen in during the winter.

From inside the tent came the muted sound of laughter and he raised his eyebrows. That didn't sound like the wild bunch.

He turned to go to his cabin and for the first time noticed the light coming from the window. What in the hell was going on? His eyes fell on a pile of split logs with an axe sticking in the chopping block and he swore angrily. Which of the hunters had the nerve to take over his cabin?

Inside, Rachael stood beside the hearth staring vacantly into the flames. The fire hissed as water dripped down the chimney. Impatiently she kicked at the logs. She sighed, thinking that she should be getting her things together. There was no excuse for her staying here now. The women would be alright and it was plain that Adam had no interest in her.

She sighed again. All those closest to her had obtained happiness . . . could look forward to a bright future, while she remained in the same state of confusion, not knowing what lay in store for her.

The door opened softly and Rachael did not hear it. But when her name was called softly, she jerked, then slowly turned around. The room was utterly quiet as she and Adam gazed at one another.

Unconsciously she stretched a hand toward him and whispered, "Adam."

He crossed the room swiftly and folded her into his arms. "I'm about licked, Rachael," he said haltingly. "I've been dying hard from the first time I saw you."

She clung to him with happy tears coursing down her cheeks. "Adam, Adam. So much precious time wasted."

AND NOW...
FOR A PREVIEW OF A COMING ATTRACTION FROM PLAYBOY PRESS

Throughout history there have been women—some famous, some infamous, but most of them unknown, like Rachael Jobe—who have spitfire courage and a lusty appetite for living. They all share an enterprising spirit and dedicated determination and will stop at nothing to capture the hearts of the men they passionately love.

FLOWERS OF FIRE

By Stephanie Blake

tells the story of another young woman, Ravena Wilding, in early 19th Century Ireland. She was torn by the love of twin brothers—one she did not want, the other she could not have. Their destinies would be inevitably interlocked as the winds of fate scattered them across the globe from the Emerald Isle to Civil War—torn America, from exotic, steamy slave plantations of the South Seas to America's Wild West.

In the following pages, enjoy a brief encounter with Ravena, a fascinating woman from a tumultuous period of history. Her love story will capture your heart.

COMING IN APRIL FROM PLAYBOY PRESS PAPERBACKS

It was a highly successful party in spite of the state of the Confederacy. Ravena felt that everyone talked too loudly, laughed too loudly and behaved too exuberantly—the same hysterical gaiety that prevailed at the French court in Poe's *Masque of the Red Death*. At midnight she asked him to take her home.

"I have a splitting headache, Roger."

"I'm sorry. Of course."

They bid farewell to close friends, paid their respects to the hostess and departed in the Wildings' carriage. They said very little until the carriage was approaching *Ravena*. Then he asked her, "Do you really have a headache?"

"Yes. It was all that noise and smoke and mindless chatter. It grated on my nerves like fingernails scraping along a blackboard."

Impulsively he said, "Do you know what would cure your headache? A brisk canter over the fields."

"At this time of night?"

"Remember how you used to sneak out of the house back in Ireland? We'd ride for an hour or two . . ." He paused—just in time. He'd come close to saying, ". . . *and make love in the meadow.*"

It was obvious from her consternation that Ravena made the connection in her own mind. She turned and looked at him. "Roger, you and I never rode together at night. It was . . ." Now it was her turn to rein back. ". . . *it was your twin brother, Brian, I came out to be with.*"

"Did I say night?" he parried blandly. "Of course, you and I rode in the daytime."

"But you said 'sneak out.' I didn't have to sneak out in broad daylight."

He touched a hand to his head. "Guess I'm a bit light in the head myself. You know how the fever comes over me without warning. I do believe I could do with a midnight ride myself. What about it, Ravena? Will you keep me company?"

She stared at him in bewilderment. The idea of her husband, Colonel Roger O'Neil, doing anything as impulsive and unconventional as riding a horse in the dark of night was preposterous.

"I—I really don't think——"

"Come on, be a sport."

A shock ran through her whole body, like the time she'd been standing near the Eiffel Tower in Paris when it was struck by lightning during a rainstorm.

"Come on, be a sport." Words spoken by a ghost. The occasion when she and Brian had gone riding to Lough Derg. She hadn't wanted to go with him. He'd coaxed, *"Come on, be a sport."*

"What's wrong, my dear?" he asked. "Why are you looking at me so strangely?"

She wagged her head slowly from side to side. All of her will had deserted her. She was a puppet activated by some mysterious external force.

"All right, Roger, I'll go with you." Mechanical voice, her eyes staring fixedly like a doll's.

Dimly aware, too, of a familiar sensation stirring inside of her—a fluttering, a keen sense of anticipation and anxiety, the sense that something momentous was about to happen to her, that she was approaching another one of the pivotal high points in the life's journey from birth to infinity . . . the identical feeling she had experienced that same day long ago.

"Come on, be a sport."

She clutched her throat as the carriage rolled up the long circular drive and stopped before the wide whitewashed steps of *Ravena*.

"Will that be all, Cunnel, suh?" the coachman inquired.

"Yes, Davis. Mrs. O'Neil and I will be riding as soon as we change. Will you saddle up Black Lightning and Ginger?"

"Yes, suh." He stared at them, muttering to himself, as they walked up the steps. "They done gone crazy, that's what . . . damn fools!"

Since McCloud had gone off to war, most of the burden of the duke's stables fell on the coachman. He drove around to the barn and put the carriage horses back in their stalls. Then he walked to Black Lightning's stall.

"You ain't gonna like this, horse, but your bedtime is over."

Davis was tightening the cinch on Ginger when Ravena and Brian arrived at the stable. She wore a loose white blouse and black velvet trousers custom-made by George Sands' personal couturier. Brian's eyebrows arched high when he saw her. How like Ravena to scorn the traditional women's riding habit! He remembered her girlhood ruse of snitching a pair of her brother's trousers to don when she was out of the house. He remembered her lace pantalets the day they had ridden out to the lough.

Jesus, but you are beautiful!

The desire to take her in his arms was almost uncontrollable. He turned away quickly.

"Let's go."

Ravena was nonplussed at his appearance as well. She had never seen Roger ride unless he was in uniform or impeccably groomed in his neat riding habit and boots.

"Why so informal tonight, Roger?" she asked.

He was evasive. "Oh . . . one has to kick over the

traces once in a while. Besides, it's so late no one will be likely to see us."

She accepted the explanation, but she was still doubtful. What was happening to Roger O'Neil, the staid, conventional, meticulous Roger that she had known for seventeen years? That Roger wouldn't have been caught in a dirty work shirt and gardening trousers even in the middle of the night.

Brian swung onto Black Lightning and Davis assisted Ravena onto Ginger. The roan reminded her of her own dear Apache. Seeing Roger astride the big black Arabian gave her another jolt. Except for the absence of a star on its forehead, the horse was remarkably like Brian's Big Red!

Goose flesh tingled on her forearms and thighs. It was eerie, almost supernatural. Once she and Brian had joked about reincarnation. He had said he wanted to come back into the world as the steed of a beautiful lady. *"I'd like the feel of her riding me every day."*

"Are you shivering?" he asked as they rode along the cowpath that led back through the woods to the fields in the north meadow.

"Some one is walking on my grave."

He cast a sharp glance at her. "I haven't heard that one in a long time."

"It was something your brother, Brian, liked to say."

"I believe you're right."

"What's so funny?" she demanded as he laughed softly.

"We are—you and I, the whole damned ridiculous human race . . . this damned absurd war, isn't that proof enough?"

She looked at him with growing disbelief. Roger O'Neil would never say anything so radical. Could it possibly be that the spirit of Brian O'Neil was trying to reach out to her through the flesh and bones of his brother? Her mind reeled.

"You're daft, lass!"

It came with the heritage, Gallic superstition—ghosts, goblins, devils, the Little People.

A stretch of rolling green lay ahead of them beyond the cotton crop.

"I'll race you," he dared.

She wanted to get away from him far more than she wanted to race. Now she was terrified. She put the whip to the horse's flank, and Ginger shot away from Black Lightning. His laughter trailed off behind her; then he was in hot pursuit.

"Go, Lightning! Go!"

"Faster, Ginger! Faster!"

It had happened before, another time, another place, reliving that wonderful day when she had been deflowered by Brian. So why was she so frightened? Because the man on her heels was not her husband, Roger; he was a phantom, a ghost!

Ravena glanced over her shoulder and saw the bigger stallion closing the distance fast. Now he was abreast of her, edging Black Lightning over so that his leg nudged hers.

She screamed and struck at him with her crop. He caught her hand, and his teeth glowed in the bright moonlight.

"Leave me alone! Please leave me alone."

Unexpectedly, he leaned across her and one powerful arm whipped around her waist. It was a game he'd played with Custer's crack horse soldiers. The next thing she knew, he had pulled her off the roan and thrown her across the stallion's neck.

Ravena fainted from sheer terror.

Not totally unconscious, she was aware of what was going on but powerless to resist. Brian reined in Black Lightning and dismounted. He carried Ravena to a grassy knoll and gently laid her down. Kneeling beside her, he began to unbutton the front of her blouse. He removed every shred of her clothing as she lay there petrified. She watched mutely as he began to undress himself.

Finally she found her voice and reason. "We can't. We mustn't."

He laughed. "And why not? It's just like the first time, remember?"

She nodded. "How could I ever forget?" She swallowed hard and blurted, "You're Brian's ghost, and somehow you've taken over Roger's body."

"The walking dead," he intoned in a sonorous voice from the grave.

She began to quake and whimper as he swung one leg across her body.

He took her hand and brought it to his manhood. Reflexively, her fingers closed around him.

"Does it feel like a phantom to you, lass?"

"Ohhhh . . ." She let out a moan, and then the fear was eclipsed by an emotion so much more powerful that it engulfed her from her scalp to the tips of her tingling toes. She was consumed in the flash fire of her desire. Her body accepted him hungrily, greedily. Her arms locked around his neck. Her heels dug fiercely into his hard buttocks. She wanted all of him.

When it was over, they lay together, still joined, basking in the aftermath of ecstasy. She was the first to speak.

"If only you could capture the beauty of an experience and put it in a bottle the way you can with a scent. When you want to smell the roses or the lilacs or the magnolia, you unstopper it and it's with you once more."

He laughed. "That would be quite a trick—instant sex!"

"There!" she exclaimed and sat up. "Roger would cut out his tongue before he would use that word in front of a lady."

"Roger is a horse's ass!" He glanced over at the

two horses, grazing in the high grass. "My apologies to the two fine beasts," he said gravely.

"How did you manage it, Brian?" she demanded.

"Manage what?"

"Taking possession of Roger's body?"

"Holy mother of God!" He roared with laughter, grasping his aching sides. "You don't actually believe that malarkey, do you? Oh, my God, you surely have your share of the dark Irish in your blood." He took her shoulders and shook her gently. "I'm real, Ravena. I'm Brian, not Roger. Brian, lass. Say it."

"Brian," she whispered and put a hand to his cheek, filled with awe. "If you are Brian. . . . You can't be Brian. Brian was killed. They found his body."

"They found a corpse burned beyond recognition. It had to be done that way. You know the law was onto me for being a member of the underground resistance movement. I would have gone to prison, maybe worse, and brought disgrace down on my father. This way, the name of O'Neil would be absolved by my demise. I'm sorry I put all of you through the ordeal, but there wasn't any other way."

She shook her head in befuddlement. "Then, where is Roger?"

"I'll start at the beginning, the night I boarded the ship at Belfast. . . ."

And he ended by recounting how Jesse Farnsworth had drugged Roger and he had commenced the great impersonation.

"I knew I couldn't fool you forever, darling."

"I guess you really didn't fool me, not altogether. I knew you weren't the same Roger I knew. Your strangeness puzzled me, frightened me at times, like tonight."

He laughed and slapped her bare bottom. "You thought you were making love to a ghost. That would shake up a woman a bit, I imagine." He started to get up. "We'd better put on some clothes before we catch our death of cold. You, that is. Naturally, a ghost can't catch cold. I'm already dead."

His back was to her as he bent over to pick up his trousers. Grinning impishly, Ravena planted a foot on his vulnerable bottom and shoved as hard as she could. He went sprawling on his face, knocking the wind out of his lungs.

When he was able to breathe again, he looked up at Ravena standing over him and gasped, "Now, what did you do a thing like that for?"

She stuck out her tongue. "Because you're a sneaky, conniving, fraudulent mick of an Irishman."

His hand whipped out, and he caught her ankle and yanked. She fell beside him in the grass.

"And you are a bitchy little Irish doxy."

Nose to nose, their eyes aglow, her breasts brushing his hairy chest, her breath quickening, she reached down between them and found him.

Ravena giggled wickedly. "I see you have the same thought on your mind, too!"

He sighed and took her in his arms. "Scandalous wench."

* * *

The next month was glorious for Ravena. She had never been happier in all of her life, and it showed.

"You are positively radiant, dear," Vanessa Wilding said to her daughter at breakfast one morning after Brian had gone to the capitol building and her father was out watching his two racers practicing.

It was curious that even at the lowest ebb of the war, the southern aristocracy never lost interest in the sport they claimed as the "Confederate national pastime."

"Thank you, mother. I feel wonderful."

The two women smiled in secret feminine empathy.

"Could it be that you're pregnant? Your father always said I was more beautiful in the early months after you children were conceived—an inner glow."

"I'm not sure, mother, but it is possible."

The duchess arched her eyebrows. "I would say it is distinctly possible. I'm pleased that you and Roger are getting along so well these days. It shows in him, as well. Why, he's been like a different man since his return from active duty. Oh, maybe not that long, but he has changed radically."

Ravena suppressed the urge to laugh. "Yes, I think he's finally outgrown his adolescence."

"A child would do you both a world of good. Having a baby makes both a man and a woman more responsible. Childless couples tend to grow selfish and think only of satisfying their own individual gratifications."

"That is a point, mother. Well, I hope you're right. I'd adore having a baby."

The duchess came around the table and bent to kiss Ravena's cheek. Tears glistened in her eyes.

"And I'd adore being a grandmother."

"But you are. What about Kevin's boy?"

The older woman sighed. "Yes, but I've never had a chance to hold the little lad. That's what being a grandmother is all about."

Ravena laughed. "Yes, hugging, squeezing, kissing. Oh, if it is true, what a spoiled little brat you'll make of him, or her."

"I guarantee it."

It was the end of the first week in August when Major Manson came running into Colonel O'Neil's office, his voice hoarse with emotion.

"Farragut attacked Mobile Bay this morning at dawn! The president has called an emergency meeting! Come on!"

"That's impossible! There must be a mistake!"

Brian displayed the proper degree of shock and incredulity.

By the time they reached the cabinet room, all of the members were seated. Brian felt a pang of remorse when he saw the haggard face of Jefferson Davis, who sat at the head of the long table, head bowed, a hand shielding his eyes. Secretary of State Benjamin made the dire announcement.

"Gentlemen, it is with deep sorrow that I advise you that Admiral Buchanan's fleet has been defeated at the Bay of Mobile. Admiral Buchanan was wounded in the action and is now a prisoner of the enemy———"

Exclamations of shock, dismay and grief sounded a dirge around the table.

"Fort Morgan and Fort Gaines are under siege, and it is only a matter of time before they, too, will be in the hands of the Yankees."

The secretary of the army pounded the table with both fists. "By God! How? How did Farragut do it?"

"With seven sloops of war, ten gunboats and four monitors. Obviously, they knew the exact locations of the pilings and the torpedoes at the mouth of the bay. Farragut steamed right up the channel under Fort Morgan's guns."

"What about the *Tennessee?*"

"Evidently Farragut was also aware of the dilemma of the *Tennessee,* and he attacked at low tide when she was mired at anchor. His warship kept ramming her while one of the monitors took up a position by the casemate and kept pounding round after round of eleven-inch shells at her vulnerable spot until the armor plate finally collapsed and the tiller chains were shot away."

Brian sprang to his feet mouthing outraged indignation. "How in hell did Farragut come into possession of such vital information? It was highly classified, top secret."

Benjamin shrugged and spread his hands, palm

up in resignation. "Top secret.... Colonel O'Neil, as an army veteran you know better than most of us that if more than one person knows a thing, it ceases to be a secret. The Yankee spy system is probably the best in the world." He sighed ruefully. "Yankee ingenuity, I believe that is the term.... I don't have to elaborate on the far-reaching ramifications of the loss of Mobile Bay. Mobile City is sealed off, and the Union fleet is in indisputed control of the Gulf of Mexico."

It was not easy for Brian to conceal his elation. *Mr. Lincoln, you have the victory you so dearly needed before the election!*

Ravena did not altogether share his elation when he broke the news to her that night.

"I can't help feeling guilty, Brian. You are a Union spy and I'm a traitor to my homeland. Don't rationalize it. We've been Virginians for six years. This land and its people have been good to us, Brian. All of our dear friends——the Coopers, the Taylors, the Collinses, Melanie, Jan——and here I am betraying their friendship and graciousness with treachery."

Brian took her hands and looked into her eyes solemnly. "I understand, and I love you more for acknowledging that you feel guilty. You're a decent human being, and it's a dirty business, war. General Grant had it right: 'War is hell.' And it's one of the worst wars that we're involved in right now. You know I'm a soldier, not a spy. It doesn't set well with me, stabbing good men like Davis and Benjamin and Roger's brother officers in their backs the way I've had to do; but my allegiance is sworn to the Union, and when my commander in chief, President Lincoln, gives me a direct order, I obey it to the best of my ability and my personal feelings have nothing to do with it."

She was staring at him strangely and with some

uncertainty. "You know something, Brian, your speech might almost have been given by Roger."

"Why not? Whatever his faults are, my brother is a man of honor, and I believe he would defend his principles to the death."

Ravena knew he was right, and yet she felt let down. "You don't mind if we don't make love tonight, Brian? I'm suddenly exhausted."

"I understand." He kissed her forehead.

It was pitch-dark when Brian was awakened by an urgent knocking on the bedroom door. Gordon's voice was excited.

"Colonel O'Neil, Mrs. Farnsworth is here to see you."

Brian sat up and fumbled for the matches on his bedside table. He lit the oil lamp and sat on the edge of the bed to clear his fuzzy senses.

"Colonel O'Neil, sir!"

"Yes, yes, I'm coming, Gordon."

Ravena was awake now. "What on earth is going on? What time is it?"

He consulted his watch. "Three-fifteen. Jesse Farnsworth is here."

"At this hour? Jesse must be losing her mind."

"I think not," he said with a note of doom.

He put on his robe and Ravena followed suit. "Wait for me."

Jesse was waiting for them in the study, a glass of sherry in her hand. Her expression corroborated his note of doom.

"Shut the door," she said.

"What's happened, Jesse?" he asked.

"The worst thing that could possibly happen— your brother, Roger, has escaped."

"My God!" Ravena turned pale and grabbed hold of Brian's arm.

OTHER SELECTIONS
FROM
PLAYBOY PRESS

HUNTER'S MOON $1.75
NORAH HESS

The love story of a woman whose beauty provoked passion and violence. Widowed at nineteen, the passionate Darcy Stevens knew only one way to survive—by selling herself to men. Yet when the chance came for a new life, Darcy decided to move to the isolated Kentucky hills and leave her sordid past behind. But violence pursued her, and soon Darcy was caught between the bold and dashing Delaney brothers—two fierce mountain men, each determined to make her his own.

PROUD PASSION $1.95
BARBARA BONHAM

A tumultuous love story filled with the historical richness and raw human emotion of *Dark Fires*. Odette Morel was beautiful, proud and innocent. Men had always found her irresistible. But nothing had ever prepared her for the terrifying events that would take place on her wedding night, events that would mark the beginning of the most daring romance a woman could ever imagine or survive. In a breathtaking tale that captures the turbulence of an era, we follow Odette as she feels the brutal excesses of the French Revolution, endures the hardships of an ocean voyage to America, and faces unthinkable dangers in the frontier wilderness. We meet the men who want to own her, dominate her, violate her—and the one man who loves her enough to die for her.

THE DRAGON AND THE ROSE $1.95
ROBERTA GELLIS

When Henry took the bloody throne of England, he pledged to marry Elizabeth, daughter of his most bitter enemy, in order to keep peace in the land. Theirs was a match of convenience, laced with mistrust and fear. But from this unlikely alliance, there slowly grew a love so strong and a passion so fierce that it changed the course of history. Set against the rich backdrop of lavish ceremonials, court intrigues, bloody battles and political machinations, *The Dragon and the Rose* sweeps the reader along by the sheer momentum of its pulsating story.

PRETTY ENOUGH TO KILL $1.50
AMANDA MCALLISTER

Donna, Rita and Jennifer were the three most beautiful girls on campus. Each had a different personal reason for trying to win the beauty contest, and each was unaware that another, deadly contest was going on in the mind of a psychopathic killer. Which would be his next victim?

WAITING FOR CAROLINE $1.50
AMANDA MCALLISTER

When Caroline asked her to baby-sit and dashed off without an explanation, Andrea thought nothing of it. After all, Caroline had done this kind of thing before. But as one day became two and three, Andrea knew that something had to be terribly wrong. Who was the mysterious prowler who had been terrorizing her neighbors? Why did he break into her house yet take nothing? Andrea didn't know what all this had to do with Caroline's disappearance but when a murder was committed in her own backyard she suddenly realized that her own life was in immediate danger!

NO NEED FOR FEAR $1.50
Amanda McAllister

There were three men in Helen's life: the Agency man assigned to protect her, whose quiet strength she came to depend on; the college professor who swept her off her feet and awakened her desire for romance; and the hired assassin who had cold-bloodedly murdered her husband and was now stalking her. There were three men in Helen's life—or was it only two?

TRUST NO ONE AT ALL $1.50
Amanda McAllister

It had been two years since that summer in Sochi when Kathryn met and fell in love with Andrei. Now here was his letter asking her to help smuggle his father's papers out of Russia. Surely the Soviet authorities wouldn't dare to harm the daughter of a prominent American journalist.... On the strength of her loving memories and without so much as a second thought, Kathryn gives up everything and flings herself headlong into a bold and perilous journey from which there is no turning back.

LOOK OVER YOUR SHOULDER $1.50
Amanda McAllister

With her husband committed to a mental hospital for a brutal sex murder, Julie desperately attempts to create a new life for herself. But in spite of a new romance, wherever she goes there are always the strange phone calls, the frightening letters and the shadowy figures following her ... everywhere.

ORDER DIRECTLY FROM:

PLAYBOY PRESS
P.O. BOX 3385
CHICAGO, ILLINOIS 60654

NO. OF COPIES		TITLE	PRICE
_____	K16355	Hunter's Moon	$1.75
_____	E16345	Proud Passion	$1.95
_____	E16364	The Dragon and the Rose	$1.95
_____	C16327	Pretty Enough to Kill	$1.50
_____	C16328	Waiting for Caroline	$1.50
_____	C16329	No Need for Fear	$1.50
_____	C16352	Trust No One at All	$1.50
_____	C16360	Look Over Your Shoulder	$1.50

PLEASE ENCLOSE 50¢ FOR POSTAGE AND HANDLING.

Total amount enclosed: $ _____

Name _____

Address _____

City _____ State _____ Zip _____

WE HOPE YOU ENJOYED THIS BOOK.

IF YOU'D LIKE A FREE LIST OF OTHER PAPERBACKS
AVAILABLE FROM PLAYBOY PRESS,
JUST SEND YOUR REQUEST TO
MARILYN ADAMS, PLAYBOY PRESS,
919 NORTH MICHIGAN AVENUE,
CHICAGO, ILLINOIS 60611.